The
Purloined Boy

Book One
of the
Weirdling Cycle

By Mortimus Clay

Cover art by Justin Gerard

HARTFORD, CONNECTICUT

For Caleb

Text copyright ©2009 by Mortimus Clay™
Cover art by Justin Gerard copyright ©2009
by Finster Press

Published by Finster Press
First printing 2009

Library of Congress Control Number: 2008942525

ISBN-13:978-0-9821598-0-4
ISBN-10:0-9821598-0-3

Cover Design:
Avoca Designs, www.avocadesigns.com
Xillion Design, www.xilliondesign.com

Cover Art:
Portland Studios, www.portlandstudios.com

Interior Design:
DeSollar Studio, www.desollarstudio.com

Acknowledgements

Thanks to all who played a role in helping Morty bring this book to market, including: Nancy Franson of Finster Press for her editorial work; Amy Park for her tireless proofreading; Mark Gilroy, of Thomas Nelson Publishers, for his sage advice; all the middle school teachers who assigned the test-market edition of *The Purloined Boy* for their students to read, including: Bill Cherniske, Tonya Snyder, Joy Press, Tammy Ekstrom, Donna L. Koropatkin, Mark Waller, Sharon Van Wickle, Lynne Brennan, Tom Hoffrage, Janet Rogers, Merri Grodecki; and last, but certainly not least, all the kids who read the test-market version of the book from: Nathan Hale Middle School (Coventry, Connecticut); H. W. Porter School (Columbia, Connecticut); Mansfield Middle School (Mansfield, Connecticut); Cornerstone Christian School (Manchester, Connecticut); The King's School (Bolton, Connecticut); Trinity Christian Academy (Barnstable, Massachusetts); Veritas Academy (Hyannis, Massachusetts); Trinity Christian School (Windsor, Connecticut); and New Testament Christian School (Norton, Massachusetts).

Contents

CHAPTER ONE

A Hint of Blue

*A**ll the doors were locked, all the windows were latched, and everything was perfectly secure the night the bogeyman came. But none of those things mattered since he was a bogey of the old school and had come in the traditional way; which is to say, through the closet.*

The closet happened to be in a bedroom, and the bedroom happened to contain a boy. He was a bright-eyed, happy boy —the sort often found in bedrooms. He was on the smallish side, with the smallish sort of feet that fit into footsie pajamas with plenty of room to spare. And he was all sleepy-woozy because he'd had a busy day. It had been filled with sunshine, and watermelons, and cousins running through the sprinkler. And he was all tucked in, warm and cozy and safe, and terrifically tight, because he was loved very much.

Now when the closet began to stir, the bright-eyed boy opened his bright-eyes and looked across the room. His Casper the Friendly Ghost night light helped him with that. It cast cool blue stripes across the floor and up the walls. It made black stripes too, because of the toys he'd left on the floor. (Let that be a lesson to you.) But he could see the closet door there, half in the light and half out of it, with its knob shining weakly.

The door made him catch his breath when it began to open.

It swung slowly and easily, but it revealed nothing. No light penetrated the black cavity it left in the wall. The doorway just gaped at him, like the mouth of a cave.

Then something shot out and disappeared into a shadow.

That got him panting. His heart started pounding in his ears. His eyes began to flit –wanting to see and not wanting. He tried to get up and run for it, but he couldn't. His covers had been tucked with such loving care he couldn't budge.

Then the sound of a deep open sniff came to him from across the room. Another sniff followed, then another. Somehow they sounded like hungry sniffs, and each was louder than the last and seemed closer.

Finally, after a rapid succession of sniffs, next to the night light, over the edge of the bed, up it came–lurid and shadow-creased–grinning and horrible–an awful head! The boy tried to scream, but nothing came out! He tried to burrow beneath his terrifically tight blankets, but it was just no good!

"I smell boy," the bogey said licking his pasty lips with a darting tongue, his yellowy eyes opened unnaturally wide. With an effortless motion, he tore the covers back. "Ahhh, yeess. Looks sweet, he does. A tender morsel. Three, perhaps four, I think. Old enough to take, but young enough to forget."

A bony hand rose and cast a knobby shadow over the boy's round white face. It was holding something. The last thing the bright-eyed boy saw was the yawning black hole of a sack lowering over him.

☆

Trevor sat up with a start. It was still dark and his burlap blanket was moist and itchy.

"Just that stupid dream again," he said with a sigh and fell back with a thud. "Ow! Stupid bed!" It made him so mad he punched it. That was a mistake since it was made mostly of wood planks and iron bolts. With a moan, he put his hand between his knees and rocked back and forth. He was definitely awake now and he knew where he was. He was in Superbia–the worst place in the universe.

Trevor didn't usually punch things. Actually, punching things was the last thing people thought of when they thought of Trevor. What did they think? They thought—*My, what a clumsy looking boy.* "Gangly" would have been a better word, kinder too. But he wasn't in a place where people cared much about words, or kindness for that matter. They also thought he looked thin. That wasn't very remarkable though, since most children in Superbia were thin. What tended to draw attention were the eyebrows. Stuck is what they were, or at least seemed to be, in two arches. They made him look scared, and that suited him, because he *was* scared most of the time. On the plus side, they kept his eyes wide open and helped him to see things other people missed. *He* didn't think that was a plus, though. Seeing things other people missed is what scared him in the first place.

He was staring at the ceiling now, his mind wandering. To his right, a blue glow from an electric torch flickered and sputtered and made some shadows dance on the cavernous vaults high overhead. Speaking of seeing things, he started to do just that. First, he thought he saw a vase, then he thought he saw a statue, then he thought he saw a giraffe. The shadows kept shifting and moving, becoming one thing, then another. Finally he thought he saw a bogeyman grinning at him.

He pulled the blanket over his head and shut his eyes tight. He began to feel sick. The feeling was so familiar he'd given it a name.

"Oh no, it's *Mr. Queasy;* I think I'm going to throw up."

It took every ounce of self-control he had, but he managed not to. When his breathing had returned to normal, he pulled his blanket back again and looked left and right and saw hundreds of beds just like his, stretching into the shadowy distance. In each bed was a child.

He whispered to the boy on his left, "Drake, you asleep?"

"Yes," Drake moaned.

"Drake...do you ever have (gulp) dreams? You...you know ...of someplace else?"

"Nope."

"I do." He started to tell Drake about them.

"Just shut up, will you?! I don't want to hear about your stupid dreams."

"But, what...what about...you know...the rumors? About Olton? They say they have families there..."

Drake raised himself on an elbow and leaned menacingly toward him.

"Shut up about that stuff, see? If you don't, Meno might hear and he'll pound you again, and this time I won't stop him, got it?"

A vision of knuckles and fists and a fat, nasty face passed before him. "Okay."

"Good. Now go back to sleep," Drake said and rolled over.

Trevor tried to, but his eyes kept opening on their own. He turned over and saw Maggie Blaise through her red hair and freckles. She was a new kid, transferred from Hall 57, she'd said. He had only known her a couple of weeks, but he really liked her, and she actually seemed to like him. She would talk.

"Maggie, wake up. It's me, Trevor." No answer. *Must really be asleep,* he decided.

Just then, something caught his attention beyond her at the far end of the hall. It was the slave who watched the children at night, reading at a tall desk. The old fellow usually wore a patch over one eye. What caught Trevor's attention was that it was turned up. Even across the enormous room, he could see that the bad eye was bleached white. It shone eerily by the glow of his electric torch.

4

Weird, Trevor thought. *Why does ol' Epictetus need his bad eye to read?*

Unexpectedly the morning bells rang, and all the curtains opened with a swoosh to let the gray dusty light of a Superbian morning pour in.

A Guardian with bored eyes and a phony smile entered and began sweeping through the aisles. "Up, up, up, children! Up you go!" he chirped.

Hundreds of kids rolled out of bed and began milling around getting ready for the day, throwing on clothes, and making beds, while more Guardians with white robes whisking entered and passed among them like ghosts.

Trevor fumbled with his blanket, working to tuck under the corner in the way he'd been shown a hundred times. *Tight folds, flat creases,* he reminded himself. He stepped back to inspect his work; *no, it wasn't right. The corner was supposed to form a perfect triangle.* He hoped they wouldn't notice, just this once. He felt a presence behind him. He looked up with a swallow. A long, thin face coldly stared back at him.

"Is that the best you can do...ahh, what's your name again?"

"T, Trevor, First Guardian Glaucon," Trevor said, looking into a pair of eyes that reminded him vaguely of empty tea cups.

"Did you say, *Trevor*? Speak up."

"Yes sir, Trevor."

"Oh, yes. Trevor. I remember you," Glaucon said to the open air. "Why don't we just tattoo numbers on them? Much easier that way. No trying to remember these confounded names...I think I'll bring it up at council," he finished, sounding pleased with himself.

Trevor hoped the Guardian had forgotten him there, but no such luck. "That bed is a disgrace, I say, a disgrace," the Guardian said, curtly. Sweeping down, he pushed Trevor roughly aside and, in what seemed a couple of motions, he produced a perfectly made bed. "There, did you see? That is how it is done," he finished contemptuously, then glided away in search of other disgraceful beds.

"Yes, First Guardian," Trevor said, feeling relieved and stupid at the same time.

Children were lining up for breakfast, and Trevor joined them. He got behind Drake, and Maggie came up behind him. Each picked up a wooden bowl and walked past serving tables where adults ladled out watery gruel. They joined some others at one of the tables.

"I hate this stuff," said Maggie. "Why can't they give us something good to eat?"

"Like...like what?" Trevor stuttered.

"Like real food. Like bacon or eggs or even toast."

"Oh, you're making it all up," said Drake, rolling his eyes.

"What are eggs?" Trevor asked.

"Mmm, eggs are really tasty. They come in a shell that you can crack, and inside there's a little yellow thing called a yolk. You can cook 'em lots of ways. I love eggs."

"You're lying," a heavy voice growled from down the table.

It was Meno, and food was dribbling from the corners of his mouth. He had two bowls of the awful stuff, one of which he had apparently taken from the skinny, sad-looking kid to his right. He glared at Maggie with hard, beady little eyes set in a massive red face. Amazingly, he had no neck; his head seemed to swell from his bulky shoulders like a huge pimple. Trevor hadn't seen him there. Suddenly he didn't feel hungry.

"Eggs are slave food and so's that other stuff. It can't be good if slaves eat it," pimple-head said.

"How do you know?" Maggie snapped. "You've never even had eggs!"

"Neither have you!"

"Have too!"

"Have not!"

"Yes I have, you big lummox! My mother used to make them for me! Oops!" Maggie's eyes went wide, and her hands flew to her mouth.

Everyone at the table froze, spoons halfway to mouths, eyes popped, looking at her in disbelief.

Just then, a Guardian glided by their table and the children looked down quickly. Silence. The only sound was the sound of spoons scraping on bowls.

After the Guardian was out of earshot, Trevor leaned over and said, "You have a mother?"

"Hey, you two, you better shut up about that stuff," said Meno. He motioned with his thumb at the Guardian. "You're lucky they're here. If they weren't, I'd pop you," he said, holding up a brick-sized fist at Maggie.

"Oooo, I'm sooo scared," Maggie crooned.

"You better be. And you, punk," he said to Trevor. "You better not get us in trouble again. If you do, I'll crack your head open like one of those stupid eggs she's talking about."

"Uhhh, okay," Trevor said, visualizing himself in a headlock.

The bells rang, and mercifully chaos broke out as everyone went to class. Trevor and Maggie lost the others in the bustle.

"Why do you let that moron talk to you that way?" Maggie said.

"Uhh, what way?"

She stopped and looked at him incredulously. "Like you're dirt, or something!"

"Oh, that," he mumbled.

Suddenly, Trevor felt a need to put the best face on it. He wanted Maggie to like him, and he realized at that moment that dirt lacked something in the likability department.

"I, ummm...I..."

She kept looking at him. Blood rushed to his face, and his eyes fell. To his relief, the press of kids going to class swept them apart.

⁙

They were reunited outside their classroom. Trevor wanted to ask her about her mother again, but when he saw Meno, a screaming need for invisibility made him duck for cover. They found some seats in the back, and he slunk down in his chair.

A rusty screech pierced the air, and an iron door at the front of the classroom opened to let in what looked like a lumpy pillow. It was their teacher, Guardian Medea. She was wearing the standard white robe of the Guardians, but her immense girth filled it so completely that every fold and ripple of her ample body was outlined for a defenseless world to see.

"Good morning, class!" she sing-songed, as she surveyed the students through a pair of thick, smudgy glasses.

"Good morning, Guardian Medea," the class answered in unison.

The scrape of a hundred chairs pushing back was followed by the sound of a classroom full of kids, marching in place. Trevor and Maggie joined in, swinging their arms back and forth, raising their knees high. It was time for the national anthem. Every voice sang out and this is what they said:

Superbia's really great!
Get up now, don't be late!
Together now, let us state:
Superbia's really great!

The tune was just as awful as the words, but Medea enjoyed it. Her fat cheeks bounced and jiggled at either end of a broad grin, and she pumped her pudgy fists in the air at the *really great!* part.

Maggie glanced over at Trevor and giggled.

After about a dozen verses of the same thing over and over, somehow they all knew they were done and sat with a thump.

"Very good, children! Very good!" the Guardian said. "How very fortunate you are to live in Superbia–the envy of the world! It is my pleasure to lecture you once again on the glories of our beautiful metropolis." She walked to a lectern and plopped down a thick stack of yellowed papers. "Today we learn about my favorite subject: sewage treatment!"

Maggie nudged Trevor. "Sewage treatment?" she whispered. Trevor shrugged.

"It is all so very, very interesting, how pipes connect every building in the city, and how they all lead eventually to the great sewage works below! It all works together and each part makes its contribution! Delightful! Simply delightful!"

What it was about times like this, Trevor couldn't say, but his mind became difficult to control. It was as if his mind had a mind of its own; and while Medea droned on about the wonders of plumbing and filtration, it got up and left the building.

It went far, far, away until it finally came to a grove of shaggy trees where a little white house with shining windows sat contentedly. A deep porch stood out front, and he walked right up the steps and into the house through a screen door. The smell of baking bread welcomed him and he looked around at a room that was strange, yet familiar. It was so bright and cheery, it made him happy just being in it. In a corner a big, overstuffed chair beckoned him to come over and sit down.

Two figures walked in. They were radiant; so bright, in fact, Trevor couldn't look directly at their faces. But he liked what he could see, and he could see that they liked him. It occurred to him that it would be very nice for one of them to read him a book. He looked up and saw one on a shelf high overhead. He extended an arm and reached for it. *Just a little higher*, he thought. He stretched his arm as high as he could. *That's it, almost got it–*

"Yes, Trevor Upjohn, what is it?" said an adult voice.

He was back.

His hand was in the air, and every eye was on him. Maggie had grabbed his arm and was trying to bring it down. "What are you doing?!" she hissed.

He sank down in his chair, and an all too familiar feeling of dread, like a lump of ice, moved from his stomach up to his throat. Mr. Queasy had come to call. Trevor was sweaty all of a sudden.

"I, uhh, I don't know."

"Nonsense, child. You have a question. Go ahead. Ask it."

"Well," he stammered. "I was wondering. Ahhh, can I go *home*?"

Someone screamed. Everyone gasped. Chairs scraped the floor, and kids edged away.

Medea staggered and braced herself with the corner of a desk. An alarm began to sound.

"I'm sorry, Guardian! I didn't mean it!" Trevor said in a panic.

"Trevor, you know we don't use *naughty* words in this school! How could you?"

She began talking to herself at this point, "Oh my, oh my, why is this happening to me? I had such a good record, too. Spoiled. Spoiled by a stupid boy! I hate boys."

"Don't blame yourself, Guardian," a girl said. "He's always saying things like that." She glared at him.

And she wasn't the only one. Trevor looked around. Everyone was staring at him. Meno was whispering to a tousle-headed stick of a kid named Willis.

"What should I do?" Medea kept saying, trying to collect her wits. "They'll be here soon. What should I say?"

A clip, clip, clip of boots began to sound from down a hall. Everyone went quiet. Clip, clip, clip. The boots got louder. Everyone got quieter. Clip, clip clip. The boots kept coming.

The door at the front screeched again. A tall, balding figure carrying a clipboard stepped in the room. Everything about his face was hollow—hollow cheeks, hollow eyes. He scanned the room.

"Ah, Mr. Gourmand, how kind of you to come," Medea said, with a nervous laugh. "Behavior Modification is always welcome here!"

The man gave a slow, solemn nod.

A little kid spoke up. "Please Guardian, don't make us go with him! He's a bogeyman!"

"Now, now, bogeymen are our friends. Besides, we mustn't hurt Mr. Gourmand's feelings, must we? He's taken time out of his busy schedule to pay us a visit."

That's right, bogeymen are our friends, Trevor reminded himself. It's what he'd always been told. He sunk down further in his chair, hoping the bogey wouldn't notice him.

"Who is it?" the bogey asked.

"Mr. Gourmand, I'm sorry for the inconvenience. Everything's under control, I..." Medea's voice trailed off under his gaze.

"Who is it?" he asked again.

Fifty hands pointed at Trevor.

"Really," said the bogey, with a toothy grin. The hairs on back of Trevor's neck rose.

"I'm sorry, but everyone here has been contaminated," the bogey said, not sounding sorry at all. "Immediate action is necessary. All the children must come with me for therapy."

Moans rose from across the room.

"Therapy! How wonderful!" Medea said, wringing her

hands. "How I remember my therapy sessions with fondness! Well, class, off you go!"

"Where are we going?" someone asked.

"To the gates," the bogey said flatly.

"How exciting!" Medea effused, with a pained expression. "A field trip! How lucky for you all. Have a good time. Bye, bye!"

Everyone got up and began to form a line behind the Behavior Modifier. They were good at forming lines; they did it a lot. Before long, they were filing out the door.

The air was thick with blame, and Trevor didn't want to look at anyone. Maggie managed to come up next to him and gave his hand an encouraging squeeze.

"Why can't I keep my big mouth shut?" he said to her as they left the room.

But just before he stepped out, Trevor looked back. He saw Guardian Medea mumbling to herself and staring blankly into space.

⁎

Once outside, they entered a forest of industrial-sized smokestacks, some rising hundreds of feet into the air. Plumes of greasy smoke belched out of them to feed heavy clouds, blanketing the sky as far as Trevor could see.

His hall was just like hundreds of others in that part of Superbia. He could see their dull, boxy shapes, with their giant numbers painted on their sides, retreating into the distance. Each one contained hundreds of children, he knew. But, none of them was outside just then. No one went out if it could be helped.

Beneath the shadows of the stacks, the children huddled together like a little, black beetle and crawled along behind the erect, white form of Behavior Modifier Gourmand. No one said a thing, which was just as well for Trevor, since no one had anything nice to say to him.

They're right. What was I thinking? he thought.

Maggie looked over and gave his hand another squeeze.

And yet, and yet–he liked his thoughts. He liked them better than Superbia. He knew he shouldn't. Everyone said so. But that house, it was so nice. And the people who lived in it, he liked them–a lot.

Who are they, anyway? A naughty idea flew into his head. He'd had it a million times. *Were they his parents? Were they his mother and father? No!* he told himself. *Don't even think it! It'll only make things worse!*

He went on scolding himself like that, all the way to the gate. That was a lot of scolding. It took all morning to get there. Superbia was a big place.

The gate was set in a tall, thick wall and was made of iron bars that filled the opening like a mouthful of black teeth. At the Behavior Modifier's signal, a man began to crank a wheel and the gate slowly rose.

They passed through the opening and out onto an empty road that stretched over a barren steppe. Trevor looked back over his shoulders and saw the city wall bend away into the distance on either side.

Gourmand now turned to address them. Slowly, he surveyed each child. When he came to him, Trevor thought he saw him lick his lips.

Finally, the Behavior Modifier cleared his throat and put a hand over his heart.

"My dear children, my dear, tender little morsels," he said with sticky sweetness. "My heart breaks whenever I hear that someone has used one of the naughty words. The naughty words are bad, very bad. They come from a sick mind, and their sickness spreads. When children hear one of the naughty words, they begin to see things and hear things–strange, crazy things and imaginary people. Now, isn't that terrible?" (Heads nodded all round.) "That is why they are forbidden!"

Everyone looked at Trevor.

"Uh...sorry, guys."

"Concerning your therapy, my tender ones. I am sorry to say it will hurt," the bogey said with a smile. "But it will be good for you."

He pointed away from the city, toward the horizon.

"There, do you see it?"

Trevor squinted. In the far distance, he thought he could see a dark line where the brown of the earth met the gray of the sky.

"What do you think that is?"

"Is, is it...the Blackwood?" a girl ventured.

"That's right, my little morsel, that is the Blackwood. And every awful story you've heard about it is all too true. It is full of creepy crawlies and hungry things. Why, it would swallow you, if it could," the bogey said, eyes widening.

The children pressed up to each other.

"Once that wood filled the world. We bogeys have pressed it back though. And someday, dear children, if we just keep at it, we'll be rid of it for good!"

Teeth flashing, he went on. "The mind that made those woods made the naughty words, you know. That is why you must be cleansed of them!

"Now, for your therapy."

Looking at the ground, he spotted a little twig with a single feeble leaf. "Look! The Blackwood sends its shoots to the very gate of Superbia!"

His hand went to his pocket and pulled something out. He threw it on the ground, and instantly smoke shot up and began spreading fast.

Everyone started coughing and Trevor began feeling odd.

"Help me, children! Help me keep our city free!" Gourmand cried.

With a hiss, a thousand roots shot out of the ground. They began climbing the wall and ripping out chunks of stone. One as big as a tree trunk wrapped itself around Gourmand and lifted him into the air.

"Fight, my tender ones! Fight for your city!" he shouted down at them.

Something came over Trevor at that moment and he felt hatred, hatred like he'd never felt it before. He wanted to hack and pull and cut. Others must have felt the same way, because children were running around frantically fighting the maniacal roots.

But, before Trevor could join in, a wind rose unexpectedly and swept the smoke away. It was a fresh wind, and when it blew the smoke away, it was as though a spell had been broken. Suddenly, everything was just like it had been before. The roots were gone, the walls stood unharmed, and Behavior Modifier Gourmand was back on the ground. Everyone stood blinking and dazed.

The air was good, and Trevor liked it. But, the bogey was having difficulty. He couldn't stop coughing.

Between coughs, Gourmand looked toward the horizon, hate twisting his face.

Trevor followed his gaze and there–on the edge of sight–over the Blackwood, the gray of the sky had thinned, and a brightness could be seen through it. A small, wispy hole had appeared in the clouds, and Trevor saw something he'd only seen in his dreams. He saw a hint of blue.

CHAPTER TWO

Epictetus

It was already dark when they finally got back to the hall. Lunch, of course, was never in question. No one would have dared to suggest stopping for a bite to Behavior Modifier Gourmand. So supper had been the hope of every stomach. They just missed it. That meant going to bed hungry, the term midnight snack being unknown in Superbia.

Standing by his perfectly-made bed, Trevor knew his prospects were very bad. He tried not to look in Meno's direction, but it seemed like his eyes were drawn to the bully unwillingly. It was as if they were made of steel and Meno was some big pimple-headed magnet. When they fell on the neckless one, they found Meno staring right back at him. The mound of meat mouthed–*You're dead!*

Trevor began shaking and his knees got weak. He thought about trying to put up a fight, but that only made him feel worse. Then he bumped his big toe on a bed leg and that sent him hopping.

Everyone seemed to know what was coming and kept their distance. Everyone except for Maggie that is. She was on a quest for adult intervention. Unfortunately because of her inexperience with the Guardians of Hall 37, she approached a particularly fussy old woman known behind the back as *Old Crusty*. Trevor couldn't hear what Maggie said but, as she spoke, she grew animated–gesturing at Trevor, then at Meno. Old Crusty simply pursed her lips and spun away without a word, leaving Maggie to sit down in a huff with a pout on her face.

The lights were being put out one by one now, and the hall was growing darker little by little. After the last one went out, the remaining Guardians prepared to leave by the light of an open doorway. Just before they did a large figure stepped in and, without a word, took a seat in a corner. The door closed, and the last bit of light was snuffed out. A whirling noise followed, and the faint blue of an electric torch came on. The face of Epictetus shone against it.

A rustle came from behind Trevor. Then that light went out too. He felt burlap against his face, and heavy bodies wrestled him to the floor. It was hard to breathe, and he struggled with all his might, but his attackers just laughed.

That's when the unmistakable voice of Meno pronounced his doom through the covers, "Time for your lesson, punk."

His education began with fists, soon advanced to kicks, then graduated to the blunt edge of a bed slat across his back. Maggie screamed.

A booming voice thundered over the others, and bodies began flying off him. Trevor fell over onto his back, and the blanket fell away from his face. Panting for air, he looked up. By a sputtering torch-light, he saw Meno dangling from what seemed to be a post. After a moment a fog cleared from his mind, and the post became a man. It was Epictetus.

He was taller than he'd looked at a distance and, what's more, a kind of electric energy seemed to sizzle from him. A deep, white scar ran from his gray-haired scalp under his eye patch to a bristling bearded jaw. A single sinewy vein-crossed arm held a pop-eyed Meno aloft like wet laundry.

With a gentleness that shouldn't have gone with that much strength, he set the human pimple down. "Child, there will be no more fighting tonight. Go back to bed," he said calmly.

When he realized the slave wasn't going to hurt him, Meno turned back on Trevor and glowered.

"Don't think this is over, punk. No slave will be there to save you the next time."

To the kids that had crowded in all around, Epictetus turned and said, "All right, children. The excitement's over. Now all of you, off to bed."

Everyone stood with mouths wide open, looking up at the enormous slave. After a moment, Epictetus said, "Shoo!" That sent them scurrying away as fast as they could go.

Maggie threw herself down on the floor next to Trevor and hugged him tightly. "Are you all right?"

He winced and let out a groan.

"Oh, I'm *sorry*," she said pulling back. "I hate those jerks. Why are they so mean?"

"Mean is easy to understand; it's kindness that has always puzzled me," said a deep voice overhead.

They looked up to see the long face of Epictetus looking down at them.

The slave bent down and placed a large, thick hand on Trevor's head. With the other, he held the electric torch up. After a moment he said, "Come. I want to take a better look at you."

They followed him to the corner where he kept his things.

There was a stool there and a writing desk with a few quill pens and an old ink bottle. Over these, there was a stand for the electric torch. The slave set the torch down and directed Trevor and Maggie to a bench.

Trevor had often wished for a better look at the torch, and now he had it. It wasn't like anything he'd ever seen in Superbia before. The crank he'd heard wound so often in the night was shaped like a twisting dragon, and the casing for the lantern resembled a mountainside. He saw now that the light came out of a hole fashioned to look like the mouth of a cave.

He was about to ask if he could hold it, but a surge of pain passed through him and he nearly fell over.

"Whoa, now," said the old man, steadying him. "I have something here that I think will help that."

The slave pulled a small, clay jar from a bag beneath the desk and removed a lid. A wonderful aroma wafted out of it.

"Take off that shirt and rub a little of this wherever you feel bruised or hurt. Use it sparingly though," he said with a firm eye. With that he stood and walked out into the darkened hall.

"Go ahead, you can trust Epictetus," Maggie said.

Trevor dipped a finger into the ointment. At first it was cool, but after rubbing it between his fingers for a moment, a warm sensation began in his hand and ran up his arm. It seemed to know where he hurt and went there and bathed his wounds in a strange, but wonderful wholesomeness. He wiggled out of his shirt as fast as he could and dipped his finger back into the jar.

"Not so much!" Maggie said. "Save some for others!"

Embarrassed, he scraped some off then starting rubbing it onto his arms and chest. Maggie helped him reach his back.

"What is this stuff?" he asked.

"It's called *basme*. Isn't it great? Smells good, too, doesn't it?"

"It's the best stuff I've ever felt." His whole body seemed to be wrapped in a warm embrace.

Just then Epictetus emerged from the dark.

"I see you've discovered the joys of basme," he said with a smile. "I think you've had enough. Basme doesn't like greedy folks."

Trevor's heart sank as he placed the jar into the slave's oversized hand.

Epictetus pulled up a stool, put a hand to his beard and stroked it thoughtfully. He looked meaningfully at Maggie.

"All the children seem to be asleep already. You'd think they'd all be abuzz with excitement."

"Everyone's tired from therapy today," she said.

"Therapy, eh? Well, that explains it. Good, no one will hear if we keep our voices low. This is as close to a private moment as we are likely to find in this part of Superbia. Well, Trevor–"

Trevor started at the sound of his name.

"Yes, I know your name," he said with a bemused expression. "Maggie's told me a lot about you. We've wondered when you and I should meet. I suppose Meno's done us a service without knowing it. That's often the way of things. Well, we have much to share, but you first. I can see you've had an eventful day!"

Maybe it was the ointment; maybe it was the cocoon of light made by the marvelous electric torch; maybe it was the manly benevolence of the old slave. Whatever the reason, Trevor felt no hesitation. He told him everything–not just the bare events of the day, but everything he really cared about–even about home–especially about home. He surprised himself with the flow of words that came out. But Epictetus didn't look surprised. He didn't even try to stop him like everybody else. Before long the dam burst and the tears were flowing.

"So, you think all your troubles are due to these dreams you keep having, eh?" Epictetus said, once Trevor had gotten a hold of himself.

"Yeah, they're driving me crazy!" Trevor said, wiping tears away with a sleeve.

"And you see a bogeyman sometimes in these dreams?"

"Uh, yeah, sometimes," Trevor said, sounding embarrassed. "But, I know bogeymen are our friends–really I do."

"They are?" said Epictetus, with an eyebrow raised over his good eye. "And how do you know that?"

"The Guardians–they always say so."

"And what do the Guardians say about your dreams?"

"They say they're bad."

"So, it sounds like you have a choice to make, Trevor. Either you must believe the Guardians or you must believe your dreams."

Trevor sat in stunned silence. To hear his problem put so simply and directly made him nervous. "But, which should I believe?" he said. "I mean, how can I know which is right?"

"Goodness knows, Trevor."

Trevor looked at the old man, blankly. "How does that help?"

"Listen closely to what I'm saying, Trevor. Goodness knows. An honest boy will know the truth when he sees it."

Trevor looked over at Maggie. She was on the edge of her seat, and there was a strange, eager look in her eyes. She nodded slightly to him. He looked back at Epictetus. The enormous slave was leaning back against the wall and looking at him with a blank expression that provided no encouragement at all. He thought about it. Which did he believe? Which was true–his dreams or what the Guardians told him?

"I think," he said slowly. "I think my dreams are true." There. He'd said it. It was what he'd always believed, but at last he'd told somebody.

Maggie was bouncing on the edge of her seat now, and a big smile had spread across her face. Epictetus leaned over and put a hand on his shoulder.

"Congratulations, Trevor."

"I knew you could do it!" Maggie said.

"What are you talking about?" Trevor said.

"That is precisely what I intend to explain, Trevor." The slave cleared his throat. "It's these dreams of yours. That is what we are talking about. They are true. It is my considered opinion that these dreams are not dreams at all. In fact, I'm almost completely sure they are memories."

"Memories?" The implications slowly dawned on Trevor. "You mean, I really do have a home and parents and all of it?"

"Now, now, slow down," Epictetus said, with a hint of a smile. "Let's not get ahead of ourselves. The universe is a mighty big place and it's always changing. You *had* a home. That much seems plain to me. There's just one more thing I must know. Tell me–this bogeyman in your dreams–how big is he?"

Trevor shuddered and closed his eyes. "Not big. Not much bigger than I am."

"Good. Now, was there anything odd about this bogeyman, some distinctive feature?"

"Uh, yeah–he had a big nose. Huge even."

"Well, that settles it," Epictetus said, looking over to Maggie again. Maggie just nodded.

"The bogey was a Snatcher," she whispered, looking a little scared.

Trevor for his part was just puzzled.

"You were stolen, child," said the slave.

"Stolen?"

"Not just you, Trevor." Epictetus looked up and swept his hand over the room. "All of these children were stolen. Trevor, Superbia is a terrible place, but it is even worse than you can imagine. I could say more, but I don't want to frighten you."

It was utterly fantastic. But, for some reason, Trevor didn't doubt it. He knew it was true. Somehow, deep down, he'd always known. His mind was racing now; he had so many questions he wanted to ask. He started with the one he most wanted an answer to, the biggest of them all.

"Epictetus, can I get home?"

The old man shifted in his seat and glanced at Maggie.

"Anything's possible, I suppose, but I'm sorry to disappoint you: it's most unlikely. First of all, there's the problem of getting

THE PURLOINED BOY

you out of Superbia. But, even if we got you out, where would you go? Do you know where your home is?"

Trevor had assumed the slave would know. "No," he admitted.

"I'm sorry, neither do I. Your home may not be in this world. I'd say it's probably not. The cravings of the bogeys exhausted our world's capacity long ago. Only a few of these children are locals. I assume you don't even know the name of the world you come from."

Trevor shook his head.

"No matter, even if you did, I have no clue how to get you back. I'm afraid records aren't kept as well as they once were."

Trevor's shoulders slumped and his eyes fell.

"Now, now, where there's life, there's hope, as they say. You saw a hole in the clouds. That's something. I'd say it's a good omen–a very good omen."

"Epictetus, how do you know so much? You're only a slave." Trevor immediately felt foolish for saying it, but the slave simply smiled.

"True, I am a slave. By law, I am the property of Superbia. But I am not only a slave," he finished with a laugh.

"Then, who are you?"

"That's a fair question. Unfortunately I can't answer it now. For the time being, the less you know the better. After all, the less you know, the less the bogeys will be able to get out of you. For although I can't see the future, I can see the past. I have seen others like you who have gained the attention of the authorities. It's always the same. Soon they will come for you, perhaps even tonight."

"Why?" Trevor said, with fear creeping into his voice. "What did I do wrong?"

"Nothing. You've done something right; that's the problem," the old man said with a grim chuckle. "Something's stirring in

23

you that threatens everything Superbia stands for. It is a germ of truth. Once caught, it spreads; first in your own mind and eventually to others. Superbia is false all the way down to the bottom, and a little truth–even from a boy–could bring it all down. That's why they must come for you."

Trevor didn't understand fully, but he had seen it–kids going missing. You wake up one morning, and someone's gone, and everyone pretends not to notice. The first he could remember was Janet. She was the best. When he was little, she'd protected him from bullies and told the best stories after lights out. Then one morning, she was gone. He'd cried himself to sleep for days after that.

Epictetus leaned forward and placed a hand on Trevor's shoulder again. "Although I can't protect you from them, I can at least arm you with a few things," he said.

He reached for the jar of basme, then he produced a small pouch with a drawstring from his bag and poured a little of the ointment into it. Then he pulled the drawstring and handed it to Trevor.

"Here, take this with you."

Trevor hefted it and turned it over. It was wonderful, like everything else the slave seemed to have. It had a little lip for pouring, and the drawstring was long enough to put around his neck. Embroidered onto the pouch was a tree of some sort.

"Basme can do more than heal. Not even I know all of its powers, and I know more than most. Use it sparingly, though. There's a rule for everything, and the rule of basme is this: it borrows from tomorrow to meet the needs of today." He paused. "How do you feel?"

Trevor thought about it and realized he didn't feel any pain. Instead, he felt warm and comfortable.

"I feel good–better than I can ever remember feeling."

"Good. But basme hasn't given you anything that you don't have a right to. It's only taken what was to be yours and given it to you now. It's taken tomorrow's healing virtue to heal you today. You've paid a price, though. Your ability to heal yourself will be weak for a while."

"How long?"

"I'm not certain. It depends on several things: how much you used, the extent of your injuries, how much healing virtue you've been given, but most importantly–how long you have to live."

"How long I have to live?"

"Naturally. If there is no tomorrow for you, then basme can't help you. Indeed, it will only speed your demise. But you're young; basme can be fatal for an old man like me."

"Now you know why you should only use a little, and only when you really need it," warned Maggie.

"Nevertheless, it is wonderful," said Epictetus. "It can do more than heal. If you're brave, it will make you braver. If you're wise, it will make you wiser. But, it can't give you anything you've no right to. It can't make cowards brave or the foolish wise. It always knows what you need, and it draws upon tomorrow's virtue to meet it. Remember though, weakness follows each use."

"Thanks," Trevor said with a gulp, as he put the drawstring around his neck and hid the pouch beneath his shirt.

"Now, I'll dare to tell you two more things. Listen closely. Soon you will be taken where you do not want to go. Someplace awful. But, take heart, not everyone who dwells there is to be feared. One will come to your aid. Just keep your ears open and listen for a small voice in an out-of-the-way place."

"What do you mean?"

"I have spoken as plainly as I can. The Behavior Modifiers have ways of uncovering secrets and you've not been tested.

How long do you think you could resist the bogeys?"

Trevor didn't know and said so.

"Good," said Epictetus, with a quick glance to Maggie. "He is honest."

"From the look of you, you're bright, too," he said looking back at Trevor. "My meaning will be plain when you need to understand it.

"Lastly," he continued, "when the time comes for you to flee, make for Olton and look for this sign." He reached once more into his bag and pulled out an enormous book. It was old and leather-bound, with gilding on the pages. Right in the center of the cover, there was a round face with tongues of fire radiating from it.

"Those who live beneath this sign will help you."

"What do you mean when you say flee?"

"I mean run. For flight is your only hope. But do not fear! Those who listen to the small voice always make it to safety."

"How will I recognize the voice?"

"You just will."

"But—"

"Enough. I have told you as much as I dare. It is late, and you will need your strength for what awaits you. Maggie, take him back to his bed."

The slave's authority was impossible to resist. Maggie stood, and Trevor got up and reluctantly followed her.

When he lay down, a sudden weariness came over him. The last thing he saw before falling asleep was Maggie and Epictetus talking quietly in the light of the electric torch.

Maggie looked toward him. "I think he's asleep already."

"He's had an eventful day and basme is strong in him. His sleep will be dreamless tonight."

Maggie kept her eye on him.

Epictetus read her mind, "Don't fret over him, my child. What will be, will be."

"I just wish there were more we could do to help him."

"I know; I wish it too. Remember, he's not the only child to save. We must remain hidden and help as many as we can. Besides, I have a good feeling about this one. I think I see something in him," the old man said, rubbing his good eye.

Maggie smiled. "Will he make it?"

"Who can say? For some reason, I believe we will meet him again. Sometimes belief is better than knowledge. Now, off to bed, Granddaughter."

"Oh, okay. Good night, Grandfather."

CHAPTER THREE

The Inspector

Cruel hands shook him awake. By the fading light of the electric torch, Trevor saw the hideous features of two bogeys leaning over him. Their eyes were just inches above his face, and their breath stank. One was familiar. It was Gourmand. The other had an enormous nose.

A Snatcher! Trevor thought.

"Look at him. He's afraid. Why, Sabnock, he doesn't think we're his friends! My feelings are hurt," Gourmand said to his partner with mock sadness. "Don't make a fuss, little morsel; it won't go well for you if you do. You're coming with us whether you like it or not."

To his own surprise, Trevor felt a twinge of courage and swung an arm. The other bogey caught it.

"Oh, ho! Feisty, is he?" said Sabnock; then he gave Trevor a vicious pinch.

Trevor opened his mouth to scream, but nothing came out.

"Tee, hee! Lost his squeak, he has!" the Snatcher quipped. "Your voice will be back in time to talk to the Inspector though. Oh ho, yes it will, yes it will! Then you'll talk and talk and talk! Hee! Hee! Hee!"

Trevor desperately looked around. Everyone was asleep. Maggie lay motionless in her bed. Even Epictetus's head was slumped upon his book. An eerie silence hung over everything, and the whole room seemed to drift as though suspended in water.

"No help from them, morsel! Hoo! Hoo! When Sabnock puts 'em out, they stays out!"

A sack was thrown over Trevor's head, then he was roughly hoisted onto a broad, hairy shoulder. An old familiar part of him spoke up at this point—*Don't fight it, it'll only make them mad!* But there was something new in him that wouldn't listen. It made him squirm and fight to get free. But a couple of whacks to the back of the skull managed to quiet the new part down and from then on he was as compliant as a bag of potatoes.

After a while, it got hard to think. He was upside down, after all, and blood was rushing to his head. By the time he was dumped onto a metal floor, he was nearly unconscious. The sound of a door banging shut woke him up.

The room, or wherever he was, was hot.

"Stoke the furnace, you piece of dung!" Gourmand shouted.

There came a sound of someone shoveling coal and then the roar of a fire and a hiss of steam. Then the floor lurched.

I'm in a steam car! Trevor realized. He'd seen the spike-wheeled behemoths on the city roads. They were only used for important business.

Over the roar of the engine, he heard voices.

"I's telling Gourmand, when I started out, we didn't have these problems. Snatchers knew their spells in those days, and a snatch never knew he'd been snatched! These new recruits just ain't cut from the same cloth."

"Bah," said another voice.

"Well, you tell me, why we's out nearly every night snatchin' what shouldn't need snatchin'? It's gettin' to be a problem. That morsel ain't ripe. He'll go down bad. Needs a couple of more years, I says and he ain't the only one. With all these morsels disappearin', there's sure to be talk."

"What difference does it make?" said the second voice. "Now

or later, it's all the same to me. I hear there are ways to prepare the younger ones that...." Trevor couldn't hear the rest of it. The engine had been getting louder and now drowned out the voice entirely.

He felt like he was in an oven. The bag made it hard to breathe, and the hot air made things worse. The combination made him sleepy again. They suddenly jerked to a stop, and Trevor felt a rush of cold air through the pores in the cloth. Hands grabbed him and slid him across the floor. The bag was opened, and he was dumped onto cold, hard ground. The dull light of morning blinded him after the darkness of the bag, and he lay in a motionless lump. He felt hands pull him to his feet, but he fell down again.

A steel-toed boot gave him a kick. "Get up. We ain't carryin' no more!" said Sabnock.

He stood unsteadily and looked up. He groaned inwardly when he saw they were at the bottom of a broad, seemingly endless set of stairs.

"Let's go, morsel. The Inspector is waiting," said Gourmand.

✼

It was another dingy day in Superbia. It fit Trevor's mood–he felt just as dingy. As they climbed the seemingly numberless steps, white-robed Guardians moved along with them, going up and down. Trevor attempted vainly with his eyes to catch someone's attention, anyone human.

"Tee, hee. Look at 'im; he thinks someone 'ill help 'im!" said Sabnock. "Well, forget about it, morsel! They like bogeys here–we're their friends. Hee, hee."

"Shut up! You talk too much," barked Gourmand.

"Oh, bother. What's he gonna say? And if I don't miss my guess, the good Inspector ain't gonna send 'im back. Tee, hee, hee!"

Finally they reached the top, and they entered the Great Hall of the Guardians.

It wasn't like anything Trevor had ever seen, and it certainly bore no resemblance to his old hall. It sat on a hill that looked as though its top had been cut off with a gigantic meat cleaver. Everywhere he looked, there were tall, white buildings with fluted pillars reaching to the sky. People were scurrying everywhere in little cliques or moving in endless lines.

As they went along, Trevor saw a sign over one entrance that read, DIVISION OF PUBLIC WORKS FOR THE MAINTENANCE OF SEWAGE EQUIPMENT, and his mind turned longingly to Guardian Medea. For the first time in his life, he wished he were in class. The building seemed important; a flurry of Guardians with clipboards bustled in and out of its doors. Lots of other buildings with equally lengthy names lined the way. Every person who passed them had a look of grim efficiency.

All too soon they came to a huge set of doors with a sign that read: OFFICE OF THE INSPECTOR OF INCORRIGIBLE CHILDREN. Sabnock got excited.

In they went and entered a voluminous waiting room filled with metal folding chairs. Children dotted the place. Most of them reminded Trevor of Meno–lumps of muscle with hard eyes. But some were the sort Trevor thought he might like to know. These looked up at him with the same wide-eyed fear he felt at the moment. Off in a corner stood a small congregation of bogeymen. Every so often one of them pointed at a child. That was usually followed by a burst of laughter.

Gourmand and Sabnock led Trevor to a prim woman at a desk beside a set of double doors.

"Take a number," she said, without looking up.

Gourmand handed her a paper and took a number from a dispenser. "1425," he said.

She wrote the number down on the paper. "Have a seat. We're on 1363."

Gourmand grunted, and Sabnock cursed beneath his breath.

Trevor found a chair, and his escorts joined the other bogeys. After that, time seemed to creep along. He was hungry, and that made things worse. To pass the time, he resorted to counting the chairs; then, the spots on the wall, and finally, the broken tiles in the dirty floor.

One by one, children were called by number into the office behind the double doors. When they came out again, the results were not encouraging. The nasty-looking kids came out with big smiles, while the ones Trevor thought he would like to know looked just awful.

Finally, his number was called. He got up and made his way slowly to the doors.

"Come on, boy. I haven't got all day," the prim woman snipped.

She opened the door just enough for him to go through, and then Trevor felt a hand at the base of his back, and he shot into the room. The door shut with a snap.

He found himself in a big space with a ceiling so high it was lost in the shadows overhead. Opposite him sat a dwarfish man in spectacles behind a desk that was as big as the man was small. Both the man and the desk were in front of a window that ran the length of the wall behind them. Beyond that, the smokestacks of Superbia receded into the distance.

"Have a seat, my child," he said, in a nasal voice.

Taking a chair, Trevor noticed a few things fast. First, the man's head barely made it over the edge of the desk. Second, his spectacles magnified his eyes and gave his face a vaguely bug-like appearance. And third, his desk had only two things on it–a piece of paper and a large green-eyed fly.

"Hmmm, 1425," he said, looking at the paper. "Do you know

why you are here?"

Trevor had his faults, but unfortunately for him at that moment, dishonesty wasn't one of them. "I'm here because I want to go home," he said, sounding braver than he felt. His voice was back, just like Sabnock said it would be.

"Yes, I see that here on the report from Behavior Modifier Gourmand," the Inspector said, with a hint of distaste. "1425, I can only assume that someone with strange, outmoded beliefs has put this idea into your head. Now, just name that someone and I will sign the release for you to go back to your hall."

"Oh no, sir, no one told me about home. I dreamed about it."

The Inspector glanced up from the paper for the first time. Oddly, he didn't look directly at Trevor, but just above his head. It was a little unnerving. That's when the fly began to buzz.

"Dreamed it, did you?" he said slowly. "Well, one must not believe in dreams. Dreams can get one into a lot of trouble."

The fly flew around the little man's head. Most people would have found this terribly distracting; Trevor did, but it didn't seem to bother the Inspector.

"1425, I want to sign the release to return you to your hall, but you are making it difficult for me. If you will just admit this dream of yours is nonsense, everything can go back to normal." The corners of the Inspector's mouth rose in a weak attempt at a sympathetic smile.

"But, it's not a dream," Trevor said. "I really do have a home, and *parents*–I think–and–" he didn't get to finish.

"Do not use that *obscenity* in my presence," the Inspector said, through gritted teeth. The veneer of sympathy had vanished. His face had gone red, and his right eye began to twitch. The fly had landed on his forehead and was scurrying around. "1425," he said, laboring to regain his composure. The fly had moved to his lower lip. "It is very common for children to have *imaginary* friends. But, we really *must* grow out of them."

"But, my parents–"

"Enough," the Inspector said, coldly.

The fly flew across the desk and bit Trevor on the hand.

"Ow!"

For the first time, the Inspector looked right into Trevor's eyes. He wished he hadn't. There was such malice in them, a cold, dull spot formed in Trevor's stomach. A grin spread across the man's face, exposing a set of alarmingly large, white teeth.

"He's a hungry little fellow, isn't he?" said the Inspector.

"Yes, but why did he bite me?" Trevor asked, rubbing his hand. There was blood.

"My child, everyone must eat."

"But, I wasn't made to be eaten by flies."

"1425, how could you possibly know that?"

With that, the Inspector began to rise from behind his desk. Up, up he rose. He didn't stop where he should have, instead he kept going up. Trevor recoiled and felt the need to scream when he saw that the Inspector's tiny torso was perched on eight, long spider legs.

The legs bent in the middle and lowered the Inspector enough to allow him to open a drawer in his desk. Out came a large rubber stamp and an ink pad.

"You had your chance, 1425. I'm sorry to say there is no hope for you," he said, sounding delighted.

Out from behind the desk he capered with lightning quickness. Before Trevor could duck, he had a handful of his hair. He pulled Trevor's head back and struck his forehead with the stamp until it hurt. Finally, Trevor managed a scream.

When the stamp was pulled away, it left a red streak of letters behind that read: INCORRIGIBLE.

"Secretary!"

The door flew open, and the formerly irritable receptionist looked in with a smile.

"Please return this child to his Behavior Modifiers for processing."

Unsteadily, Trevor reentered the waiting room. A cheer rose from the nearby bogeymen. Gourmand and Sabnock were congratulated with back slaps and loud guffaws. For their part, his escorts walked briskly up to him and began to blindfold him and tie his hands.

"Look, Gourmand. He's bleeding!" Sabnock said trying to hold back a giggle.

"I thought I smelled something good," Gourmand said. "Come on, let's get him out of here before the others notice."

"What did I do?" Trevor asked, pitifully.

"None of your lip!" said Sabnock, with a slap across the back of his head.

Then began a walk Trevor thought would never end. He couldn't see a thing, and he was pulled and jerked by a rope. He needed to stop, to rest. He was dizzy from the rough treatment, and he hadn't eaten since breakfast the day before.

Finally, they came to a halt. Gourmand barked something Trevor didn't understand, and there was a sound that he guessed to be hinges turning under a great weight. They stepped into what seemed like a small room by the closeness of the sounds. Then, with a jerk, the floor started to move and slowly to turn. This was accompanied by the sound of grinding metal and a sinking sensation. The turning and sinking gave Trevor the impression that he was on top of a giant screw. Mr. Queasy came back with a vengeance. He was glad his stomach was empty.

Now there were other sensations–the echo of an opening widening beneath him, and a hot, wet blast of steam against his legs and up his body.

With a final blast, the spinning stopped, and Trevor nearly fell over.

They were now in what sounded like a large space, with voices shouting all around.

A deep voice shouted above the din, "More larder for the Pantry, eh?"

"Right," came Sabnock's voice in response.

"Track 93, mates. Be quick, she's 'bout to roll out!"

Trevor was pulled by his rope into a stumbling run.

"Last call for boarding!" a voice cried ahead.

The bogeys picked up the pace, practically dragging him along. He bumped into cursing bodies and tripped over things on the ground. Each time, he was pulled mercilessly to his feet. At last, a blast of steam enveloped him, and the rope went taut. Without warning, he was airborne, feeling as though his arms would come out of their sockets. Two sets of hands grabbed him and pulled him onto a hard, flat, rumbling surface.

"In you come, morsel," said Sabnock. "Now, off with that blindfold. I'm tired of draggin' you 'bout."

As soon as it was off, Trevor wanted it back. By a smoky light, he saw that he was now in the rattling room of a railway car simply packed with bogeymen. Jostling oil lamps suspended from the ceiling cast their faces in a horrid yellow light.

Behind them, glassless windows revealed a dark subterranean world. It was a cavern of incredible proportions reaching into the distance. Above, a black, murky ceiling curled with smoke, and below stretched a vast canyon of sheer rock. At the bottom of it wound a black river, and over it arched numerous rickety bridges on which other trains chugged this way and that. Crude, lopsided homes with lights burning red in their windows teetered precariously on rocky outcroppings and cliffside hollows. And on the plateaus that dotted the landscape, bonfires burned, ringed by little, dark figures dancing madly, casting long shadows.

But, amid the terrors, yet there were wonders. Great spikes hung from the roof, and others grew from the floor like teeth in a huge mouth. Some came together to form pillars, threaded by veins of silver and gold, and crusted with bright stones that flashed in the fire light.

Trevor stared blankly, mouth hung open.

"Impressed, morsel? Welcome to the Sewage Works of Superbia," Sabnock said, laughing.

CHAPTER FOUR

The Pantry

Trevor wasn't the only one who was hungry.

"Hmmm, needs to be fattened up a bit," Sabnock said to himself, as he poked Trevor's middle. Trevor jerked back and bumped into a nearly toothless and very wrinkled old bogey woman sitting right behind him.

"A fine, tender-looking morsel you have there, my lads," she said, with a gummy grin. "Mind if I give him a pinch to see if he feels as good as he looks?"

"Hands off. We're taking this one to the Pantry. The Royal Court gets the first choice of all the fresh meat," said Gourmand.

"And a leg for each of you, I might add! It's not fair that all you high and mighty ones get all the best grub!" she hissed. But, then, with sugary sweetness, she changed her tune, "Come now, lads. I'm just an old woman, worn out in the service of his Majesty; surely that's something? I've not had fresh boy for it seems like ages. I'm a good cook, too, when I have something to cook. I know how to feed hungry fellows like you. Why, before his accident, my ol' husband was the fattest bogey in the Works!" Lowering her voice, she added, "Let's have this one between us, eh? You can have nearly the whole boy; all I need is one little arm to gnaw on, what do you say?"

Trevor drew his knees to his chest and looked anxiously back and forth between his captors. Sabnock seemed to be considering it, but it was hard to know what Gourmand was thinking. Some nearby bogeys were eavesdropping, and they didn't look too pleased with the course of the conversation. Trevor overheard someone mumbling about "corruption in high places." As the hag went on about her culinary abilities and all the wonderful ways to prepare boy, a particularly nasty looking bogey had enough. A knife glinted as it came out of a sheath.

Gourmand finally spoke, with one eye on the knife-wielding bogey, "Keep your drool in your mouth, crone. Lucian will have our tongues if we take this little delicacy for ourselves. He doesn't look kindly on poachers."

At the mention of *Lucian*, every face went rigid. Everyone awkwardly turned away and, for the rest of the trip, they all worked very hard pretending Trevor wasn't there.

✻

"Next stop, the Pantry!" a bogey in a conductor's cap cried from the front of the car.

The Pantry wasn't anything like a normal pantry most folks know about. It wasn't a little room, like is usual with pantries; it wasn't even a building. Instead it was a big, gaping hole in the side of a cliff. The hole was so big, ten railway cars like the one Trevor was on could have passed though at once. Across it, a thick, iron wall of immense height stretched from one side to the other. The architect must have been a person of perverse humor, for the wall had been made to resemble a great, ugly face with a mouth for a door. Above that was a nose with a watchman in each nostril. Higher still, two eyes stared ravenously downward beneath a furrowed brow. And last of all–thankfully–above all that, two long horns curved outward and upward.

It was before this fearsome visage that Gourmand, Sabnock and Trevor exited from the train and stepped out onto an open space known affectionately by the locals as "The Plate."

After the train had pulled away, a droning sound enveloped them.

Trevor noticed that the whole surface of the wall was moving and flickering. Numberless tiny specks shifted about and made what looked like a gossamer curtain. Something flew by his ear, and he heard a buzz. With a stab of horror, he recognized the specks were flies—large, vicious green-eyed ones like the one that bit him in the Inspector's office.

A wad of them peeled away from the wall and swarmed to meet the new arrivals. Trevor tried to shield his face, but the bogeys just laughed.

"Patience, lovelies, wait for the scraps," Sabnock said, with genuine affection.

The three of them walked through the mouth of the Pantry up to a small desk where a grotesquely fat bogeyman sat, picking his teeth with a fork.

"Saucy, you ol' flea bag, how are you?" said Sabnock.

"No, really, I couldn't eat another bite!" the fat bogey quipped.

"Good, he ain't for you anyway. He's here for processing," said the Snatcher, suspiciously.

"Fine. Can't you take a joke, you little sneak? But, truly, I am full!" Saucy said, pushing himself back from his desk. "Too bad you fellows missed the fun last night. The cook was in his best form, and the eating was grand! Ah, the holidays are my favorite time of year. But I know you boys on the surface missed out on the festivities. I don't envy you," he said, shaking his heavy jowls. "I did once, you know, being around all that lovely food. But what's the use of looking, and smelling–" he said, with an eye toward Sabnock–"but not eating? I admire your self control. We owe you a lot down here. If not for you fellows, we'd all go hungry. Anyway, everyone's stuffed. We won't need fresh boy for at least a week. It's a good thing you're here though. We need to replenish the Pantry. It's nearly empty. Just a few ol' stale, wrinkly women down in the corners. Anyway, let's have a look at him."

The bogey extended a flabby arm. Trevor shrunk back, but Sabnock shoved him forward. Two disgusting, dirty-nailed hands grabbed him and pulled him in. Saucy began to probe Trevor's middle, arms, and legs. He prodded, pinched, and poked. It hurt, but Trevor did his best not to let on.

"Hmmm, not quite ripe, is he? We're getting a lot of that lately. His Majesty hisself is looking into it, I hear."

"We don't pick-em; we just snatch-em!" said Sabnock, defensively.

"Don't get worked up about it," Saucy said, as he stamped something on Trevor's hand. "I'm just telling you what I've heard. Now, here's your claim tickets. Don't lose 'em—you won't get your portions without 'em. Take the morsel to my man over there, and he'll store him for you."

Trevor's rope was handed to a bent over, half-blind old bogey with a wispy beard. He mumbled something that sounded like, "Follow me, me Lords." Since bogeys are naturally suspicious of one another, that's just what Sabnock and Gourmand did.

After many twists and turns down shadowy, torch-lit passages and tunnels, Trevor was finally thrown into a lightless and windowless stone chamber. A metal door was slammed shut behind him.

Sabnock's voice came from outside, "Pleasant dreams, morsel. Until we meet again! Tee hee! Hee tee!"

In the total darkness, Trevor groped forward until he found a corner. With his back to it, he slid slowly down until his bottom found the floor. There he sat for a while, in shock at first, feeling numb. The gravity of his predicament came crashing down on him, and he felt fear and utter terror like he'd never known before. He wished he were any place else, even with Meno. Tears welled up in his eyes, and he began to shake uncontrollably.

After what seemed like hours, a small light appeared at the foot of the door. It was blindingly bright after the total darkness. It was a little door within the door. A plate slid into the room, along with a metal cup. Then, the light blinked out.

"Here's your food, little morsel," came a craggy, muffled voice through the door. "Clean your plate now, you mustn't go hungry!"

"Just trying to fatten me up," Trevor mumbled to himself, between heaving sniffles.

He was right, of course, but he'd not eaten since the previous morning and fattening up or no, he still needed some nourishment. His stomach grumbled.

The stuff actually smelled good. He felt his way over to it in the dark, and probed the contents of the plate. It wasn't bogey food, thankfully, but real, human food. There were beans, some biscuit and a little piece of chicken. He ate the vegetables and biscuit. He wasn't in the mood for meat at the moment, for understandable reasons. After drinking the surprisingly tasty tea he found in the cup he felt a little better, and he even managed to stop crying.

The effects of basme were completely gone now. The hurts from his pounding by Meno were gone, too, but he'd gotten a whole new set during his abduction and his blind run through the train depot. His whole body seemed to have become one throbbing sore.

He reached for the pouch under his shirt. A wonderfully fresh smell of something natural and wholesome filled the room when he opened it. Instantly, his mood lightened. Then, he realized someone outside might notice. He listened intently but heard nothing.

Epictetus's warning came back to him. *Use it sparingly, and only in great need,* he'd said. That seemed like ages ago. The throbbing made it difficult to think. "If Epictetus didn't give it to me for a time like this, then what did he give it to me for?" Trevor said to himself.

So, he reached his finger in and took a small dab of the stuff. Maggie would be pleased at his moderation, he thought. As he rubbed the ointment between his fingers, he felt the warm sensation of the night before, but it was noticeably weaker. He wondered why.

It must be that I'm using it too soon. But, what else can I do?

Then a terrifying idea occurred to him, *Since this stuff takes from tomorrow to care for today, maybe I'm running out of tomorrows! Maybe I'm going to be lunch for fat ol' Saucy or some other bogeyman!*

He panicked.

It's not good to make an important decision when you're in a panic–but no one was there to tell him so. That's why he reached into the pouch and took a great gob of the stuff, far more than he should.

A reassuring surge of warmth coursed through him. It went up his arm and rose to his head. He rubbed the ointment on his bruises and immediately felt a change. The pained ceased and the throbbing stopped. He felt warm, relaxed, and strangely content for a boy condemned to be eaten by bogeymen. He felt so good in fact, he curled up in his corner and fell asleep.

CHAPTER FIVE

Zephyr

Trevor felt a wet, little tickle on his forehead. It went on for a while, but once he crossed the line that separates dull half-sleep from dim half-waking, he sat up with a jolt. Something flitted through the air with a little, "Yow!"

He felt his forehead; it was moist. It didn't feel like perspiration, though.

Then he thought he saw something, something very small, yet very distinct. There, sitting on its haunches and looking up at him, was the tiny form of a mouse.

It was small, even by mouse standards, and had two oversized intelligent eyes. The really unusual thing about it was that it glowed. And that wasn't the only unusual thing.

"Don't be afraid," it said.

It talked.

Trevor blinked and rubbed his eyes, but the mouse didn't go away. Instead, it moved quietly around his plate, sniffing at the remains of his food, taking a nibble here and there, and passing a few droppings.

"Hey, that's mine," Trevor said.

"Don't worry, I won't eat it all," the mouse said, in a cultured accent. It turned its nose up at the meat and started in on a crumb. "Besides," he continued, with a mouth full of biscuit, "you've eaten already and I need so little you'll hardly notice I've eaten anything at all."

"Who are you?"

"Ooo, good. You ask questions," he said, sounding pleased. "Hasn't Epictetus told you about me?"

"No."

"Didn't he tell you to listen for *a small voice in an out-of-the-way place?*"

Trevor nodded.

"Well, here I am—I'd say my voice is on the small side, and this is about as out-of-the-way as it gets. My name is Zephyr. And yours is Trevor, I believe, or would you rather I called you *Incorrigible?*" He nibbled on a bean.

"Uh, Trevor, please."

"Good. Incorrigible isn't a good name for a boy. That's why I licked your forehead clean. I got rid of that horrid remark the Inspector stamped up there. Besides, it would never do where I'm taking you."

"Uh, taking me?"

"Hmmm, Epictetus said you were intelligent, but I'm beginning to wonder. Yes, taking you. I've come to rescue you. Or would you rather I leave you here to be eaten?"

"Uh, how can you do that? You're a mouse!"

"Uh, uh, uh—my, are we not articulate?" Zephyr said, with an eyebrow raised. "Look at me. Do I look like an ordinary mouse?"

"No. You're so small, though."

The mouse sighed heavily. "That's what they all say," he said with disgust. "I suppose it can't be helped. You'll just have to believe me; what else can you do? There's a saying I heard once—*more than meets the eye.* Very fitting—that's me—more than meets the eye."

He slipped off the plate and came up to Trevor, wrinkling his nose. "Ooo, you smell like basme. You seem to have smeared it all over you. Too bad; those Snatchers have good noses. I'm surprised one of them hasn't come down to investigate. Hmmm," he said, twirling his whiskers and making them curl up at one end.

"I didn't know what else to do; I hurt so much."

"Still, it is regrettable, and if I don't miss my guess, you've had far more than you should."

Trevor felt embarrassed. Deep down, he knew he could have gotten by with less.

"Come, come, let's deal with the problem and not fuss over it. That smell has got to go." With that, he puckered up and began to blow. A fresh breeze passed over Trevor's body and, in a moment, the smell of the ointment had completely disappeared.

When the mouse was done, he sniffed and said, "Humph, that's better. Now, by my reckoning, this time tomorrow you'll be too weak to move. In the meantime, you'll feel remarkably vigorous. Now is the time for action." He then stood up on his hind legs and placed his front paws behind his back, as though he were about to give a lecture, and said, "But before we go, you must ask your questions. Since we're in a hurry, I'll only answer three of them. But, I warn you, I'll only give you answers you already know."

"Questions, what questions? And why should I ask them if I already know the answers?"

"Good. That's two out of three, and they're excellent questions."

"Hey, I didn't mean those to be my questions, I think." Trevor said scratching his head.

Ignoring him, the mouse went on, "To your first question—*What questions?* Good questions. You shouldn't expect good answers if you don't ask good questions! Now, to your second excellent question—*Why should you ask them if you already know the answers?* Because, my boy, asking helps you remember the answers! Here's a bonus. My, I'm feeling generous today! *Liking* the answers takes work. It's an acquired taste. That's why so few people ask *good* questions. They don't like the answers they already know."

Trevor didn't know what any of that had to do with him. What he did know is that he did have a question he desperately wanted an answer for. It was the only thing on his mind, so he asked it.

"Okay, here's a question even Epictetus couldn't answer. "Can...can I get home?"

"Bingo! Best question yet!" exclaimed the mouse. "It's the greatest question of them all. I'm proud of you, my boy. Since you asked *the* question, I'll give you more answers than you expected or wanted." The mouse sat down on the edge of the plate and let his feet dangle. "To get home you must first know where you are. One should never expect to find home until he first finds himself. Now, it's my turn to ask you a question. Trevor, do you know *where* you are?"

Trevor thought about it. He knew he was someplace called, *the Pantry*. He thought it was beneath Superbia, but where was that? The more he turned the matter over in his head, the less sure he was of the answer.

The mouse waited patiently.

Finally, Trevor said, "I don't know."

"Excellent!" laughed the mouse, clapping his front paws. "That's right! You're lost. I was afraid you were going to say something stupid like, *I'm in the Pantry*. Well, now that *that* is settled, we can start your journey home. I know the way. If you follow me, I'll take you there."

Trevor fell to his hands and knees and drew close to the tiny mouse.

"Really? You can do that?" he said.

"Certainly, my boy; I'd be delighted. Leading children home

is my favorite thing to do. But," the mouse added, with a warning finger, "you mustn't expect to get home today, or even tomorrow. The journey home is long–longer than you can possibly imagine."

Trevor felt the slightest twinge of disappointment. "How far is it?"

"If I told you, you couldn't fathom the distance. But, you can reach it–yes, you will reach it, *someday*–if you persevere." Zephyr cleared his throat. "Now, every journey starts the same way. It begins with beginning." He put the back of one paw to his mouth and said confidentially, "You'd be amazed at the number of children who want to get home, but never begin." Then, with a nod implying that Trevor wasn't *that* sort of child, he continued, "To begin with, we need to get you out of here."

"How?"

"Weren't you listening? If you follow me, I'll lead you to safety." The mouse slipped from the edge of the plate. "Just keep your eyes on me and go where I go." He went to the door and said, "Open it, Trevor."

"What? It's locked, isn't it?"

"Not the big door, silly–the little one your food came through."

"What good will that do?"

"It will let me out, of course."

"What about me?"

"You'll follow me, naturally."

"But, that's impossible!"

Zephyr heaved a noisy sigh.

"Yes, it's impossible for a boy to pass through that door. But, it is possible for a mouse. And if you follow me, you can do whatever I can do. Now, open the door."

Trevor blinked at the mouse.

"Trevor, I'm the only way out. Doubt that and you're a bogeyman's breakfast."

Trevor opened the door.

"Now, don't think of anything else but following me, and then just do it. Don't think about the door. Don't think about yourself. Just think about me." The mouse scurried through the opening, then turned and looked back. For his part, Trevor was on his hands and knees looking out at him. And there they were–a mouse and a boy, a boy and a mouse–just looking at each other.

"I'm waaaiiting–" sing-songed the mouse.

Trevor visualized himself crawling forward and bumping his head. He didn't move.

"Follow me," Zephyr said, with a voice that seemed to push every other thought out of his mind.

Trevor swallowed hard, blinked twice, and then crept forward. As he did, the opening seemed to grow until it was out of view. To his amazement, he didn't bump his head. He didn't feel anything at all. After crawling a few feet he was on the other side of the door, looking back in wonder at the little opening. It wasn't any bigger, and he certainly wasn't any smaller, but he was outside!

"Good job, my boy! You'd be surprised at the number of children who take their eyes off me and end up bumping their heads!"

Trevor wasn't surprised at all.

"From here on, just keep your eyes on me. Don't look left or right. If you do what I say, you'll be as small and as quiet as a mouse. If you don't, you'll just be yourself."

So, off they went. Trevor felt just as big and clumsy as ever; but it didn't matter at first, because his cell was in a remote part of the Pantry, and the place was nearly empty. Zephyr moved stealthily, keeping to one side, and stopping only to peer around corners. It looked as though he knew his way around. When they came to a corner where their passage intersected a much larger one, the mouse turned to Trevor.

"Here's your first test. There are a couple of bogeys in the next tunnel. They're busy talking–that's good for you. I can get past them quite easily and, if you keep your eyes on me, so can you. But, if you don't, you'll just be a boy sneaking down a hall, and any fool would be able to see that."

"This is crazy–" Trevor whispered.

It was too late. The mouse had already slipped around the corner.

Something interesting was happening to Trevor. Just a couple of days ago, he would have been frozen stiff with fear and just sat there until someone found him. But, something new was stirring in him. He just took a long, deep breath and stepped around the corner.

He went into a much larger space, better lit too–with torches lining the walls. Up to this point, Zephyr's glow had been the only light. The mouse was moving quietly from one shadow to the next. Up ahead, voices were rumbling. He felt an urge to look up. It took every ounce of willpower he had to keep his eyes on the mouse. As they got closer, he heard the scrapes of wooden chairs on stone and the sound of mugs rapping on a table, along with some loud, slurpy drinking, and grunts of approval. He felt a sudden urge to turn and run away. Still, he kept going. They were very close now; he could feel the bogeys there, with their sweaty bodies, like a kind of wet heaviness to his right.

Why don't they see me? he wondered.

One of them gave a long, rattling belch, followed by a laugh that sounded like a bark.

"Zimri," another protested, which made the first laugh even harder.

"Be serious. Is the rumor true?"

"Course it is," said Zimri, composing himself. "They's roustin' third division."

Abruptly Zephyr stopped. His little ears twitched. Apparently, what had been said interested him.

Trevor nearly stepped on him. *Come on! What are you waiting for?!* a voice screamed in Trevor's skull.

"When's it supposed to happen?" asked the first bogey.

"Any time," continued Zimri. "All very secret-like. Spies everywhere, they says."

"Ah, don't believe that spy talk," said the other. "I thinks the higher-ups is just makin' busy work."

Perspiration began to form on Trevor's forehead, and his heart pounded so loudly he wondered if the bogeys might hear it. The sweat started to trickle down his nose and collect at the tip. One big globule formed quickly and fell with a tiny plunk on the floor.

Oh, please, please, get going, he repeated over and over in his head, at the mouse.

"Say, what's Arsenal's chances in tomorrow's match? I've got a five spot riding on 'em," said Zimri.

"A five spot? That's all?"

Zephyr finally lost interest and started moving again.

Oh, thank you, thank you.

The mouse moved breezily, almost carelessly, reentering the shadows on the other side of the bogeys. He glowed as warmly as ever, and Trevor lumbered behind him as awkwardly as ever. The bogeys continued arguing about matches and bets and where the best grog could be found, and still didn't see them. They had gotten well past the guards and would have gotten around the next corner unnoticed if something regrettable had not happened.

A loud gong rang.

"The alarm!" said Zimri.

Chairs scraped on stone.

"There's been an escape!"

The gong rang again.

"Down this way!"

Again it rang.

Zephyr didn't pause. He didn't run or even look back. He just kept on his steady pace. Trevor was mighty tempted to look though. He knew the alarm was for him.

Finally, from some place deep to the rear, a voice yelled out, "There's a mouse in the Pantry! A spy! A thief! A mouse! A mouse!"

It was just too much. Trevor thought they'd been spotted. It wasn't so–the guard had simply noticed Zephyr's droppings in Trevor's cell. (They'd had problems with Zephyr before.) So that was the reason Trevor took his eyes off of the mouse and looked back.

At first, he saw nothing but a table and two empty chairs. Then, some bogeys emerged from an opening farther down.

"There!" one of them yelled, pointing at him.

With an icy chill of dismay, Trevor looked back at Zephyr. The mouse was looking up at him with his fists on his hips and a cross expression on his face.

"Put me in your ear!" Zephyr shouted.

There was no time to ask why or think about what it meant; he just did it.

The mouse fit perfectly. With his paws, he grabbed hold and leaned back like an engineer on a train.

"Run!" he yelled.

Trevor sprang forward and was off running as fast as he could.

"Too bad you took your eyes off me. Now we have to get out the hard way. Turn right here!"

Something unusual was happening. Trevor felt like something was pushing him. Soon he was moving faster than he had ever run before–much faster. The walls whizzed by. He noticed a blowing sound coming from his ear.

"What are you doing?" he shouted.

"I'm blowing you along," Zephyr said, between breaths.

Trevor looked back and saw the bogeys way behind him. But, as soon as he did he started slowing down.

"No looking back! Keep your eyes ahead and run!"

A spike of fear shot through him, and Trevor leapt forward again. His speed returned. Keeping his feet under him became the main problem. He was going too fast for his legs to keep up. He stumbled and nearly fell.

"Stop trying to help yourself! Let me do the work," said the mouse. "Just go through the motions!"

He tried barely letting his tippy-toes graze the ground. To his astonishment, it worked! In fact, he started going even faster! The wind rushed through his hair, and he felt like he was flying!

In spite of the desperate circumstances, as strange as it sounds, he couldn't help wondering why he needed to do anything if Zephyr was doing all the work. *Why run at all? Why not just let yourself be carried along?* So–wonder of wonders–he stopped trying. Immediately, he lost speed and with a herk and a jerk, he stumbled and fell to his hands and knees until he slid to a stop.

"Ow!"

"What did you do that for?" said the mouse, who'd managed to hang on.

"Why do I have to run if you're doing all the work?"

A pack of bogeys shot out of a passage. "There he is!"

"This is no time for a lesson, boy!" Zephyr said. "Get up and run!"

Trevor staggered to his feet and began limping and hobbling as best he could. Then he heard the sound of Zephyr blowing, and soon he was the fastest limping, hobbling boy who had ever lived.

They turned this way and that, up passages and down others. The alarm had raised the prison, and new bogeys joined the chase with shouts and curses. Basme was still coursing through him, and miraculously, Trevor's injuries mended on the fly. His bruises were soon gone and so was his limping. He was running faster than ever.

Suddenly, out of the corner of his eye, he saw something shoot at him. It grabbed at his foot, and he fell again.

Zephyr flew from his ear this time. Trevor caught a glimpse of his glow, arching through the air. He rolled to a stop. Everything went dark without the mouse.

Two vise-like hands grabbed his ankles, then an all-too-familiar voice carried up to him through the blackness.

"Oh no you don't, morsel! Tee, hee! You're *mine*, now–*all* mine. No fancy pants Royal court, no snooty Gourmand either."

"Sabnock!" Trevor blurted out.

The bogey's hands were working their way up his body–feeling for Trevor's neck.

"Hoo! Hoo! Remember me, do you? Well, ain't that nice. I remember you too, morsel. In fact, I was comin' to pay you a little visit. Imagine my disappointment when you wasn't where I put you! Thought ol' Saucy had taken you for hisself, I did! But, I never forgets the smell of dinner, oh no! *Trust your nose*, that's what my mammy taught me. I knew you was about here, somewhere." In the dark, he tapped his nose appreciatively. "Ol' faithful is what helped me find you, it did."

Trevor struggled and squirmed, but the bogey was unbelievably strong.

"Now, now, hold still. I's feelin' the need of a little afternoon snack, I is."

The bogey was on Trevor's chest now. His hands had found his neck and were beginning to squeeze.

"Help!" Trevor managed to squawk.

A light flashed, illuminating the hideous face of the bogey. Then, a sudden wind blew him off and sent him crashing into a wall, head first.

A voice came from the direction of the light.

"Are you all right, my boy?"

To one side, Sabnock lay still on the floor. On the other side was a tiny glowing mouse.

Trevor sat up, holding his neck.

"I'm okay," he croaked.

The sounds of their pursuers echoed down to them.

"Let's get going," Zephyr said.

Trevor put the mouse back in his ear. The pursuit clamored into view just as he did. With a spur of fear, Trevor ran yet again.

"Turn here!" Zephyr commanded, when they came to a large passage.

As they turned the corner, Trevor saw an opening with several bogeys building a hasty barrier across it.

"Keep running! When you get to the bogeys, jump!" shouted the mouse.

Trevor didn't know what to say. He didn't know what to think. He couldn't jump that high–just like he couldn't run this fast. There was no time to question–so, he just did it.

Up he went, sailing over the astonished bogeys.

As he did, he noticed something. Perhaps it would be more apt to say he noticed the absence of something: there was nothing on the other side. He was flying over a narrow road and into a great chasm.

Unexpectedly, his feelings changed from the thrill of an escape to the terror of a fall.

"Don't be afraid!" yelled the mouse, as they sailed into the darkness.

CHAPTER SIX

Down the River

Trevor fell feet-first into a black void opening to swallow him.

Looking up, he saw bogeymen gathering on a ledge, waving spears, and shouting down.

Zephyr was blowing hard. Just a minute ago, it had sped them up; now it was slowing them down. They were falling as slowly as a leaf on the wind.

"What's going to happen to us?" Trevor said, mind racing.

There was no answer. In a flash, he realized you can't talk and blow at the same time. With that thought, he was happy to wait. But wait for what?

The wait ended with a light splash into dark water.

Trevor didn't know how to swim—since swimming is a lot of fun and very useful—the Guardians never thought to teach it. As he sank, a cold wave of fear surged up from his gut.

Zephyr gave a bubbly shout into his ear. "Stand up!"

He hadn't thought of that. Down went his feet and up came his head—just enough to bring his chin above the surface. Fortunately, the water was shallow. Unfortunately, it smelled just awful.

"Welcome to the Sewers," Zephyr said. "Never fear, nothing unclean can harm you so long as I'm here. Now, give me your hand."

Trevor reached up to his ear, and the mouse stepped onto it.

"Let's have a look at you."

He held the mouse in front of his face.

"Hmmm, you don't look too much the worse for wear, although you do need a bath. I think I'll risk a little more light so we can have a look around."

What had been a weak glow grew in intensity until the mouse shone with the radiance of a candle flame.

Something slithered away along the surface of the water. Flotsam and jetsam bobbed all around, and Trevor clenched his mouth shut and hoped he hadn't swallowed anything when he was underwater.

"What do we do now?"

"We swim out of here, naturally. What else?" Zephyr answered.

"But I can't swim."

"Don't worry; the water stays shallow. It will be more like walking than swimming. Where we're going isn't far. Besides, we'll be going with the current. It should only take a few hours."

"I'm cold," Trevor said, shivering.

"Not for long. A few minutes of swimming will warm you right up. Here, put me on your head so you can use both arms."

The mouse was right; nothing gets the blood moving like swimming, even if it is more like walking. The bottom was slimy though, and uneven, and Trevor had a hard time keeping his head up at first. Dank water was up his nose and dripping from his hair before he learned (with Zephyr's encouragement) to support himself by stroking the water with his arms, rather than putting all his weight on his feet.

Somehow, Zephyr managed to stay dry all the while.

If it hadn't been for the dark, stinky conditions it would have been a pleasant trip. Zephyr made wonderful company. They spoke of many things. And, unlike most folks, the mouse happily took an interest in people other than himself. So, their conversation centered on Trevor–his time in his hall, his likes and dislikes, and his dreams of home. To his astonishment, the mouse knew all about him and even corrected his memory at points. He knew of where he had lived in Superbia, his friendship with Maggie, and all about his troubles with Meno and Willis.

"Zephyr, did Epictetus tell you about me?"

"No, I've watched you."

"You could see me?"

"I'm a mouse, remember? No one notices a mouse. I've watched you from the shadows. Why, I took an interest in you from the first time I saw you. You're a special boy."

That made a warm, happy spot form in Trevor's chest. He was immensely pleased with being called special.

"Zephyr, do you only help special children, like me?" he said cheerfully.

"Boy," the mouse said with annoyance, "every child is special. Do you think specialness is in short supply? It's the most common thing in the world."

Trevor suddenly felt small. A little flicker of resentment passed through him, and he went cold and stiff.

"To answer the question," said the mouse, "yes and no. I come to all children, but I'm more help to some than to others, and I'm no help to certain children."

"What do you mean?" Trevor asked grumpily.

"I offer my help to every child, but most don't want it."

"Why?" Trevor said, suddenly intrigued.

Zephyr twirled his whiskers thoughtfully. "Hmmm, different reasons," he said. "Some don't think they need saving. They've believed the lies of the Guardians."

"Epictetus told me about that."

"The Guardians are good liars–if there can be such a thing as a good liar. And the lies work–for a while, at least. But some people keep on believing them even after they've stopped working. Why, I've seen children sitting on the cutting board of the Chief Cook of the Pantry as he sharpened his knives, convinced that being served for dinner meant that the Cook was preparing a nice, little meal for them. And even when they see that bogeys eat children, they go to their ends thinking what may be true for other people, couldn't possibly be true for them. It's very sad, really. Like you, they believed specialness is in short supply."

When Trevor heard that, he didn't know what to say.

"There are other children," Zephyr went on, "who know they've been lied to; but knowing so has ruined them. They're not about to be fooled again! Oh, no! They're full of suspicion and won't believe anyone. Why, when I show up to help them, they think I'm just a clever ploy to fool them again. When I try to reason with them, they stop their ears and shout things like, *Fool me once, shame on you; fool me twice, shame on me!*"

"I don't know why," Trevor said, "but when I saw you, I just knew you were good."

"That's good for you, my boy, but it's not enough. It is a start, but something more is needed for me to help a child. You see, there is a third kind of child–the most miserable of all. This child knows he's been lied to and he knows deep in his heart that I'm good and have come to help him, but he still can't be helped."

"Why not?"

"Because he doesn't believe he can do what I can do. He may try, but it's just no use. He's the kind of child who bumps his head on the door."

Trevor heard a little, mousy sniffle. He felt a wave of sadness pass over him for the third kind of child, too. Then he realized how close he'd come to being one. They traveled in silence a while.

Eventually, they saw some lights shining ahead. Zephyr directed them toward some shoals on one side. The lights seemed to be floating somehow and were coming right at them. As they grew Trevor saw that they were torches and that they were hung from poles, and these were attached to a large, flat-bottomed boat. The sound of a steam engine and the slap of paddles echoed off the sides of the canyon as it drew nearer. Zephyr dimmed his light.

"Let's move behind that boulder, my boy," he said.

"What is it?" Trevor asked.

"A royal barge, from the look of it."

"Are they looking for us?"

"Doubtful. Word of your escape will take a while to reach the docks. More likely, it's a pleasure cruise. Members of the court sometimes travel the river on holiday."

"Lucian isn't there, is he?"

"Lucian? You've heard of him, eh?"

"One of the bogeys who took me from my hall mentioned him. When he said his name, all the bogeys got scared."

"Well they should, too. He's a nasty one—the nastiest. Let's have a look-see, shall we?"

"Are you serious?"

"Of course I am. Now, don't worry—they won't see us. I've got a little trick up my sleeve that will keep us hidden."

With a feeling of foreboding, Trevor pushed off and drifted toward the boat. The river was wide at this point and they were going with the current. As they drew nearer, the slap of the paddles grew louder. The boat was churning upstream and coming at them. The distance closed with alarming quickness. Trevor's feelings of foreboding grew as the boat drew nearer. They were becoming feelings of dread. They descended on him and numbed his mind, then welled up within him and made him sick. Trevor realized they were heading straight for the bow of the boat, and that they were going to be crushed.

He began to try and move to one side, but it was no use. They were going too fast; there wasn't time. But, before the light of the boat had reached them, Trevor heard the sound of blowing from the top of his head and felt a gentle whoosh. They were swept to one side. Zephyr had saved them again.

Now he got a clear view of the craft. It was long and low with a steam engine in the middle and a big paddle wheel in the aft. The passengers were beneath a canopy toward the bow. Long, black streamers and flags flapped limply from posts at the corners. What looked like bogeys, judging from their long-armed silhouettes, moved up and down the craft, apparently on guard.

"Let's get a little closer, shall we?" whispered the mouse.

No!, thought Trevor. But, before he could speak there came another blow from the top of his head, and they cut silently through the water, right up to the side of the boat.

Now he could really see things. The bogeys he had seen were guards, and he was right beneath one who was prowling like a cat, back and forth, looking into the darkness. Somehow, the bogey didn't see them. And those poles Trevor had seen with the flags, well, those were topped with human skulls. The canopy itself was crawling and moving and flickering in the torchlight, and there was a buzzing sound that accompanied the chugging of the engine.

Flies, Trevor realized with disgust.

What was under the canopy was worse. A pilot steered the vessel by an oversized wheel, and behind him stood a ring of important-looking figures. Most were bogeys—tall, menacing ones with breastplates flashing and long swords at their belts. One of these was all too familiar; it was Gourmand. But to Trevor's surprise, there were humans, too. Guardians, in fact. And he recognized one. First Guardian Glaucon was there, and along with the others he was bowing repeatedly to a large, black hulk.

The bogeys were bad enough, but what was really alarming was the lump they were all looking at. The little hairs on Trevor's arms began to stand up. The thing was as big as a miniature mountain, and it was surrounded by a smoky shadow. Trevor felt himself attracted to it and repelled by it at the same time. He couldn't take his eyes off it, yet he could hardly bear to look. It wasn't a bogey; whatever it was—it was too awful, too terrible. Fear and pain radiated from it in waves that seemed to ripple the very air, and it was the darkest thing in that dark place. It was almost like a hole in the blackness. Later, when asked about it, Trevor would say, "It was like a shadow that could swallow you."

"Don't be afraid," said a little voice from the top of his head. Instantly, Trevor felt a blanket of safety descend over him. Everything that just a moment before had made him want to scream for mercy, now seemed indifferent and strangely far away. For the rest of their time there, it was as though he were observing the whole scene from a distance.

"My Lord—" Glaucon said, as he rubbed his hands and bowed over and over to the shadow. "I am sorry to say that the reports are true. There *has* been an increase in recidivism. The figures from the Inspector of Incorrigible Children clearly demonstrate it. But, I hasten to add that the Guardians are not to blame. We have known for some time that the Snatchers' spells were losing their potency. We have—"

"My Lord," interrupted Gourmand, "don't allow this worm to change the subject. He assured us that the Guardians were fully capable, through their ministrations, of compensating for our recent problems. Now, after we have increased their budget time and again, and after we've redirected morsels destined for the Pantry to teaching and administrative posts, he dares to come with his excuses, and he even has the audacity to ask for more resources! I, for one, am tired of hearing hungry bogey-children cry themselves to sleep! I say enough is enough!"

A chorus of, "Hear! Hear!" came from the other bogeys.

Spreading his hands and bowing, Gourmand added, "If it pleases my Lord, restore the old ways and the old allotments."

Glaucon fell to his knees, followed by the other humans.

"No, my Lord, have mercy! Think of the social costs! Think of the long-term consequences!"

"Consequences!" roared Gourmand. "This is the consequence of failure!" He gave the Guardian a vicious kick. The human rolled over, groaning.

A soft, oily voice came from the black mountain, "Come now, Gourmand. Business before pleasure. Please, please, no more kicking the First Guardian."

It was an odd voice, and oddly out of place. It was more like an adult speaking to a beloved child than something menacing. Still, it sent a chill up Trevor's back.

"My good bogeys, I have always doubted Glaucon's claims for Guardian teaching methodology. And I can assure you, I will compensate you for your sacrifices in good time. My heart breaks at the very thought of hungry bogey babies. But the occasion for our little meeting is the curious weakening of the Snatchers' spells.

"Ahem, First Guardian Glaucon, you may rise."

"Thank you, my Lord," Glaucon said, getting to his feet while holding his side and looking side-long at Gourmand.

Gourmand feinted at him. The Guardian cringed.

The shadow continued, "But why have the spells weakened? That is what we should wonder. Very odd, is it not? And then there is the matter of children disappearing. I am quite concerned. These children must be getting help. Can you not see the hand of a conspiracy in this? I am afraid there is only one logical explanation—the Guild is back to its old tricks."

The biggest, most heavily-muscled bogey Trevor had ever seen stepped forward.

"Those shopkeepers, my Lord? Surely not!"

"You forget, Azrazel, that I have some knowledge of the Guild?"

The bogey's eyes went wide, and he quickly bowed and backed away. "Forgive me, my Lord."

"You are pardoned, my good bogey. But do not underestimate shopkeepers. I suspect they are doing more than tending shop. No, I am certain they are to blame for these disappearances."

Gourmand stepped forward. "If that is so, my Lord, why not round them up and make an end to the problem?"

"If it were so simple, think you not that I would not have done so long ago? One troublesome detail stays my hand."

"But my Lord, what could possibly prevent your Majesty from doing as you please?"

"Nothing!" the shadow screeched, with a voice that cut to Trevor's very soul.

Everyone on the boat fell to his knees. Even Trevor felt a need to kneel, and he wasn't even standing on anything.

"My will is never frustrated," the shadow said, long and low. Then he resumed with deliberate calm. "No, my friends. I bide my time in order to perfect my malice. Measures long in preparation are nearly complete to rid us of the pesky Guild. The time is ripening. Azrazel, is Third Division mustered?"

"Nearly, my Lord."

It was at this point that a fly that had taken notice of Trevor became a problem. Zephyr's attention was fixed on the conversation, but the fly's attention was directed toward the base of Trevor's neck. It flew in a lazy loop and settled down on his unprotected skin. Before Trevor could whisk it away, it took a generous bite.

"Ow!"

"Silence!" commanded the shadow.

Everyone on the boat rose to his feet.

"A spy," the shadow declared, with silky malevolence.

Goose bumps rose all over Trevor's body, and he felt the hair on his head begin to stand straight up.

The bogeys began to stir and scan the dark surface of the river.

"Down you go!" whispered Zephyr and Trevor felt himself plunged beneath the surface.

He just had the presence of mind to take a breath as he went under. Up through the murky water he saw a huge bogey, torch in hand, looking down toward him with a puzzled expression. Trevor had let go of the boat and was again being carried downstream by the current. The bogey shrunk in size as the vessel churned upstream. The space between them grew. As it did, Trevor's lungs began to beg for air.

"Not yet," a mousy voice bubbled through the water.

When he couldn't take it a second longer, he burst through the surface. The boat had become just a sliver of light receding in the distance.

"That was close. Really, my boy, you must learn to exercise a little self-control," said the mouse.

"But it bit me!" Trevor said, heaving for air.

"Of course it did. But trust me, a bogey's bite is much worse."

Trevor didn't feel like arguing, which is just as well since the mouse was right. He just felt cold, colder than he had ever felt. Not physically cold, although he was shivering. He felt cold and gray on the inside.

They were drifting in the dark now, since the mouse hadn't started glowing again. It was in that utter blackness—with his head just above the water and a mouse perched on top—that Trevor asked his next question.

"What was that thing?"

After a pause, Zephyr said, "*That* was Lucian."

"What *is* he?"

After another pause, the mouse said, "He was a man, once."

"A man?"

"Yes, but let's not speak of him."

Trevor thought the mouse sounded different, sort of distant.

After a moment, he dared to ask, "What were they talking about?"

"About me. And Epictetus—and those like him. But mostly about you, my boy."

"Me?"

"Not to worry—not you specifically—but children like you. They need you. You see, you keep Superbia in business. The bogeys want you for food, of course, but the Guardians need you, too. You feed their delusions; not to mention, you keep them from being eaten. It is a strange, but profitable partnership. The bogeys snatch children and place them under the care of the Guardians. The most pliable and complicit children become Guardians themselves, and the rest are sent to the Pantry.

"But there are some of neither party who work to save as many children as they can. I am one, and Epictetus is another. There are more, but not many. But as you heard, they know of our little conspiracy and, from the sound of it, they are about to act. When I get you out of here, you must warn the others."

"How *do* I get out?"

"We'll use the drain."

"What's that?

"It's just what it sounds like. We're nearly there."

As they drifted along, Trevor noticed the current speeding up. Zephyr had begun glowing again, but dimly. Whitecaps were forming, and he could hear a faint roar ahead. His heart began to race.

"Up ahead!" the mouse shouted.

Trevor couldn't see anything, but he could feel something vibrating the air and filling it with mist.

Without warning the water fell away before them, and they were swept to one side. In the faint light, Trevor saw a chasm to the left with a wall of rushing water spiraling down. They had been sucked into a vast loop, and they were heading lower. The water began to rise to the right.

"Zephyr! What's happening?"

"No fear, my boy! Perfectly normal! Everything is going according to plan!"

It was a good thing Trevor couldn't see very well, because the terror of the sight might have frozen him and made it impossible to follow the instructions he was about to receive. As Zephyr had predicted, they had come to the Drain–the great whirlpool at the end of the river. Their velocity was increasing the closer they got to the bottom.

The rush of the water was deafening now, but somehow Zephyr managed to shout over it.

"WHEN I TELL YOU, TAKE THE DEEPEST BREATH YOU CAN HOLD!"

The swell was all around him, and Trevor was having difficulty keeping his head above it. Just before he was about to go under, Zephyr shouted.

"NOW!"

In went the air, and down went the boy. Down, down, down he shot in a mighty surge, twisting this way and that, spinning along with the press. It seemed he couldn't hold his breath a second more when he saw a dim light through the dirty water. He sped toward it, then burst out of the darkness into a gray expanse.

It was open air, and his grateful lungs sucked in its life-giving oxygen. But he was falling now, along with water. The fall ended with a smack that stung and pushed the air back out of his lungs. He was under water again and being forced down. He struggled desperately against it; fortunately an upward current took over, and his head broke into the open air once more.

He found himself in the shallows of a large pond, panting for air. A shoreline shone weakly in an evening twilight.

Amazingly, Zephyr was still with him.

"Make for those rocks. We should be able to spend the night hidden there."

Trevor pulled himself onto the land and crawled a little way to a small space between two boulders. The sand there was cool and soft. He collapsed onto it, and a sudden weariness came over him. In an instant, he was asleep.

CHAPTER SEVEN

Water Rat

"Ooo, how's my little bugaboo?" the woman said.

Baby-talk; he hated baby-talk. It was a sweet voice, though; but couldn't she see he wasn't a baby? He looked up at the giant face beaming down at him and said–

"ACK!"

Ack? What's *ack* supposed to mean? That's not what he'd meant to say.

The woman's eyes sparkled, and a loving smile spread across her face.

"Does Twevor-wevor want his ducky-wucky?"

Ducky-wucky?!

She held a huge, plastic duck in front of him and wiggled it.

"A chubby, *wittle* ducky for my cubby, *wittle* bugaboo!"

Chubby? Who's chubby? Trevor held up a chubby, little hand to push the giant duck away.

Wait! *Chubby little hand?* He looked at it. It *was* chubby–a *chubby*, little hand with five *chubby*, little fingers! He looked closer and saw that it was attached to a chubby, little arm and that was attached to a chubby, little body! And there, around a chubby, little tummy was some sort of blue plastic donut thingy. Worst of all–he was completely naked!

"ACK! ACK! ACK!" he said, waving his arms and slapping the water–by which he meant, *Hey, what's going on here?*

"Ooo, Twevor wikes his bathy-wathy!" the pretty giant said, pouring water over his head.

"ACK!" Trevor protested.

The sound of something ringing came from a distance.

"Oh, that darned phone!" the giantess said, pushing herself to her feet. "Mommy will be right back."

When she left, she didn't close the door behind her. A cool breeze came through it and blew over his wet, little body. There he sat, shivering, with water dripping from his nose and earlobes, when a rustling began in the linen closet behind him. He tried to look, but the stupid plastic donut made it impossible to turn around. He could hear the knob to the closet turning, though. Then he heard the latch unhitch and the door slowly creak open. A shadow grew over the room as the swinging door blocked the light from a window.

"Sniff, sniff," Trevor heard, and a chill ran through him that had nothing to do with any breeze.

He desperately wanted to say something, anything–even *Ack!* But when he opened his mouth, nothing would come out.

Lips smacked beside his ear.

"Ahhh, yes. A plump one. A sweeeet, teeender morsel."

Long-nailed fingers grabbed the edge of the tub, and slowly a broad face rose behind them. Two blood-shot eyes looked at Trevor hungrily over a grinning mouth full of yellow teeth.

"Toooo bad. It's a shame, truly it is. The young ones are so tender. But no, Lucian has forbidden it. Snatchers *must wait until the morsels don't need their mommies any more,* he says. But just this once, just for me. He needn't know. This one is barely a mouthful."

A quaking hand began to extend toward him. Trevor drew back, eyes wide, chubby cheeks quivering. A sound of someone coming rescued him. The bogey pulled his hand back and twisted his ugly face.

"Bah, you won't be so lucky next time, morsel."

With a sudden quickness, the bogey was back in the closet just as the giantess entered.

*

Trevor's eyes sprang open.

He was cold and damp. He was hungry, too, and he felt oddly weak. It was all very unpleasant.

He noticed that he was situated between two large boulders that made for a small enclosure, and he was lying on fine gray sand that clung to his wet hands and clothes. Sitting on one of the large rocks was a little mouse sniffing the morning air and looking down at him.

"Good morning! How did you sleep, my boy?"

"Terrible. I dreamed about a bogey."

"Naturally, with what you've been through. Now, how do you feel?" the mouse said, with an emphasis on *feel.*

Trevor told him.

"To be expected, to be expected," Zephyr said, with a faraway look as he twisted his whiskers. "Cold and hunger don't worry me as much as the weakness does. You've slept long, and the morning's half gone. You must get into the city before you are too weak to walk."

"Why? We worked so hard to get out of it!"

"Not into Superbia, my boy. We must find help and a place for you to stay. We can only find those things in Olton."

"Olton! Epictetus told me to go there. Where is it?"

"Oh, it's not far. It's right over there."

Zephyr pointed at a long wall of very old and worn brick, running along a dark stream.

Trevor stood and for the first time took in his surroundings. Looking upstream, he saw the pond he had fallen into the night before. Behind it rose a sheer cliff face to a plateau far above. On top of that, the walls of Superbia climbed higher still. About midway up though, between the pond and the city, there was a small opening, like a little mouth, spewing out black water. He realized that it must have been the way he'd gotten out of the Sewers.

To one side, the plateau met a long slope, and down that slope a ramshackle town seemed to tumble. Alongside it ran a crumbling wall. It was the very wall that stood before them.

"Before Superbia, this foul stream was sweet and clear. This was rich land in those days, filled with farms and small groves."

"You sound like you actually saw those things."

"I did," Zephyr said wistfully. "The town used to run right up to the water, and there were festivals, in honor of my folk. But these days, people hate the river. And who can blame them? It is a source of disease and evil. It's good for nothing but carrying garbage away."

Without warning, a small door in the wall opened and released some refuse into a little tributary that went down a rocky bank to the water below. Along the length of the wall were several doors like it.

"That's your way in, my boy. You must go through one of those garbage chutes."

"What, aren't you coming with me?"

"No, I am sorry, but I must get back to the Pantry. There are other children to help."

"But, I thought you were taking me home!"

"Oh, I am. But not today. Remember, I told you the trip home is long; longer than you can possibly imagine, and you're in no condition to make it. You need to rest and heal. When I think you're ready, I'll come back for you."

"How long will that be?" Trevor said, heart sinking.

"Could be years; could be longer than that; could be tomorrow. Who knows?"

"Y–Y–Years?!"

"Perhaps. You maybe an old man before I get back. On the other hand, I may only be away a few days. When the time is right, I'll be back."

"I can't believe it! How could you do this to me?"

"Do what to you?" the mouse said, with irritation. "Save you from certain death? Oh, yes, that is a terrible thing."

"No, not that!" Trevor said, feeling a little chagrined. "What am I supposed to do in the meantime?"

"Wait."

"Wait? But I thought I was going to be traveling."

"Ah, I see you've not done much traveling. Traveling is mostly waiting–waiting for the train to arrive, waiting for the tide to come in, waiting for the rain to stop."

"That's different!"

"How do you know? Have you ever journeyed home?"

"No."

"Well, I have and I'm telling you there's no difference at all. When you're ready and the time is right, I'll come for you. There are plenty of worthwhile things to keep you busy in the meantime, and I suspect time will fly. In fact, by the time I return, you may find that you don't want to go home as badly as you think you do.

"Go now," the mouse said. "The cesspools filled overnight and someone I know is clearing them. If you don't get through one of those doors this morning you will have to wait until evening or even tomorrow, and considering your condition that may be too late."

Trevor looked at the wall and said sulkily, "Which door? There's so many." When he looked back, Zephyr was gone.

He searched for the mouse in vain and called the mouse's name over and over, but it wasn't any use. He was alone. Gloom started to billow up inside him and he nearly started to cry.

Then he sat down with a plunk on one of the boulders and thought about quitting.

After wasting precious time in that way, he suddenly remembered Zephyr's warning about having to wait until evening if he didn't act quickly. He forced himself to stand against the protests of his stiff limbs and shuffled unsteadily toward the wall. Since the bank was rocky and there were no paths, it was hard going.

When he got to the nearest door, he saw that it wasn't the normal size. It was only chest high and the lower part of it disappeared beneath shallow, dirty water. It was wide though, about as wide as the span of a man's outstretched arms from fingertip to fingertip. He noticed that it was actually two doors that opened in the middle and swung outward. Neither had a handle or knob of any kind.

While he was wondering if he should knock, another door farther down opened. Stumbling and tripping, he made for it as fast as he could. He reached it just as it swung shut. Disappointed and out of breath, he sat down right in some mucky water.

After a minute, he heard another door open. Up he jumped and staggered toward it, only to see it clap shut again before he could reach it.

That's when the thought pierced his mind that someone must be on the other side, going from door to door. He trudged on, as fast as he could, to the next door. He guessed right and halfway there, that door swung open releasing a surge of black water. When he got there, he leapt in. The press was so strong it nearly swept him away. But he was able to steady himself and, as he did, he saw a pole pushing debris through the opening.

"Help! Wait!" he yelped, when he saw the doors beginning to close.

The pole propped them open, and a man's face appeared. When Trevor got near, the pole extended and he grabbed hold and a laughing voice said, "Sweetie, look at the size of this water-rat!"

A meaty, calloused hand pulled him out of the water and onto a landing. The hand was attached to a thick body, and that was connected to a balding head. A wide smile and two sparkling eyes greeted him. Trevor liked the man immediately, but the face he liked seeing even better was Maggie's. She stood right next to him, bouncing on her toes.

"Trevor!" she squealed, throwing her arms around him and squeezing him hard. "I knew you'd make it! I told Grandfather you would."

"Sweetie, he's soaked—he's getting you wet," said the man.

Trevor didn't know what to say, he didn't know what to think. He just stood there with his mouth hanging open, not sure if he could believe his eyes.

"Come on," Maggie said. "You need to get out of those awful things. I've got clothes to help you fit in here. Grandfather sent them." She held out a bag with the ends of clothes sticking out of it. "Quick, let's go over there. You smell terrible; can't give you a bath though, but at least we can do something about the way you look."

She shuttled him into the shadows of a nearby building where he began to peel his soaking garments off. When he pulled his shirt over his head, he dully noticed his pouch of basme was gone. He'd lost it in his escape.

Maggie had turned away while he changed, but she kept talking. "You're wondering how I got here, aren't you?" she said, not letting him answer. "Oh, I'm so excited. You're my first catch! I told Grandfather that I was old enough to fish, but he almost didn't let me. I'm a real Fisher now!"

"How *did* you get here?" Trevor managed to squeeze in.

"Not now," said the man who had come alongside them. "The buildings have ears. It'll have to wait until we get back to the Ward."

"Uncle, I'm so excited; he's my first catch!"

"I know," the man said, with a smile. "We'll throw a party for you both. Maggie, you've not introduced us."

"Oooh, I forgot. Uncle Max, meet Trevor Upjohn. Trevor, meet Uncle Max."

"Just call me Max," said the man.

"Ah, thanks," Trevor said awkwardly.

"Maggie, wait here with your catch. I've got a couple more doors to clear. It won't take long."

Maggie grabbed Trevor's hand tightly and said, "Oooh, you're coming to Trothward! You'll like it there—everyone does—it's such a wonderful place. You'll see Grandfather again!"

"Who's that?"

"Epictetus," she said proudly.

Trevor's sense of bewilderment grew. It must have shown.

"You'll understand when we get to the Ward," she said, looking amused.

"Today's market day," she said with a conspiratorial whisper that made Trevor lean toward her involuntarily. "The streets will be full, and we should be able to get there without being noticed. Don't talk to anyone though; you'll give yourself away. Let Uncle Max and me do all the talking. There are Guardians here. There's even some bogeys."

"Bogeys?" Trevor said nervously. "Do people like them here?"

"Like them? No! They hate them. You won't hear any of that—*Bogeys are our friends* nonsense here. But that doesn't mean there aren't collaborators. Then there are the Guardians, they're all over the place. Anyway, I better not say anymore," Maggie said, looking around. "Here, eat this." She pulled a little package from a pocket. "Grandfather thought you might be hungry."

"Thanks." He did feel hungry, famished even. A fruity smell met his nose as he opened it. It was something he'd never had before–a kind of sweet bread. He hardly tasted it, it went down so fast.

"Pretty good, huh? Better than that stuff they made us eat in Superbia. Mother made it, she says it's good for you, too."

With some food in his stomach he felt a little better, but a wave of weariness swept over him unexpectedly. Max returned in time to grab him when he nearly fell over.

"What's the matter?" he asked.

"It's the basme. Zephyr said I used too much."

Max and Maggie exchanged worried looks.

"We've got to get him to the Ward as quickly as we may," said Max. "He must walk while he can. We can't risk drawing attention by carrying him."

They steadied him by each arm and began leading him down a narrow alley. When they stepped out into a street, a riot of color assaulted Trevor's eyes. Every house was so brightly painted that even the dull gray sky couldn't keep them from seeming to shout–*look at me!* They rose up three and four stories high and hung over the street precariously like stacks of matchboxes.

"We've got to be careful," Maggie whispered. "This is a bad neighborhood. The Guild doesn't have many friends here."

"What do you mean?"

"Shhh, not now!" she scolded.

They went up another alley, winding uphill, block after block. Each street it brought them to had more people on it than the last, and the houses kept looking better and even brighter. A couple of times, Trevor saw the billowing white robes of the Guardians from a distance. Max went out of the way to steer clear of them. But mostly the streets were filled with children playing and women calling to each other from open windows. Once they passed some boys playing a game with a ball and a stick.

"Playing *slap the pig* by the look of it," said Max when he noticed Trevor's longing stare.

There was so much to see and hear and smell! There was food–lots of it: people were sitting out eating, delicious aromas wafted from open windows. There were even shops where he could see people making things–breads, and pies, and other delicious looking things. His stomach growled.

Finally, they got to the top of a hill, and the street leveled out. A wide space opened before him, and the muffled roar of ten thousand voices all talking at once and saying different things swept over his head. They had come to the grand old market of Olton and it was market day! A sea of open-sided tents filled his sight. Dust rose from the feet of men and animals and gave the whole scene a ghostly quality. Trevor paused for a moment to try and take it in, but Maggie grabbed an arm and pulled him along after her.

As they began to weave their way between tables and through the crowd, Trevor couldn't help but feel a little frightened by all the yelling going on around him.

"Why is everyone so mad?" he shouted at Max. He had to shout to be heard.

Maggie gave him a steely look, but Max just laughed and said, "They're not mad, Trevor–not most of 'em anyway. They're a-haggling. Enjoying themselves, I'd say. It's market day, and that's rare enough these days."

There was so much to buy! And so much of it was food

Trevor could hardly stand it. There were salted meats on hooks hanging high for all to see, and tables laden with fruits and vegetables. But what he liked best were the confectioner's wares–the iced pastries were so tempting he began reaching for one without thinking. Maggie slapped his hand and shouted in his ear, "They cut off the thumbs of thieves here, you know." He shoved his palms into his pockets and tried to think of something besides food.

Fortunately, there was more than food to see. Some booths had bolts of cloth–all brightly colored and foreign looking. (Maggie tended to linger at those tables.) There were tinkers with racks of pots, pans, and knives all clinking as they swayed. The booths pressed hard together, one following another–one for books, another for trinkets, another for spices. Every so often someone shouted at them and bandied their wares, but Max just waved them off.

More than business was going on. There were musicians–acrobats too! Trevor especially liked those. There were groups of older men listening to and arguing with each other about things Trevor didn't understand or care about. (Max was most interested in these.) But, most fascinating of all (besides food, that is) were the groups of girls and boys running around and teasing each other. One girl ran right up to him and said, "Tag, you're it!" and ran away. He wanted to take off after her, but Max pushed him along.

They eventually came to a very large and important looking booth, larger than ten others put together, with a green banner lined with golden leaves. Hundreds of people milled all around it while sleek, bearded men wearing green robes and gem-encrusted necklaces worked the tables and bargained with customers.

The tables were filled with an odd assortment of things that

Trevor couldn't see any point in. There were little branches that Maggie informed him were a thing called mistletoe and clear glass bottles, each filled with what appeared to be water and a single golden leaf. There was one thing he did think he recognized–in one place there were several little clay jars. A long line of people were standing by them.

"Basme!" he said.

One of the bearded men glanced sharply at Maggie.

"Come on, let's go over here," she said, moving him away.

They bumped right into some angry looking people.

"Blasted Guildsmen," said one to the others. "These prices are outrageous!"

"Aye, they've got a monopoly; there's the reason. The authorities should come down on 'em!" said a prune-faced woman.

"You know why it won't happen," said a grizzled man. "Greased palms. They're all in it together." A chorus of grunts followed.

"Come on," Maggie said, sounding disturbed.

A commotion arose in the distance that caught everyone's attention. Something was moving at the far end of the market and was coming towards them. As it did a wave of silence washed over the crowd, and a pregnant stillness followed that was very odd for a place so large and full of people. Feet stopped moving, robes ceased their rustling, dust began to settle. Then from far away, Trevor heard what sounded like chains jingling and a hoarse voice rhythmically shouting time. He strained to see.

Eventually, the crowd pushed back to make way for a long line of bare-chested men chained at the ankles, moving at a quick trot. It occurred to Trevor at that moment that these were the first men he'd seen who weren't old. They were young and strong, and sweat glistened on their muscled arms and backs. He saw more than men, though. Accompanying them on either side, carrying whips and cudgels, were a troop of swarthy, square-jawed bogeys. Max pulled Trevor back out of view.

"What is it?" asked Trevor.

"Press gang," whispered Maggie.

"What's that?"

"Shhh!" she said, with a finger to her lips.

Trevor noticed that everyone around him was staring at the ground. Even though he thought he should, he couldn't make himself; he had to see what was happening. The men in chains filed by. Most looked haggard and worn, but some looked just a little older than himself. The heavy breathing of men and the clanking of shackles and the harsh voice of a bogey keeping time were now the only sounds.

Some bogeys were scanning the crowd, intently looking into it. Abruptly one of them shouted, and instantly the entire line came to a halt. He pointed in Trevor's direction. A stab of dread pierced him, *They've found me!* he thought. Trevor looked from side to side for a place to run. Suddenly some bogeys pushed violently into the crowd. A woman screamed. An older boy standing near tried to bolt. The bogeys shot past Trevor and went after the boy. They were on him in a flash, like a pack of apes. The crowd pulled back and turned away. The screaming woman fell to her knees, "Please! Please, he's only a boy! He's too young!"

The bogeys pulled the boy to his feet and, with one quick tug, ripped the shirt off his back. One of their number was at his feet, clasping his ankles in iron cuffs. The boy just stood there, eyes wide and teary, shoulders and chest beginning to heave. No one could meet his gaze but Trevor, and when their eyes made contact something electric seemed to pass between them. The words, *Please, please help me!* formed in Trevor's mind. Involuntarily, he took a step toward the boy.

A heavy hand appeared on his shoulder. "No. Come along, we must get going," Max said sadly.

"What's happening?"

"Not now," said Maggie.

As he turned to follow, Trevor felt as though someone had suddenly sucked all his strength away. He collapsed to his hands and knees.

Maggie bent down, "Come on, we're almost there!"

He tried to get up, but he collapsed again. He felt one of Max's thick arms reach around his middle. "We'll have to risk it. We've got to get him back before it's too late." Vaguely, Trevor felt himself leave the ground.

He didn't see much after that, nodding off the way he was. He knew Max was carrying him because he felt his cheek rubbing against the man's muscled shoulder, and every so often a bump in the man's stride would jostle him awake briefly. That's when he would see Maggie's worried looks.

Foggily he heard her finally say, "There it is!"

He just managed to peek a look. They had come to the middle of a narrow, dirty alley and were standing at a door. It was situated in what appeared to be an old wall, and it was shut. It was full of carvings, and at the top, right in the center, was a many-rayed face. After he saw that, everything went black.

CHAPTER EIGHT

Trothward

At first, Trevor didn't want to wake up; then, when he wanted to, he couldn't. It was as if someone had set an enormous boulder on his forehead. He couldn't budge a muscle. But sometimes voices came to him—faint and garbled. Other times, he felt as if he were outside, lying on the ground. That's when he thought he heard singing and saw lights moving through his eyelids.

Finally, his eyes fluttered open. He found himself in a deep, downy bed in a darkened room. Dying candles on a nearby table cast leaping shadows on the walls. Next to the table, in a chair and sleeping upright, was Maggie.

The flickering light made her face dance an eerie jig, and she looked strange and uncanny. The oddness of it made him wonder about her and an unwelcome thought popped into his head—*Just who is that girl, really?* She'd kept secrets from him, after all, big important ones about all sorts of things—Epictetus, the Guild, all kinds of stuff. *Could he trust her? Friends don't keep secrets from friends, everyone knows that.* The distance between them seemed to grow somehow. Then a flame suddenly shot up in a fireplace and momentarily bathed the room in light. It revealed a simple red-haired girl. She was Maggie again, that's all, and she was his friend.

A growl rose from the general vicinity of his stomach. *Feed me!* it demanded. Happily, there was a platter with some bread and cheese on the table, along with a cool, sweet drink in a frosted, metal cup left by some thoughtful person. He gratefully gulped it all down like he hadn't eaten in days.

When he had finished, he looked over at Maggie a second time. Still asleep. *Let her,* he thought. He didn't feel like talking–and talking was something he knew she was always in the mood for.

He looked around and, for the first time, fully took in his surroundings. Opposite the bed was a hearth with a fire that had burnt low. Above the hearth was a mantel, and over that was a bronze face. It was round and had tongues of fire coming from it, just like the one on Epictetus's book. It looked down on him with a blank stare that gave him a creepy feeling. With a shudder, he turned away. Then he noticed the most remarkable feature of the room–it was lined with paintings.

Those nearest to him were the normal sort–portraits of people he didn't know and of things he didn't care about, mostly potted plants. But the people looked friendly and the plants, looked, well–*planty*. But as he went on, things became interesting. People and plants got sort of mixed up. In one painting, there was a boy with leaves for hair–not leaves in his hair, mind you; leaves *were* his hair. Then, in another, there was a girl with reeds where her arms should have been. More alarming were the trees with eyes and the shrubs with noses; some were grotesque and knobby, but others were beautiful and graceful. Those were feminine, he was sure. Further on, the paintings showed the plant-people and the people-plants doing things together. In one, they seemed to be playing a game with dice and stones; in another they were dancing beside a band of pipe-smoking rabbits who accompanied them on fiddles and drums. *Weirder and weirder,* Trevor thought. Then he came to the largest of the paintings. Here he saw the creatures in a large circle around a huge tree covered with golden fruit. As he stood considering its meaning, it seemed like the figures began to move. They began a ponderous dance, slowly bowing to the tree, then cross-stepping, then bowing again. He rubbed his eyes and shook his head. When he opened them again, things had gone back to normal. *Too weird,* he thought and turned away.

Now he was standing in front of a large curtain. It was long and black and it ran the full length of the wall. It was made of some heavy material that seemed to swallow what little light there was in the room. At one end, a crimson tassel hung at the end of a silver rope. "Maybe there's another painting behind it," he said to himself. On impulse, he grasped the tassel and pulled. The curtain opened with an easy swish. What was revealed made him stand in blinking astonishment.

Before him was a wide arch and beyond that was a sparkling garden reaching into the night. Its far side was lost in shadow. A vast, gentle lawn stretched out, shimmering in a dancing light. The light didn't come from a fire, or even an electric torch, but from hundreds of heavy, golden fruits swaying like lanterns on the branches of an enormous tree at the center of it all.

It was the tree in the painting; he was sure of it. Its enormous trunk was smooth as silk, and its thick boughs reached outward and upward into the nighttime sky. It was covered with dark, green foliage lit from beneath by its bobbing lights. And when a breeze rustled the leaves, they flashed and flitted like tongues of fire. Trevor's insides were warmed at the very sight of it.

"Beautiful, isn't it?" sounded a deep voice behind him.

Trevor turned to see Epictetus standing a few feet from the open door of his room. He didn't look like a slave anymore. He was dressed in a robe that flowed both violet and black as its folds moved in the dimness. His silver hair and beard glistened, and his eye patch looked like it was made of gold. Trevor didn't know what to say.

Epictetus walked up to him and placed one of his large hands on his shoulder. "Come, let us enjoy the tree together."

As they stepped out into the garden, the sweet fragrances of growing things rose to greet them. Trevor now noticed that his room was just one of many surrounding the garden; archways like his repeated into the night. But unlike his, all the other curtains were shut. The stillness gave the impression that it was either very late or very early.

After walking in silence through the lush greenery, they came to a bench and sat down.

A heavy quiet rested on the place, and Trevor wasn't sure if he should talk. But after a minute Epictetus turned and said quietly, "I imagine you're full of questions. I know I would be if I were you. Now is a time for answers, those I know anyway. The bogeys cannot reach us here."

Trevor didn't know where to begin, he had so many questions. He began with the first that came to mind. "Epictetus, who are you?"

The old man smiled, "You already know that; you had it right the last time we spoke. I am a slave."

The blood rushed to Trevor's face, and he lowered his eyes, "I'm sorry."

"Don't apologize, Trevor. You had it right. I am a servant; I serve this house." He paused. "I know that seems odd to you because you come from a place where ruling and serving are thought of as different things. But here, ruling is serving and serving is ruling. I am called Master here because I am the chief servant." There was a twinkle in his good eye when he finished.

Trevor looked around. "What is this place?"

"This, Trevor, is the last stand of a great garden that was once much larger. Long ago, before our current troubles, you could walk from the Pupille Sea to Redoubtable Hills and never approach its borders."

"Those paintings in the room I woke up in, they're of the garden, aren't they?"

"Yes, they are. They're very precious. The oldest of them actually come down to us from those days, others are just based on accounts in books."

"Uh, some of them were–uh, kind of strange. The people, I mean. Some of the plants, too."

"Yes, I know what you mean," Epictetus said, his voice trailing. "I admit they seem odd to me as well. The world we live in is so different from what it once was. But, if you and I could see things correctly, we would think that it is our world that is truly strange.

"What you saw were the Folk. What the Folk were, I couldn't say. But they lived in the garden and dwelled in the trees and the flowers much like we live in houses–but they're gone now. Their houses remain, and are still beautiful in their way; but it's not the same–now they're empty and cold."

"What happened?"

"They abandoned them when the bogeys came. Some say they're still in them; they've just fallen asleep. But, others think that they have left our world and will never return."

Trevor looked at the tree and asked, "What about this tree, did they live in it, too?"

"No," Epictetus said gravely. "This tree is different. It is the one and only–the Troth–the Great Tree, the oldest of trees. It is unchanged; the coming of the bogeys did nothing to diminish it. This house that surrounds it is called Trothward–the Ward of the Troth. It was built to watch it and protect it, although I am of the opinion that the Tree protects the house more than the other way around."

Trevor looked at the fruit and asked, "Where does the light

come from?"

Epictetus sat up and caught his breath. "That, Trevor is a question I didn't think someone your age would come up with. Why do you ask?"

"Well, it just seems like the fruit isn't making the light–it's more like the light is shining on them."

The old man's bushy eyebrows rose, and he broke into a broad grin. "Very good, very good. That's exactly right. The light does come from someplace else."

"Where?"

"Not so much where–as when," said the old man meaningfully, almost whispering. "The future."

Trevor looked at the tree and its shining fruit without understanding.

"The tree, Trevor, is in two places at once. It is here, of course, but it is also here Tomorrow–not just the next day on the calendar–but all the tomorrows–all the way to the Tomorrow when the clouds are gone."

Trevor still didn't get it.

"Here, maybe this will help. Remember the basme I gave you? Do you remember the secret of its power?"

He thought back to their earlier conversation in his hall. It seemed a lifetime ago. "Yes, I remember," he said, feeling a twinge of embarrassment recalling his misuse of the ointment. "Basme's power comes from taking tomorrow's virtue to meet today's need."

"Correct. Don't feel badly, Trevor. I know what you're thinking. Why, I've misused basme myself–too many times to recall. I suppose that is why I tried to impress its power on you so strongly. But I didn't bring it up to scold you. I only want to teach you something. You see, the Troth has the power of the future. It takes the future and joins it to the present. Do you see what that means?"

Trevor shook his head.

"It means we have a *reason* for hope. If the clouds are gone in the future, that means the bogeys are gone, too."

Epictetus paused and let his words sink in.

"There is just one thing that troubles me." A shadow crossed his face and he grew quiet, and his shoulders appeared to droop slightly. But, after an uncomfortable silence, his face brightened and he seemed to set his jaw beneath his beard. It was as though he had intended to say something, but decided against it. "Well, time is getting on. I've time for one more question before the day begins."

"Sir, I'm just wondering, why does a great man like you watch children at night, and why are you helping me?"

"Tsk, tsk, tsk," Epictetus wagged his finger in mock disapproval. "No fair, you've asked two questions when I invited only one." But then he smiled, and put an arm around Trevor's shoulder. "By answering your second question, I'll answer your first–I'm looking for children like you–children who remember things they don't understand and who feel out of place because of it. My granddaughter helped me find you. She's very proud of you; you're her first catch."

"I heard her say she's a *Fisher*."

"Yes, she is–although it is much sooner than her mother had wanted. Fisher is the name we give people who try to save children like you. As to how I came to be in your hall; well, let's just say I've got connections in high places. I was able to arrange it so that I can watch children sleep at night. In fact, I've just returned from your old hall and I'm delighted to report that they hardly miss you. That's the way of it there. When a child disappears in the night, no one asks questions because no one wants to know the answers. Now, if you'd like, you may stay with us."

With the old man smiling down at him, getting home seemed much less pressing than it had. *Besides*, Trevor told himself, *Maggie's here–and even the food's good.*

"Well, I suppose it's okay. Zephyr did say that I'd have to wait a little while before he came for me. So, thanks. I'll stay until it's time to go home, if that's okay?"

"Yes, Trevor, that's okay. Stay as long as you like."

✻

"Oh, Trevor, you're so lucky," said Maggie. "Fresh Fish usually have to wait weeks before their Feast, but you woke up just in time!"

Trevor had learned that he wasn't the first "catch." There was a steady trickle of children into the Ward, and each month there was a banquet in their honor called *The Feast of the Fresh Fish.*

"The Guild has lots of ways in and out of Superbia," Maggie said, knowingly. "We use them to get kids out. Our people are everywhere. We even have people in the Guardians."

"Everybody keeps talking about *The Guild*. What is it?" Trevor asked.

"The Guild has been around *forever*," she said. "Its real name is *The Venerable Guild of the Sun Eaters,* but that's way too long to say, so we just call it *The Guild*. Grandfather is one of the Masters of this house. There are other houses in places like Ophir, but this is the most important house because of the Troth, and Grandfather is the headmaster here," she said proudly. "You'll learn more tonight. But first, we have to get you ready for the fun!"

She took him by the hand and led him up some stairs, then down some others, around some bends, then through a long corridor lined with doors. The whole time they didn't pass a single window. They went through some big rooms full of people sitting around talking and an even bigger room where some men were practicing with swords. Trevor wanted to stop and watch, but Maggie tugged him along. "Come on! There'll be time for that later!"

The place seemed to go on and on. He vaguely remembered seeing it from the outside. All he could recall was a door in a wall in the middle of a dirty, little alley. How could it be so big?

"It's hidden, that's why," Maggie explained when he asked. "Grandfather says it has to do with bent light or something. Whatever–I don't understand it, but who cares? Just so long as the bogeys stay away. You're going to love it here. It's so fun! Finally, we're here."

They entered a vaulted room where a couple of women worked at looms.

"Mother, I've brought Trevor for his robe," Maggie said.

A tall woman with long, black hair and a dignified air rose and came to meet them.

"Welcome to Trothward, Trevor," she said with a smile, and then she kissed his forehead. Her lips were softer than anything he had ever felt, and she smelled of lavender. He blushed.

"I am Abigail's mother." Trevor looked at Maggie quizzically. "Ah, I see Abigail has not told you her true name." She gave Maggie a disapproving glance. Maggie found something of keen interest on the floor and didn't return her mother's look. "Not only am I *Abigail's* mother, I am the daughter of Epictetus, who is Master of this house, and the wife of Marcus, who is yet to return. I am Lady Rowena."

A boy entered the room from a door behind the Lady. He had a round, friendly face to go with a round, stumpy body; his hair was mussed up, as though he had just pulled something over his head, and he had on a brown robe much too long for him.

The Lady turned to him, "Theodore, good. Stand over there so we can finish."

Theodore looked at Trevor and smiled. "Hi," he said.

"Janet," the Lady continued, "fetch a robe for Trevor."

The other woman brought him a light blue robe. He felt he knew her somehow.

"Hello, Trevor," she said.

"Janet?"

"Yes, it's me."

She extended her arms toward him, and he stepped into them in stunned disbelief. It was her!–the girl he had loved so much back in Superbia–the one who had gone missing so long ago. She was a young woman now.

When he managed to step back and wipe the tears from his eyes–he hated when he did that, he felt like such a sissy –he took a better look at her. She was beautiful; her soft brown eyes looked at him kindly, seeming to enjoy his tears. She was nearly as tall as the Lady, but without the coolness.

"I didn't think I'd ever see you again," Trevor said, feeling suddenly awkward and looking down.

"I didn't think I'd see anyone again when the bogeys came for me. But after Zephyr saved me, I thought I might see some of my little ones again."

"Zephyr! You met him, too? I'd never have gotten out without him."

"Neither would I," said Janet. "We've got a lot to talk about, but first you need to get ready for the feast. Here, put this on."

Trevor pulled the light blue robe over his head, and then Janet directed him to stand next to the other boy on a little platform. The Lady was working on his hem and cuffs.

"Hi, again," the other boy said. "I'm Theodore, but people just call me Tubby. That's because I'm shaped like a tub, I guess."

"Theodore, you shouldn't let them say that!" Janet scolded.

"Oh, I don't mind. And it's true, I *am* shaped like a tub.

Anyway, it's better than being called *Theodore*," he said, sticking out his tongue and wincing.

"What is it with these children? No one wants to be called by her given name," the Lady said with a stern glance up at Maggie.

"I'm Trevor."

"I know, everyone knows your name–you're famous!"

"Famous?"

"Yeah, people have been talking about you for days, ever since you got here."

"Days?"

"Yeah, you were the worst-looking fish people had ever seen! We thought you were going to die or something. Leave it to Maggie to bring in a sick fish!"

"Hey! I didn't make him use too much basme; that was his fault!"

"Oooh, isn't *Fisher Girl* touchy?!"

"You're just jealous 'cause I get to Fish and you don't!"

"That's 'cause Epictetus is your grandfather! It's no fair–you're only a year older than me!"

"Children!" the Lady said, standing. "Enough! If I had my way, no children would fish! Now, let's talk of pleasant things, shall we?"

After an awkward silence, Trevor asked, "How long was I asleep?"

"Three days," Maggie said, sounding irritated.

"Three days?! No wonder I was so hungry when I woke up."

"All right, Tubby–I mean Theodore, or whatever your name is–you're done. Step down. Trevor, now it's your turn. Over here," the Lady said.

"Say, I'm hungry," said Tubby, rubbing his stomach. "The feast isn't for hours. Let's go get a snack."

"You're always hungry," Maggie said, crossing her arms and

looking away.

"I'd like something to eat," said Trevor.

"There," said Tubby, with a wink at Trevor, "it's settled. We'll go to the kitchen when you're done and get some grub."

"Oh, please. Giles won't let you anywhere near his popovers. What you need is a little intelligence if you expect to get anything. I'd better lead the way," Maggie said.

"Whatever you do, don't make Giles angry again," the Lady said. "He's got too much on his mind with the feast to bother with you three. There. Done. Step down, Trevor, and give the robe to Janet. It will be ready by the time you get back."

Maggie beat Tubby to the door. Trevor ran to keep up.

"And stay out of Giles's way!" the Lady shouted after them.

Trevor could hear and even smell the kitchen before he could actually see it. There were the raps of wooden spoons on metal pots, and the voices of people calling to each other for things you'd expect to find in a kitchen—salt and butter and such. The smells though; they were so delicious on an empty stomach that they seemed to grab his nose and reel him in like a fish on a line. He found himself leaning forward a little as he went along.

The passages were getting wider, and they were now filled with people with baskets of potatoes and corn and other things on their heads. Things began to get a little tight, and Maggie and Tubby jostled for the lead. When they rounded a corner, they came to two tall doors painted silver and carved into the shapes of two huge fish. They were swept behind a particularly wide woman carrying a kettle and through the righthand door. As soon as they were through, Maggie grabbed Trevor's hand and yanked him to the side. Tubby came along, not looking too happy about it.

"Follow my lead," she said, and without waiting for an answer, she pulled Trevor along after her.

The sight that met Trevor's eyes was glorious! Food everywhere! It wasn't some little affair with a hearth and a kettle. There was an army of cooks in white aprons, carrying platters, and tending fires. One whole wall was dedicated to man-sized cauldrons, bubbling away and being stirred with oar-sized spoons. There were tables for cutting and others for sorting. Another wall was given over to ovens, where bakers were shuttling loaves and buns in and out.

In the center of the room stood a large, round table, and in the middle of that sat an enormous bowl of the pear-shaped fruits from the Great Tree. They still shone, and their light illuminated the faces of the cooks who were cutting and preparing them. Some were peeling them and putting the peelings in boiling water. Others were cutting the fruits and arranging them on trays. Still others were pressing them for juice. But whatever was done with them, they gave off a soft green light.

Maggie edged toward the ovens. When a wooden shuttle sent some piping hot rolls sliding across a cooling table, she said, "Now's our chance!"

As they neared their goal, a voice rang out, "And what do you think you're doin'?!"

A round man with rosy cheeks and a furrowed forehead came over, wiping his hands on his apron.

"Hi Giles! Tubby and I are just showing this new kid around," Maggie said cheerily.

"And helpin' yourselfs to my best hot buns!"

Tubby, who had been looking very uneasy, attempted to slide away unnoticed, but Giles was too quick for him.

"Oh, no you don't, Theodore! You'll not escape me this time!" With that, the big man moved with surprising agility and got ahold of Tubby's left ear between his thumb and forefinger.

"Oww! Oww! I didn't do anything! Honest, we were just looking!"

"We just wanted to show Trevor how good the food is here, Giles, that's all," said Maggie, with a big smile.

Giles' eyes lit up. "Trevor, is it? Well now, that's different!" He let go of Tubby's ear and stuck out a plump hand toward Trevor, which Trevor promptly took and shook.

"We've been worried about you. Touch and go, I hear it was! Well, seeing as you just woke up this very morning, I suppose—"

"Pleeease, Giles," begged Maggie.

"Yeah, please," said Tubby, rubbing his ear.

"Oh, all right. In honor of Trevor. But only one each!" A clatter of pans hitting the floor made them all jump and sent Giles blustering away. "No, no! Not over there, over here!" he shouted to someone who was looking chagrined and holding a basket of carrots near a pile of cookware.

"Giles is great," said Maggie, as she handed out two buns each. "He tries to sound tough, but his heart is as soft as his belly."

The buns were piping hot. "Ow!" Trevor said.

"They're best this way," Tubby said, stuffing a piece of bun in his mouth.

Trevor tore one open with his thumbs. A wisp of steam rose from it, and the delicious smell of hot yeast filled his head. He took some of the fluffy middle and ate it. It had a buttery taste, and it melted like butter too. He closed his eyes. "They're great," he murmured between bites.

"Wait 'til the feast," Tubby said, with his cheeks puffed out like a squirrel's. "This is just the beginning! And since you're the only fish this month, you'll get the first pick of the food!"

"I'm the only catch?" Trevor said, chewing slowly.

"Usually we have two or three," said Maggie. "But it's been a slow month. Good thing I caught you or there'd be no fish at the feast," she finished, directing her words toward Tubby as though they were darts. Tubby just rolled his eyes.

"Then we would have had to listen to old fish tell their stories. I hate when that happens. It's boring," said Tubby. "I wish they'd let me be a Fisher; I even wish I could be a fish. I mean, you guys have had adventures. And then you get to tell everybody about them."

"What do you mean?" said Trevor, who had stopped chewing.

"He means we get to tell everybody about how you got out of Superbia," said Maggie. "It's the most important part of the feast, Grandfather says. We learn all sorts of important stuff about what the bogeys are up to."

An old familiar feeling began to form in Trevor's stomach that had nothing to do with food. "You mean I have to get up in front of everybody?"

"Well, you don't actually have to get up. You'll see. But you do have to tell your story."

"Yeah, I can't wait," said Tubby. "I especially want to hear the part about how Maggie almost killed you!"

"I didn't almost kill him!"

While they went on arguing Trevor felt a sense of trepidation growing. Talking to a bunch of people he didn't know was almost as scary as being captured by bogeymen. Suddenly, he didn't feel hungry anymore. In fact, he had gone from looking forward to the feast to dreading it.

CHAPTER NINE

Fresh Fish

Trevor, Maggie, and Tubby stayed together all that day, exploring the Ward, playing hide-and-seek in the Great Garden with a bunch of other kids, and generally having a good time. If not for his lingering apprehensions about the Feast, Trevor would have said it was the best day he'd ever had.

But, the time for the Feast finally arrived, wanted or not, and they went to get their robes. Lady Rowena had them ready and, after some final adjustments, the children went to the Feast together.

When they got there, hundreds of people were already entering an enormous chamber through many doors.

"This is the place!" Maggie announced. "It's called The Hall of the Green Fire."

"Green fire? Why?"

"You'll see why," said Tubby. "Hey, I gotta go. I see my mom calling me."

As Tubby pushed his way through the crowd, Trevor noticed that people were looking at him. He also noticed that he was the only person in a light blue robe. The combination made him feel uncomfortable. He asked Maggie about it.

"Yep, light blue is the color of Fresh Fish. Since you're the only fish this month, you're the main course," she said with a giggle. Trevor could tell how excited she was by how she kept bouncing on her toes.

Just then Max came up. "Follow me, Fish and Fisher," he said with a bow. Maggie laughed and grabbed Trevor's hand, "Come on!" she said with a tug.

Max's broad shoulders made way for them, and they snaked through the crowd. As they went along, people stopped to look. "Oh, look—it's Abigail and her fish," someone said. Maggie nodded to the someone and giggled louder and bounced higher. Trevor, for his part, was beginning to feel like a trophy.

After they got through the initial press, things opened up a bit and Trevor had a chance to take it all in. To one side, a huge fire roared in a long hearth. *It doesn't look green to me,* he thought. Overhead, oak timbers spanned an arched ceiling of stone. Suspended from the timbers, iron-wrought chandeliers skewered with torches burned bright. *They're not green either,* he noted. Beneath these, long wooden tables draped in white cloth splayed out like spokes in a wheel, each situated so as to give every chair a clear view of the head table. When it dawned on Trevor that that was their destination, his heart skipped a beat.

When they got there, Max pulled out a couple of chairs for them toward one end. "Here you are, Miss Fisher and Master Fish," he said. "Just hold tight, the festivities are about to start," he concluded, with a wink toward Maggie.

"Thank you, Uncle Max," she said, sitting up straight and nodding slightly to her uncle. At that moment, Trevor felt she looked very much like her mother.

He looked out over the feasting hall and saw clusters of people talking loudly, and children running around unsupervised. *So many people,* he thought. Just then, his old friend, *Mr. Queasy,* opened a door in his stomach and came in and sat down. "I think I'm going to be sick," he said.

"Oh, no you're not," Maggie said out of the corner of her mouth. "Mother worked all afternoon on your robe. The least you can do is keep it clean."

Out of the crowd, some girls came up, giggling behind their hands. One said, "I like this fish, he's cute!" Trevor went red and turned to Maggie.

She rolled her eyes and waved them away, "Go away, little girls! Go back to mommy and daddy!"

"What's a-matter, Abigail?" another said. "Afraid of a little competition?" The rest giggled even louder.

Now Maggie got red.

Suddenly the lights went dim, and the room began to quiet down. People began finding their seats. The hall was packed, and only the head table remained empty. There the torches burned just as brightly.

Two tall doors opened at the back, and a solitary figure entered. Now the room went completely still. The figure began striding up the center aisle. He was a barrel-chested man in a gold-festooned uniform, and he walked with a polished ebony walking-stick. As he drew closer, Trevor noticed a fat, white mustache that sat up on his lip like a porcupine. The only sounds now were the martial clip, clip of his boots, and the tap of his staff on the marble floor.

"That's Brendleback, Captain of the Men-at-Arms," Maggie whispered.

When he reached the head table, he turned toward the assembly with statuesque dignity. With a voice like a mixture of thunder and gravel, he called out, "All rise for the Masters of the Guild!"

Chairs pushed back and everyone stood. Three grandly adorned men entered, followed by a retinue.

The first was the youngest of the three, and Trevor thought he recognized him from the market. He wore a dark green robe draped over a well-fed body, and his black beard glinted with oil and was combed into a fork. Two smiling eyes peeped over round rosy cheeks. On his robe, around the hem, collar, and cuffs, golden leaves wound in an intricate embroidered pattern.

"Good old Paracelsus," said Maggie, with a smile. "Everyone loves him. He's the Master Alchemist, you know. The Alchemists are the reason the Guild is so rich."

Second came Epictetus, looking even grander than he had that morning. His robes were scarlet, and like those of Paracelsus, they were embroidered around the collar, hem and cuffs. But instead of leaves, his robes depicted fish, one after another, head biting tail. The eye patch he wore now was encrusted with white gems that flashed when he turned to the crowd. He smiled when he saw the children.

The last was the oldest of the three, and he wore a dark blue robe. His hair was snowy white, and his eyes seemed to be set just a little too close together, giving him a slightly confounded expression. He squinted from beneath enormously bushy eyebrows that jutted out like the brims of a hat. And his beard was so immense and thick that it seemed to weigh him down and bend him over. His jaw made a chewing motion like an old man makes when he's lost his teeth, which–Trevor came to find out–he had. About midway up the aisle, he veered left and knocked into a table. Hands went out to help him, and Maggie's mother moved alongside to steady him, but he shook them all off.

"I'm all right, confusticate it! Who put that blasted table in the center of the aisle?!"

"That's Ichabod," Maggie said, looking embarrassed, "–our Master Illuminator."

The Lady Rowena stayed with him and helped him find his seat. Trevor noticed that his robe was embroidered like the others, but with tongues of fire.

Other regal looking people came in now and joined the others at the head table. When everyone had found a place,

Brendleback struck the floor twice with his stick and everyone but Epictetus sat down. Trevor sat late and with some awkwardness, but thankfully, no one seemed to notice.

"Guild Fellows, welcome to The Feast of the Fresh Fish!" Epictetus said, in a voice that filled the room.

Many hearty chuckles came from the tables. Maggie laughed a little too long and drew a few looks. She covered her mouth and sank down in her chair.

"We are come this evening to honor Fish and Fisher! Great deeds have been done, and later those deeds will be told! But now, let the feasting begin!" With that, Epictetus clapped loudly three times, and a set of doors off to one side flew open. In came men wearing tall white hats and bearing wide trays stacked high with food. Girls followed with pitchers for pouring. A cheer went up, and Epictetus sat down.

Although Trevor had seen some of the preparations, he didn't expect this. The volume of food was stupendous! He'd been raised in Superbia, after all, where variety meant having a biscuit with your gruel. Maggie explained what he saw and where it was from. There were vegetables and fruit from the lands south of the Desert of Zin. The sweet breads and rolls were baked in Trothward, of course, but the butter and honey were from beyond the Bounding Heath. And the smoked fish and scallops came from the Pupille Sea. There was more, lots more, but describing it all would be tedious.

Trevor piled the food on, and no one stopped him. Then he ate it all and piled it on again, and still no one stopped him! Just when he thought it was all too good to be true, they brought out dessert! There were pies and cakes and pastries and candy. But best of all were the flavored ices!

Throughout the evening, Trevor felt a growing sense of comfort even as his belt became less comfortable. He'd forgotten all about having to tell his story when the food arrived, then the entertainment began and kept the thought away. Some musicians with wooden flutes and a drum accompanied a juggler who mesmerized everyone with his ability to juggle anything: balls, cups, even flaming batons.

Then, people began looking in Trevor's direction, whispering to each other. He half guessed why, and Mr. Queasy reintroduced himself. Now he wished he hadn't eaten so much.

Unexpectedly, the lights went out and the juggler extinguished his batons. Light burst in from an outer room when the doors flew open to let in the cooks. Another cheer went up. This time they came with platters of glowing fruit, the light of which would have reminded Trevor of a summer's day in a forest if he'd ever had the opportunity to see one. The green light shone up on the faces of those carrying the trays, and the effect made it seem like each man was bearing his own head on a platter.

Platters were set on tables. The fruit had already been cut into bite-sized portions. Handing a tray to him, Maggie said, "Take a piece and pass it on." Goblets were then filled by girls from pitchers of shining juice.

Trevor looked around the room. Everywhere, faces were lit from beneath as by green candle flames. He leaned over his cup and looked down. There, he saw himself reflected, all green and round looking back.

Maggie elbowed him.

"Now you know why it's called The Hall of the Green Fire," she said, with a slice of fruit in her hand. She popped it in her mouth and followed that with a swig from her cup.

He noticed that everyone else was doing the same thing, so he took his fruit and ate.

It was like a burst of flame had ignited in his mouth! Without thinking, he grabbed his cup and took a sloppy swallow. That made it worse! The heat got hotter and the fire slipped down the back of his throat and continued on to his stomach. Perspiration formed on his forehead, and he shot a panic-stricken glance at Maggie.

She smiled back at him with a mouthful of green teeth! It unnerved him exceedingly.

What's going on? Who are these people? he wondered.

By the time the heat hit his stomach, he felt a more alarming sensation.

Suddenly, he began to feel as though he were growing. It felt like every part of him–from his head to his feet–began to expand. He looked at his hands and legs; they didn't look any different. But the feeling of growth went on. Maggie seemed closer somehow. Then, after a moment, he felt like he was beginning to press up against her. He looked over at her; she wasn't any nearer. Still, the pressure increased and continued to grow until it got uncomfortable. He felt he might panic and run screaming from the room if it kept up.

Then there was a pop and the pressure eased.

"Hello, Trevor," said a familiar voice.

He looked over at Maggie, but her eyes were closed. Then he noticed everyone else's eyes were closed, too.

"Maggie?"

"Yes, it's me," she said, not moving her lips. "We're sharing our minds."

"What?!"

"Don't be afraid. It'll only last a while. It's the fruit. It's making us one."

"What do you mean, it's making us one?"

"Don't worry, silly. It'll be okay."

While she spoke, Trevor began hearing other voices. More

and more people seemed to be entering his head. It was getting loud in there. It should have been a cacophony, but to his amazement, he could make out each voice distinctly and understand them all at once.

Among the voices, he heard the voice of Epictetus cry out. "Guildfellows! Now we are truly gathered. It is time for tales of daring to be told. This evening, we will hear the stories of my beloved Granddaughter, Abigail Blaise and her catch, Trevor Upjohn. She is this month's only Fisher. I am very proud of her, as you can well understand."

In his mind, Trevor could sense the pride, like a mighty red swell. There were feelings from other people, too, some not so pleasing and hastily covered up. Who they belonged to, Trevor couldn't tell; they came and went so quickly.

"Ahem, well now, Granddaughter, begin your story," said Epictetus.

And Maggie did. But she didn't use words. Instead Trevor felt himself swept up into a memory not his own. The fruit of the Tree not only made it possible to hear her mind, it made it possible to see her mind, and even feel her emotions. He was one with her when she volunteered to be a Fisher at a dinner table shared by her mother and grandfather only a few months before. At this point, there was a change of perspective. It was abrupt and jarring. He now saw Maggie from the outside. She looked small and vulnerable. He felt he was now in the Lady Rowena's memory, and he was now seeing Maggie through her eyes. But the scene shifted again, and a calm confidence settled on everything. Maggie looked stronger and taller than before. He was now in Epictetus's memory, and he saw her through the old Fisher's eyes. Then he heard Epictetus say, "Abigail, you have my support. I know your father would be pleased." Then he was again in Maggie's mind and felt her heart nearly burst with joy.

And so the tale was told. Although it was Maggie's story, others contributed to it, filling it out and making it richer and more complete than it could have been otherwise. And it was done so seamlessly and effortlessly that the shifts in perspective were hardly noticeable after a while.

After weeks of tedious training and growing impatience, Maggie got into a hidden compartment beneath a horse-drawn grain cart. After a long, cramped, and bumpy ride, she looked out of a peep-hole and saw the gates of Superbia rising above her. Her heart beat faster when she heard the boots of a guard walking around the cart and talking with the driver about spies and refugees and other undesirables who had been caught sneaking in and out of the city. "Carts much like this one are being used," the guard said. There was a muffled conversation in low voices that Maggie couldn't understand, and then the guard said, "I knew we could work things out." Then more loudly, "All clear here, let them pass!" And Maggie felt the floor shift beneath her, and they were moving again.

They finally came to a stop, and the compartment was opened. With a shock, she saw the white robe of a Guardian and a hardened face, but then Maggie saw a quick and subtle hand gesture that was a mark of the Guild and a wave of relief washed over her.

She was taken straight to one of the children's halls, and there she saw Trevor for the first time.

It is quite a shock to see yourself through another's eyes, and it was the weirdest thing Trevor experienced in a day of weird experiences. There he was, taller and goofier-looking than he ever knew, but there was a certain charm as well. Some odd feelings began to rise up that he wasn't sure what to make of until he realized they weren't his own feelings at all: they were Maggie's. They were quickly suppressed. Trevor glanced over at her, but he couldn't see her face because she had turned away.

The scene shifted again, and Maggie was talking quietly with her grandfather late at night after everyone was asleep.

"Are you making friends? Any prospects?" he asked.

"It's hard to get to know kids. There's a bully here named Meno, and most of the kids are afraid to talk about naughty things because of him. But there is one kid that I think there's hope for."

"Good. Remember, do not be too direct. You might frighten him. Let him come to you. Watch and listen. If he is truly remembering, you'll see the signs."

Epictetus reached into his bag and pulled out a pouch.

"Be quick about it and get back to bed," the old man said, handing the pouch to Maggie.

She crept quietly into the dining hall, and from there back into a darkened kitchen. In the back, she found a tall bag of meal. She opened the top and poured the contents of the pouch into it.

In a flash, Trevor understood. She had added something to the food–something that would help children remember where they came from, something to counteract the spells of the Snatchers. It all made sense now. That's why kids were remembering home, more than ever before. The Guild really was behind it all.

What came after that Trevor already knew–his embarrassment in class, the trip to the gates, the fight, his conversation with Maggie and Epictetus that night. Maggie's story ended when she woke up and found Trevor missing.

Here Epictetus spoke up. "For those of you who don't know, when a Fish falls into the hands of the authorities, Fishers are immediately removed from Superbia as a precaution. But I think Abigail's story is largely told. Now it is your turn, Trevor."

It wasn't nearly as bad as he thought it'd be—no knocking knees, no quavering voice—just remembering. Mr. Queasy didn't even come back. He managed to leave out the parts where he cried. He hoped no one noticed. When Zephyr entered the story, a wave of pleasure swept over the room. Trevor could tell they had seen him before and knew what to expect, but there were feelings of awe and devotion at the appearance of the little mouse, too. As he told the story, he found himself enjoying the reactions of the listeners to his narrow escapes. He could feel their feelings toward him were changing. His stature was growing in their minds, and he knew it. He had never known what it was like to be admired before, and he discovered that he liked how it felt.

And so the Feast ended much better than Trevor could have foreseen. Shortly, the effects of the fruit wore off and he returned to his own perspective on things. But the perspective of those who had heard his story had been changed for good. People looked at him differently. There was one person in particular who took special note of him; and unbeknownst to Trevor, he had become part of that particular someone's very elaborate calculations.

CHAPTER TEN

Hot Cocoa

Far away from the lights of Trothward, in a musty room in darkest Superbia, there sat a fat, old man in a shabby red suit. He wore a paste-on beard that had been white once, but had gone gray from dust and cookie crumbs. "Ho, ho, ho! Sweet children, dear children," he said to three boys huddled in a doorway. To a shadowed figure standing behind them, he added, "Bring them closer, Mr. Gourmand; bring them closer."

The boys were the villainous sort so common in children's books, but who are, quite inconveniently, based on real boys who sit next to nice children at school. You know the kind—the ones who take pleasure in torturing small defenseless animals when they can find them, and when they can't, they turn on their classmates. There was Trevor's old nemesis, Meno, and his partner-in-crime, Willis. And tagging along behind them was someone Trevor had never suspected of complicity in his sufferings—his old bunkmate, Drake. A man in a red suit with fluffy cuffs was the last thing they had expected to see when they were awakened in the night by the Behavior Modifiers.

"Ho! Ho! Ho! No need to fear, my delicious little morsels! Come and have some cocoa with me!" There on a dais—next to the fat man (who the children felt looked oddly familiar)—was a table with a tall pitcher on it and four steaming mugs.

"Go on," said Gourmand, nudging the boys.

The children crept forward warily and sat down. Each eyed

his drink suspiciously and then looked at the man. "Don't you recognize me?" They shook their heads. "Why, I'm Santa Claus, of course! I've come all the way from a place called The North Pole to pay you a visit! Ho! Ho! Ho!" The boys stared at him with vacant eyes. "Go ahead and drink. I think you'll like it; no, I know you will." He picked up his mug and took a loud, slurpy swallow. "Ahhh, deeeelicious. See? Have some."

Drake looked at the steaming mug of brown stuff. It smelled good. Cautiously, he picked it up and brought it to his lips. Looking over the edge, he saw that Meno had gulped his down already and was wiping a frothy mustache away with his sleeve. Willis was drinking from his mug, and there was a big smile on his face when he set it down. Opening his mouth, Drake let a little of the hot liquid touch his tongue. It burned, but the thick drink was sweeter than anything he could remember tasting. He greedily drained the cup, oblivious to the scorching heat that scalded his throat. When he finished, he wanted more and he wanted it right then.

Now, when the brightly-dressed, fat man spoke, Drake thought he had never heard a voice so pleasant and agreeable.

"Ho! Ho! Ho! Want some more? There's plenty!" cried the jolly man, pointing to the steaming pitcher.

"Yes, more!" Willis demanded, thrusting his mug at the man in red.

"What's the magic wooorrd?" the man asked, with an indulgent smile.

"Pleeeaassse!" the three sang in chorus.

"Ho! Ho! Ho! I am so glad you like my cocoa. I made it especially for you. But first, let's chat a while, shall we? If you're good, and promise to help dear old Santa, he'll give you more cocoa, all right?"

"Why can't we have some now?" Meno said.

"Because Santa says so," the fat man said, a little irritated.

"But–" Willis chirped.

"Because Santa says so," the red man said, through gritted teeth.

"Uhh, okay," Meno said, slumping in his chair.

"Good. Such wonderful children; don't you agree Mr. Gourmand?"

"Yes, Santa. Wonderful."

"Now children, Mr. Gourmand and I would like you to perform a little service for your beloved country. It is a small, teeny, weeny thing. You see, my tender morsels, there are some very bad people spreading some very bad ideas among the children of Superbia. They tell them about an imaginary place called *home*." (He made little quote signs with his fat fingers when he said *home*.) "They say *home* (quotes, again) is lined with *candy* and filled with people called *parents* who provide their every wish."

The boys were shocked to hear an adult using naughty words–even with quotation marks.

"When children believe these ridiculous fibs, they're stolen from their beds in the middle of the night under the pretense of taking them to this make-believe place. Once there, all kinds of horrible, awful things are done to them. I won't go into it because I don't want to frighten you, but I will say this–those children are never seen nor heard from again.

"The good news is that the noble Guardians have uncovered their conspiracy. We know who many of the leaders are, and we could try to apprehend them one at a time, but the others would just run away and reorganize their terrible plot. That's why we must come on them all at once and arrest them all."

"So? What does that have to do with us?" interrupted Meno.

A look of annoyance passed over the jolly man's face, but he composed himself quickly. "Ahhh, he's a sharp one, sharp as a pin; wouldn't you agree Mr. Gourmand?"

"Yes, Santa. Very sharp."

"My young fellow," the fat man said to Meno, "Santa is looking for a few good boys to help him. You see, we know where their hideout is, and we want to surprise them and capture them all at once. There's just one thing standing in our way. At the center of their hideout is a bad thing–a very bad thing. It's magic–wild magic–and it will spring to life at the slightest hint of an attack. It is this wild magic thing that Santa needs your help with."

"If it's magic, won't it be dangerous?" asked Willis.

"No, no, no, my sweet. No, for some strange reason it doesn't harm children. But children, properly equipped, can harm it." The man in red reached into a great, felt bag and pulled out a brightly wrapped box. "This, my delicious children, contains magic so powerful, it can even overcome wild magic. It has taken years to make and it is very precious. All Santa needs you to do is smuggle this box into the hideout where the wild magic is and open it. That's all. What's inside the box will do the rest. But you mustn't open it before that– oh, no. If you do, it will turn on you. And you wouldn't want that. That would be most unpleasant," he finished, in a low voice.

"How are we supposed to get to this hideout?" Meno asked, suspiciously.

"Nothing could be easier, my sweet. All you need do is say five simple words, and before long the villains will come for you and take you right to it. Just repeat after me. Say–*I want to go home.*"

The boy's mouths fell open.

"Won't we get in trouble?" squealed Willis.

"No, no, no. Santa's arranged everything," the fat man said, impatiently.

Still, the children looked uncertain.

"Can you say it for a little more cocoa?" he said, reaching for the pitcher at his elbow.

After considering the pitcher, Meno mumbled, "Uh, I want to go home."

"Awful. Simply awful. If that's the best you can do, I suppose I will have to find children who like my cocoa."

"No!" Meno blurted. Then with enthusiasm only gluttony could muster, he said again, "I want to go home."

"Better, but not good enough. Say it with conviction!"

"I want to go home!"

"Getting there. Now, all of you!"

"I want to go home!" they all said.

"Again!"

"I want to go home!"

"Good, good my sweets. That's the way. Ho! Ho! Ho! Now, if you are good boys, I'll arrange a big party for you with all the hot cocoa you can drink and treats besides. Isn't that right, Mr. Gourmand?"

"That's right, Santa."

"Well, that's all my sweets. Mr. Gourmand will take you now."

Gourmand whistled and two Behavior Modifiers stepped into the room.

"Go with the bogeys, tender ones."

The boys looked longingly at the pitcher of cocoa.

"But, the cocoa—you promised," whined Drake.

Suddenly, the jolly man's face twisted and got as red as his jacket. All thought of cocoa fled their minds. But just as quickly, his face softened and a creepy smile slowly spread across it. "Ho! Ho! Ho! What was I thinking? Yes, yes, of course I did. Have some more." He reached for the pitcher, and messily poured the drink into their mugs. "Now drink up, but no more until you have finished your task."

The boys downed their drinks, getting as much on themselves as in their mouths.

"Now, off with you!" the fat man commanded with a wave of a chubby hand.

✧

Once the children were out of the room, Gourmand turned to where the fake Santa had been, but instead there was a hulking shadow.

"My Lord Lucian, a most clever disguise. Wherever did you come up with it?"

"Yes, it was, wasn't it? It is from a fable of their home world. I knew it would elicit their trust. And the drink worked nicely, too."

"Forgive me, my Lord, for my impertinence; but what of the Troth? How will such stupid boys get close to it? Won't it be guarded?"

"My dear bogey, a most reliable source has confirmed what I have long suspected. It is unguarded. They believe it is invincible. As to those morsels finding it, I am told children are taken directly to it as soon as they arrive. Any imbecile could do what we need–even those imbeciles. Ahhh, isn't it delicious, my carnivorous companion, using those succulent sweets as bait?"

"Yes, my Lord. But will it work?"

"Of course, my friend, the Guild positively drips with compassion–it's their greatest weakness. They couldn't bear to turn them away."

CHAPTER ELEVEN

Ichabod

"Well, you've got a big day, there's no mistake about that," Max said. "Master Epictetus tells me I'm supposed to take you to see the Illuminators. Thinks you might have a natural inclination for their work, he does. I feel I should warn you, though, Master Ichabod can be a tad difficult, not to mention forgetful–not that I normally speak ill of my betters. But I thought you should know.

"'Tis a pity, if you ask me–you wasting time with the Illuminators. Fishing is where the action is. You've only seen a tiny bit of what we do. But when you've had your fill of them, you'll be back, I'm sure. From your story, it looks to me as though you're more cut out for our line of work."

Trevor walked alongside Max as he ambled through Trothward's seemingly endless corridors. The day after the Feast, he had learned that Max wasn't even Maggie's real uncle. He had been her father's shield-bearer. They had only started calling him that when her father hadn't returned with him from the wars in the south between the bogeys and the few remaining kingdoms that hadn't submitted to Lucian.

Trevor was living with Maggie's family now, since it was customary for Fresh Fish to live with their Fishers until it was determined which order of the Guild a Fish should join. After that, a Fish became a Guildfellow and moved into the wing occupied by his new order. Not that Trevor planned on staying in Trothward very long; his goal was getting home. But he had to wait for Zephyr to do that. So he'd decided to make do and fit in as best he could until then.

He was just beginning to learn his way about the place. There was a lot to learn; it rambled on and on. One thing that helped was its shape. It was really just a big square built around the garden. "The technical term for it is quadrangle," Maggie had told him that morning, in her most annoying—*I know more than you*—voice. "I know what a quadrangle is," he had fibbed. Their words had been a bit sharp at the breakfast table, and they had both come away with some internal bleeding.

What he had been able to piece together from his own observations and his talks with others was this: Trothward had four sides (just like a square) and each of the sides was home to one of the orders of the Guild. The Alchemists were the largest, and they were on the southern side; the Illuminators were the smallest, and they were on the east; the Fishers were on the west; and finally, everybody else—the cooks, gardeners, men-at-arms, and all their relations—were on the north. No matter how many people lived in it, each side was the same size. That meant that some parts of Trothward were more crowded than other parts. Each side had three floors above ground, but Max hinted that there were some floors below ground, too. One of the more curious features of the place was the windows—or rather the absence of them. There were plenty looking in toward the Troth and the garden, but none looking out. When Trevor asked about it, Max told him, "We already know what's outside, and we don't like it. It's what on the inside that's worth looking at. Besides, looking out means looking in, and we don't need them bogeys peeking in anywhere."

It was all pretty simple and easy to imagine, but there was one element to the design that complicated things. At each corner of the square, on the outside, there was a smaller garden with a wall around it, and at the far end of each of these smaller squares sat a Master's residence.

To get to the Illuminators' wing, Max was leading Trevor through the Alchemists' quarter. It struck Trevor as an odd place. It was full of workshops that emitted strange noises and stranger smells.

"Max, what are they doing?" Trevor asked.

"Doing? Why, what Alchemists always do. They're trying to make gold."

"Gold?"

"That's right. Mostly, they make things from the Troth, basme and such, and they sell those things in the market, as you've seen. They make a whole lotta gold that way. Not that I'm complaining. They've made us rich. Things are pretty comfortable these days, in spite of troubles with bogeys. But, they've got this crazy notion that they can make real gold out of just about anything you could imagine: wood, rocks, even lead. Don't know why. They sell their goods far and wide, not just in Olton, but even in Hareton, and as far away as Ophir–even as far as the Redoubtable Hills, and that's as far as you can go. In my opinion, they should be satisfied with that–but that's just my opinion. Ahh, we've finally arrived!"

They had come to a set of glass doors that went nearly all the way to the ceiling. Streams of brilliant, white light poured through them and settled at their feet. On the lintel and doorposts, tongues of fire licked at the edges of the glass. Trevor reached out to feel the heat, but there wasn't any.

"Go ahead, touch them. It won't hurt," said Max.

To his surprise, the flames were cool to the touch. They only produced the slightest tickling sensation.

Unexpectedly, the doors swung soundlessly inward.

They entered a long, white passage. There were two strange things to it. First, except for the doors lining either side, it was completely empty. And second, the light was so alarmingly bright there were no shadows to be seen.

"It hurts my eyes," Trevor said.

"You'll get used to it," Max said, squinting.

"Here, try these," said a cheerful voice from behind them.

Trevor turned to see a portly man with a black beard and a broad, pearly smile with a single, golden tooth. On his nose was a pair of glasses with smoky lenses. In a plump hand, he held out a second pair.

He peeked over the rims with a pair of jovial eyes. "Go ahead, you can return them later. I'm sorry my good Max, I've only one extra pair."

"That's all right, Master Paracelsus. I won't be here long. I'm just taking Trevor here to see Master Ichabod."

"Trevor? Not the boy with the remarkable story from the feast? Well, this is a pleasant surprise! How I did enjoy that story, young man. You must be a special child to have come through such danger with nary a scratch! Here, do take these glasses; you will need them here."

Trevor felt a surge of pleasure. He gratefully reached out for the glasses. "Thanks," he said. As he took them, he couldn't help noticing that each of Paracelsus' fingers was encrusted with several golden rings.

"I do hope you will join me in the Alchemists' quarter when you are done with your time here. There, you will learn something of practical value, I assure you—unlike here, where more is forgotten than remembered. It is such a shame to see what the Illuminators have come to—but we must not judge them too harshly. One must be generous. As for Ichabod, I am afraid he can't help himself. It is a pity."

"Ahem, well now," Max interjected awkwardly. "Fancy seeing you here, Master."

"Yes, it is odd, isn't it? But sometimes my research brings me to the Illuminators' Library. Not that I find much–but we mustn't despise little things. Even they can be put to use. But I am on my way back to my workshop." He nodded to Trevor. "Until we meet again, my remarkable young man." Then with a flourish, and a billowing of robes, he strode away.

Max watched his departure with a puzzled look. "Hmm, well, where were we? O, yes, Master Ichabod."

He led Trevor to a set of large, wooden doors that swung outward at their approach, and they entered a vast windowless room.

The light was dim, and Trevor had to take off his glasses to see. The place was huge, but it was as cramped as an overstuffed closet. Boxes and books were stacked precariously in towers so high he couldn't see over them; and there were so many of them, and they were set so closely together, meandering canyons had formed. The stuff had a musty, old smell, too, like it been sitting there, decaying, for years. It was so depressingly shabby, Trevor hoped they had come to the wrong place.

"Here we are!" said Max, trying to sound cheerful. "I was told Master Ichabod would meet us." He glanced about. It didn't look like his stocky frame could fit down any of the man-made valleys. "Well, I'm sure Master Ichabod is here–somewhere," he said uncertainly. "No doubt he'll be along presently and you'll have a fine time," he continued apologetically. "Well, I suppose I should be off to see about my duties. Bye, bye," he finished, not looking sure if he should really go. He backed out reluctantly and, as if on cue, the doors slammed shut right on Trevor's nose.

"Ow!" He fell back into a tower of boxes which began to

teeter. "Oh, no!" he said as he steadied it. He had barely avoided disaster. On the other side of it was another tower, and another and another into the distance. They would have gone down like dominoes. "Whew, that was close."

The space left to him was barely enough to turn around in without bumping into something. He considered what to do. One of the trails looked like it went toward the center of the room so he took it. After several turns, he came to an open space.

He found two chairs next to a small table set with a couple of tea cups. There was also an electric torch on the table, like the one Epictetus used, except this one didn't look like a mountain, and it didn't have a dragon. What it did have was a glassy face at the top, and that's where the light came from. It was burning brightly.

There was one more thing on the table, and it was this that attracted his attention. It was a book. Now, he was in a library simply chock full of books–so another book shouldn't have been noteworthy. But he felt drawn to it. It had a black, weather-beaten binding that was cracked and ancient looking. The edges of its pages were yellowed and irregular, as though someone had torn each and every one of them individually. Inexplicably, his palms started itching and he felt a strong need to pick it up. When he did, an almost electric thrill went through him.

What he saw in it was page after handwritten page, written in a bold, confident hand along with incomprehensible diagrams full of lines and figures. At first, he thought he could read some of it, but as he went along the writing seemed to change. It began to move and rearrange itself. Letters hopped over each other, making one word, then another, and then becoming nonsense and back again. He set the book down and rubbed his eyes. But when he picked it up again, the same thing happened.

"Epictetus was right–you are a nosy boy," said a wheezy voice over his shoulder.

Trevor jumped when he saw Ichabod's frowning face was leaning over him.

"I–I'm sorry."

"Sorry?! Don't be ridiculous," the old man said scrunching up his nose repeatedly. "What do you have to be sorry for?– Wait! You didn't understand it, did you?" Ichabod said, sounding suddenly eager. Trevor shook his head. The old man grunted. "Figures, I've been trying to make sense of it for years, but I've not been able to read a single sentence. In a way I wish you had; I should very much like to know what it says."

Ichabod had probably been taller than Epictetus at one time, but now he was bent and stooped. He had a steaming kettle in his hand.

"Come along, come along, let's get acquainted, shall we?" he said, as he shuffled toward one of the chairs.

When he got to it, he began to sit, ever so slowly, then his legs gave way. He landed with a bump and nearly spilled his kettle. When he looked up, his eyes opened wide, bewildered.

"Whaa –? Who are you? What are you doing in my library?!"

Trevor remembered what Max had said about Ichabod's memory. "I–umm, I'm Trevor, sir. I was sent by Master Epictetus to help you, remember?"

"Trevor? Who the blast is Trevor?" Suddenly a light came on in his eyes. "Trevor! Oh, the new boy. Why didn't you say so? Don't just stand there like a clod, have a seat and have some tea. Take anything in yours?"

Trevor sat. "Take anything?"

"Yes, yes–in your tea?" he said irritably. "Oh, I forgot. You're new here. Back in Superbia, you're lucky to get tea at all, I suppose. Well, I like to indulge myself a little, take sugar in mine.

Want to try some?"

Ichabod offered him a little cube of white stuff. Trevor took it and carefully licked it, then nodded vigorously that he would very much like some sugar in his tea. Ichabod passed the bowl, and Trevor put five or six of the cubes into his cup. Ichabod grunted.

"Sir," Trevor said tentatively, "what good is a book you can't read?"

"What? What's that? What good is a book you can't read? Not much, I can tell you," he said.

"But why can't I read it?"

Ichabod looked at him crossly. "Why can't I read it?" he mocked.

It was the sort of thing Trevor was used to hearing an eight-year-old say. Coming from an old man, it was a little unnerving.

"Let me ask you a question, Mr. Nosy-Bosy," Ichabod said, sounding even more like an eight-year-old. "Have you ever wanted to write something down that you didn't want the wrong person to read?" Trevor nodded, tentatively. "Well, there. The man who wrote that didn't want the wrong person to read it. The good thing is that we're the right people. The bad thing is that we've forgotten how to do it. Unfortunately, we have a number of books like it," he said, sounding more like an old man with every word. "It's a sad story, really. We Illuminators are a bit out of form lately. You shouldn't like to hear about it, I would think."

Trevor wasn't sure if that was a question or a statement, so he just nodded.

"Bah! I was afraid of that."

After a pause in which Ichabod fussed with pouring his tea, he said, "When I was younger, things were better—but not by much. You have to go a long way back to see the Illuminators in their prime. Those were the days," he said, with a hint of a smile. "There were only the Illuminators then; no Fishers and no blasted Alchemists." He muttered something under his breath at this point. "Ah, yes, those were the days. But, of course, that was before the greatest Illuminator of them all."

"Who was that, sir?"

Ichabod paused in mid-pour over his cup. He looked up, dumfounded. "What's that? You don't know?!"

"Uh–know, sir?" Trevor said, looking at the tea. It was getting dangerously near the brim.

Ichabod slammed the kettle down, knocking much of the tea out of his cup.

"Why, everyone knows about him! I would have thought the Alchemists would have said something at least!" Suddenly his eyes narrowed. "That's it, isn't it? They want me to tell you," he said accusingly. "One more humiliation for the Master Illuminator–that's the idea. One more; it's cruel, that's what it is, cruel." Ichabod slumped back in his chair and looked despondent.

"I–I don't understand," Trevor sputtered.

"I don't understand," Ichabod mocked, rocking his head back and forth. "Why, that it's all *our* fault! But it's not, I'm telling you! It's *his* fault!"

Trevor edged away as much as he dared.

The old man looked so sad and tired, Trevor felt a twinge of pity for him–not enough to really feel uncomfortable. But it was a twinge.

"Ah well, one more humiliation won't kill me," he said at last. When he reached for his kettle again, he noticed the tea that had spilled. "What in the world? Who spilled my tea?" he said, looking around. "Was it you?" He eyed Trevor suspiciously.

"No, sir."

"Must be something wrong with my cup," he said, lifting it and wiping the tea on the table with a hem of a sleeve. Then he took the kettle and poured some tea into Trevor's cup. "Good thing I made this," he said. "Thought it might prove useful this morning; not that I thought of telling stories. Troth leaf tea loosens the joints, and that is something an old man can appreciate, but it has many uses." He then picked up the electric torch and wound it. It had begun to go dim, but as he wound it flashed intense, white and clean. He set it down in the middle of the table. Then, he took a long sip from his cup. After that, he sat up, cleared his throat, and closed his eyes.

After an awkward silence, he opened one of his eyes and looked at Trevor. "Well, aren't *you* going to drink *your* tea?"

"Uh, sure," Trevor said, uncertainly.

He raised it to his nose and breathed in. It had a strong, heady smell. It was a dark drink, with what he thought was a tinge of green. He put it to his mouth. It was hot! He blew on it and a little of it lapped his lips. It was pungent, but not unpleasant. Indeed, it finished sweetly as it lingered. He took a slurpy sip. Immediately, he felt the change.

"That's better," Ichabod said, without moving his lips. "Now I can tell the tale properly."

CHAPTER TWELVE

The Greatest Illuminator of Them All

"In the beginning," Ichabod intoned, "when the world was younger and bogeys were only found in tales told by old wives, and there were no clouds in the sky save those that brought rain and then went on their way, there were the Illuminators."

He spoke directly into Trevor's mind, and his voice rose up lilting and almost musical, as though he was reciting something from memory. Strange, beautiful images formed as he spoke, and Trevor felt himself lifted from his chair and carried high into the air. Up he climbed, over rolling mossy hills to rocky places and higher still. Up, up he rose until he came to a range of mountains standing in a line, like sentinels at the edge of the world. And there, on the foremost of them, he came to rest on a high wind-shorn shelf. From there, he looked back down on the very world Ichabod described. Stretching out before him were patches of farmland and forest, standing golden and green beneath the clear blue sky.

It was all like a dream; but it wasn't a dream. And standing right next to him on the ledge was a younger version of Ichabod. His beard was not so immense, neither were his eyebrows quite so unruly. Both contained hints of black. He was tall and straight and breathing deeply.

"What happened?" Trevor said.

"Eh, what's that? Why, I'm showing you a memory, of course. Not my own, obviously. Someone else's whose name has been forgotten. It came down to me over many generations, passed from father to son. Since I've no son of my own, I might as well show it to you as anyone. Now, come along."

With startling quickness, the Illuminator grasped Trevor's hand and stepped off the cliff. With a jerk, Trevor followed. The shock was only momentary. A wind rose up to meet them, and it lifted them high into the air. They now passed over streams and lakes flashing bright, as well as small castles standing on green hills beside tiny thatch-roofed villages. There were people too, looking like ants crawling on the roads.

Finally, after he had lost count of the little hamlets he'd seen, they came to the largest yet, standing next to the eaves of a forest. At the center of the town was an open green, and flanking it on one side was a long building with a sharply pitched, many-gabled roof.

It was the roof they were heading for, and they weren't slowing down. Trevor cringed and clamped his eyes tight. There was no crash though, only the feeling that they had come to a stop. When he opened his eyes again, he saw that they were now standing in a long, dark room. Before them was a broad table draped in cloth, and behind it sat a line of men in tall, wooden chairs. They were like kings, some old, some not so old, each with a beard across his chest and dressed in a robe of white. The oldest sat in the center, his back hunched, his head jutting forward like a bird's. The bird-ness was reinforced by a long, hooking nose and a pair of piercing eagle-like eyes that looked out from beneath a balding brow.

"My fathers, long past," said Ichabod softly.

Impressive as these were, the most striking figure in the room was the man standing before them. He was tall and straight, and a light fell on him from a smoke hole in the roof. He had a short, black beard, braided at the end and streaked with two silver lines. His eyes were hard and humorless and hungry. And when he laughed, his eyes didn't, they just kept the same hungry look. His chin was raised, and he looked disdainfully down his nose at the men behind the table.

The whole scene made Trevor uncomfortable. He didn't like confrontations and this certainly had the look of one.

"Wha–what's happening?" he asked nervously.

"Shhh!" Ichabod scolded. "Listen and learn."

The standing man began to speak, softly at first, in a voice that began like a growl and finished with a roar. "Cowards–here you sit–satisfied with the crumbs that fall to you. Your servile lore is contemptible to me. I will have more!"

The bird-like man at the center stiffened and his eyes narrowed. "Lucian, your ambition has breached the bounds of virtue once again. Can you not speak respectfully? We all acknowledge your talent; we are not so proud as to deny genius when we see it. But we warn you, check that ambition of yours lest you burn yourself by venturing too close to the flame."

"Virtue?" the man named Lucian said, contemptuously. "What do you know of virtue? Virtue is for men–men who aspire to greatness! Men who do not fear to rise and take and rise yet higher! Men who refuse to bow and scrape!"

"Yours are the brazen words of one who has not learned his limits," said the bird-man, scolding. "Yet, why do you rail so, young Lucian? Do you truly believe that you are the first to desire the lore of the Shining Ones?"

"Ah, the Shining Ones," Lucian said, pronouncing the words as though he were spitting them and not speaking them. "Why do they not share this precious lore of theirs? Why do they keep it to themselves if they are truly our benefactors as they claim?"

"You know full well. It is too great for us. To lay hold of it would be certain death."

"So they say," Lucian said slowly. Then lowering his voice he continued, "They speak of our welfare, but what they really mean is our place. These warnings and whispers are nothing more than craven falsehoods intended to keep us from rising to meet them and perchance surpassing them."

Commotion filled the room as men turned to each other and spoke heatedly. The man in the center raised a hand, and after a moment all grew still once more.

"Beware Lucian, lest you call down the sacred fire upon yourself and in so doing, burn your fellows as well."

"The sacred fire? That's it! Don't you see? That is the true secret of their power. Would that it did fall on me! I tell you, I would receive it gladly–it would not harm me. No–I would master it and make it do my bidding!"

The room erupted in shouts. Some reached for swords, others fell back stunned. The old man rose, eyes aflame, hand pointing, shaking.

"Blasphemer! You will be the ruin of us all!"

"Ha! Spoken like the coward I always knew you were, Musonius! Not only do I call for the Sacred Fire to fall on me, I will do more! I will ascend the Unseen Stair, and with these very hands, I will retrieve it and bring it down. I will bring a new day!"

At this point, men stepped out of the shadows to lay hands on Lucian; but he thrust out his arms and power came from him, throwing his would-be captors back, knocking them to the ground.

"If I fear not the Sacred Fire, think I am at a loss when facing your hired lackeys?!"

With those words, he spun on his heels and strode out of the chamber.

The scene faded, and Trevor found himself alone with Ichabod.

"Master, who were those people, and who was that man?"

"Eh? Didn't I just say? Listen more closely, boy. They were my sires of old, and that bold one was the ruin of the Illuminators!"

"But what happened after that?"

"Questions! Questions! Just watch and learn, will you?"

The scene changed again, and once again Musonius was in his chair, but this time he was alone. He was reading a book by the light of a tiny pillar of fire that stood on the table at his right hand. Again, a stream of light came from the hole in the roof. The light then dimmed, as though a cloud had passed over the sun; then there was a blinding flash that filled the chamber and made sharp-edged shadows leap and recede. Next came a crack of thunder so great it shook the pillars of the room, sending dust falling. Musonius rose to his feet just as a youth came running in.

"Come quick, Master!" he said.

They ran to the door, and Trevor and Ichabod followed.

Outside everything was cast in shades of red and gray. People came streaming into the streets, pointing up. Where the sun had formerly shone bright and golden, now it pulsated dull crimson and over-large like a bleeding wound. Clouds of red and black smoke trailed from it against a darkening sky.

"There!" the youth said, pointing.

From the throbbing light, a small flaming dot shot leaving a streak of blackness and fire behind as it fell.

"The arrogant fool!" Musonius said in dismay.

Down the fireball fell, away toward the hills standing miles distant in a rainbow arc, speeding up as it neared the ground. When it struck, a plume of earth and smoke flew up like a tiny spout–but there was no sound at first. Then low, and growing in volume, came a noise of a crash, accompanied by a hot wind blasting. It ripped tiles from roofs and made trees bend and snap. From the edge of sight, a heaving ripple of earth came like a wave of the sea, casting up rocks and trees and hills. Then a flood tide of destruction came upon them. The outer buildings of the village collapsed first, then the rest in a wall of dust and fury. The scene went dark, amid the wails of despair and death.

Silence followed like night after day. Trevor stood trembling. He wasn't cold, and he wasn't shaking from what could properly be called fright. It went deeper than that. His emotions rose up within him all at once and mixed together so that he couldn't sort them out. It was too much, and he'd gone numb. But his body hadn't; it was vibrating like a coiled spring.

"Master–" he dared whisper. In that quiet, it sounded like a shout.

"Hush!"

The darkness rose like a curtain, and they found themselves sitting on a large wagon behind a man driving a team of horses. Next to them sat Musonius, worn and thinner than before. Their wagon was only one in a long line, along with men on foot and horseback. The sky was bleak and overcast, and dust rose from the road. As they passed through desolation, the shattered remnants of a forest surrounded them. Trees lay on the ground everywhere, as though an axe of immense proportions had passed through them all, cutting them down in one swipe. The weather seemed cooler, too, and most people were wearing tattered and dirty clothes.

A commotion came from up ahead, and the line staggered to a stop. A strange figure was coming toward them, towering over man and horse, and walking with a fast loping stride.

"A-hoy! Be Musonius in this rag-tag tussle?!" the figure said.

Through the dust stepped the oddest man Trevor had ever seen. He must have been eight feet tall, and the horses shied away at his approach. He had a bristle beard and a very prominent jaw, and in his mouth was cocked a corn-cob pipe that emitted a green smoke. The longest part of the long man were his legs, and those were wrapped in a pair of thigh-high boots. His clothes were blue, and his shirt was rolled up at the sleeves to reveal a pair of generously muscled forearms.

"Grandfather!" Musonius called. "Here, my old friend!"

"I do declare! It is you! Why, I've been lookin' fer days! Lucky I heard tell you was in these parts. How fare you since the Sundering Crash?" His pipe jumped and bobbed as he spoke and as he came near, he stuck two over-sized thumbs behind a pair of suspenders and gestured with his elbows for emphasis. It almost made him look like a flightless bird.

"Not well, my friend. Everyone is suffering–those who have survived that is. Perhaps those who died fared better. Who knows, with winter coming on?"

"Aye, it'll be a hard one–but you'll come through it, hardship or no. But are you in these parts a seekin' what I think you're a seekin'?"

"Grandfather, I'm sure you already know. Have you any word from the lands ahead?"

"I do, I do. Not that you'll like to hear tell of it, I'll warrant. Yes, I've been to the hole."

"I don't imagine there could be remains from such a fall?"

"Remains? There's more than that. Spoke to him myself, just this mornin'."

"What?! He is alive?! You've seen Lucian!? How can that be?!"

"Well, speakin' to him is one thing, and seein' him is another. But he's alive, if alive is the proper word for it. Changed, he is–

for you're right—no man could have survived that crash."

Musonius sat, as if at a loss for words. After shaking his head and looking blankly into the distance, he spoke in low tones. "Once word of this spreads, vengeance will be on every man's lips. So many have suffered loss, so many children and wives dead; I don't know if I will be able to hold them back. Even if he has survived that fall by some power unknown, he will not survive the wrath of the people. Tell me, Grandfather, what did he say to you? Was there any remorse?"

"Remorse?" the giant said, with a grim laugh. "Hardly. No, not him. Just, 'Go away!' and 'Begone!' and things of that sort. He didn't come out into the daylight, but just shouted from his hole. Never liked the man, awful bossy if you ask me. None of my affair, I told myself, so I just came lookin' for you, knowin' you was about. Anyways, I'm here to tell and now I'm done. I got my gal awaitin' and I need to help her get ready for the snow." The giant took his pipe out of his mouth and breathed deep. "I can smell it comin'. Won't be long till there's a blanket of white all around."

"How far, Grandfather?"

"You's makin' in the right direction. Lookin' at what you've got here and your speed, I'd say a week's hard goin'. Just keep your eye fixed on Eyrie Top there, and you'll make it fine."

After that they parted ways, and the giant set off at a startling pace and was out of sight long before the smell of his pipe faded.

The scene shifted yet again, and this time Trevor knew better than to ask the questions that flooded his head.

Now there were no trees, not even on the ground. There wasn't a hint of life as far as the eye could see. Ahead the ground rose, and above stood a ridge of rock and ruin from which wisps of smoke trailed. Men were working their way slowly up the rise, carefully picking paths between the stones. The earth here was scorched and tormented. Flows of slag lay gray and cooling all around, and the air was full of sulfur and the odor of burning stone. The sky was the color of slate, and the first flakes of a snow were falling. Trevor noticed that most were ill-equipped for the cold. Several had swords and were using them like staffs to help them up the slope.

Ichabod took Trevor's hand, and together they floated over the edge of the rise even as the foremost of the men arrived. Before them lay a great empty bowl of earth, all twisted and smoldering. Only black and gray colored the chaos. But in the center, a dark hole pierced the ground.

The scene changed, and now many men stood around the mouth in the earth. Musonius was front and center and he spoke into it.

"Lucian, can you hear me?! It is I, Musonius! We have heard report that you are alive, as astonishing as that seems to us! Answer if you yet live!"

A voice came from the gaping earth, "I hear you, chief of vultures. Why have you come? Is not my ruin enough for you, or have you come to mock me?"

Upon hearing the voice of the one who was to blame for the deaths of so many, a frenzy of shouting broke out and nearly all rushed the hole with swords drawn and teeth bared. Musonius called for them to stop but none could hear him. When they crowded the opening and began to press their way in, a deep rumble shook the earth and a voice sounded like thunder from below.

"NO!"

Rock and dust flew back, and bodies were thrown in the air and away from the hole. Musonius shielded himself behind a boulder, and when the rain of men and rock had ended the voice spoke again from the depths.

"No man shall look upon me and live! Stay where you are!"

After a short time in which the wounded were tended to, Musonius stood and called out. "Lucian, mighty deeds you have ventured, none denies! But the suffering of thousands follows in your wake! Give you any thought to them? And what of the quest you boasted of and the power you sought? If it is in your hand, by some unlikely chance, surely it could be used for making things new? And even if you have it not, will you not use your great lore for the righting of your wrongs?"

"You betray yourself, Musonius! How quickly your mind turns to the boon I sought! Admit it, it was for that you came, thinking me dead! I am sorry to disappoint you, for I am not dead, but neither do I have it! But I nearly did; and such a boon it was! I had it in my hand, and it would have been mine if not for the one who rose to oppose me."

Lucian's voice had gone from outrage to grief in an instant. Then, quick as lightning it raged once more. "As for righting my wrongs—press your grievances upon the Shining Ones! They are the ones to blame for your woes!"

Those who had picked themselves off the ground looked upward as though fearing a blast from the sky.

"Have you no reverence, even now?" said Musonius.

"Reverence is but a noble-sounding word for fear. The Shining Ones have their advantage, and they jealously guard it. They share it not because they know fear as well. They fear me, and any who will join me. But take comfort in this, if you must have payment; I have suffered greater loss than you can know! Even now my body writhes with pain. But know this, too—I would go again, yes, a thousand times again! I have climbed the upward way, and I have gazed upon blazing fields and seen the eternal sky! I have even touched the Sacred Fire! And all was nearly mine!"

At this point, the voice cracked with emotion.

"Very terrible he was to overcome, Lucian! But I gave him more than he counted, and only after great struggle, did he best me and cast me down."

The voice paused, but when it began again it grew in strength and power. "But now I am changed. Think not that I have returned empty, nor that I regret my attempt. Do you marvel that I survived the fall? Marvel no more! I am like them now! The Fire did that much–and I only felt it for an instant! Now, no mere man can slay me! Think not that I have failed–I am only delayed. For a thousand lives of men, I will labor if I must! I will ascend again! I will not be denied!

"Now, Musonius, take your vultures and go! There is no corpse to pick at here. Begone while I yet feel an unwelcome flicker of mercy! And return not again!"

Then things went finally and utterly black.

CHAPTER THIRTEEN

Two Masters

Trevor heard a loud snore. His eyes burst open, and there in the chair across from him was Ichabod, chin on his chest, fast asleep.

What happened next?!, Trevor wondered; he had to know. He leaned toward the old man. Yep, he was sound asleep. Cautiously, he nudged the Illuminator's knee. "Sir, wake up. Ah, please wake up." Nothing.

It was awkward. Should he try to wake him up? What kind of mood would he be in then? Trevor was afraid to think about it. Should he just get up and leave him sleeping there? No, that didn't seem right either. Politeness is a close cousin to fear, and since Trevor had more than his fair share of the latter; he sat there a while hoping the grumpy, old man would wake up on his own. It didn't happen. After what seemed like an eternity, but was really only a few minutes, he made up his mind to risk it. He reached over and nudged Ichabod's knee like he had done before. Still no good. "Ah, sir, please wake up," he said, a little louder than before. Still nothing. After a few more attempts, each one more forceful than the last, he was clutching the knee and rocking it back and forth hard and shouting as loud as he could, "Master! Master, wake up!"

Finally, with a snort–and a kick that knocked the table and sent tea splashing–Ichabod sat up, eyes wide open. "Eh, what's going on here! What's that shouting about?! And who the blazes are *you*?!"

"It's me, Trevor!" Trevor said, too exasperated to be cowed by the old man's wrath.

"Trevor? Trevor? Why do I know that name? Oh, the new boy! Of course, of course. But what are you shouting for? There's no shouting in libraries! If you can't behave yourself, you'll just have to go back to the Fishers! I tell you, I can't abide shouting in my library!" he finished, shouting.

Trevor could see there was no use in arguing. "I'm sorry sir, but you fell asleep. I was just trying to wake you."

"Fell asleep? How absurd. If you can't tell the truth, then I *will* send you back to the Fishers. Admit it, you were frightened by the story of Lucian, and that's what made you shout. No shame in that, although I would have expected more from a boy of your age."

Trevor was confronted with one of those moments when truth and expedience just can't seem to be reconciled. It happens a lot in life. He hated admitting he had been afraid when he hadn't been. He'd been genuinely afraid often enough that it galled him to say he was when he wasn't. But, since there seemed to be no other way of getting to what he really wanted to talk about, he said, "Yes sir. I'm sorry, it won't happen again."

"Well, let us hope not."

"Yes, sir."

"Good. Let's get back to that memory. Seems like the effects of the Trothleaf tea have worn off. I need another dose." Ichabod reached for his cup. When he saw that both it and his kettle were flipped over and their contents running all over the floor, he said testily, "What's this? Did you spill the tea when you were shouting a moment ago? Come now, fess up."

Trevor knew the truth would never do. "Yes sir, I'm sorry, but I was so scared I kicked the table."

"Humph! Well, at least you're honest. I should be angry and

send you away, but confession is good for the soul, and I don't want to discourage it in the future. You are forgiven, young man. But mind that nervous nature of yours, and let us have no more kicking of tables. Wasted good tea, it has."

It was hard to say it, but Trevor mumbled, "Sorry, sir."

"All right, all right, where were we?"

"We ended when Musonius was talking to Lucian."

"That's all? Blast! The tea's worn off and I'm out of Trothleaf. Of all the rotten luck. Now you'll want me to tell you the old-fashioned way, how tiresome."

He studied Trevor with a wary expression, looking like he was wondering if he was worth the trouble. He began to speak. As he did, he closed his eyes and leaned back in his chair. His voice took on a new tone; it was so different that it seemed to be a different person talking. Gone was the irritable impatience–replacing it was a deep ponderous formality. Trevor didn't know it, but Ichabod was reciting something he'd been forced to memorize by his father when he was a child. His father had learned it from his father and so it went back, from father to son, to the very man who had crafted the tale. It was a good imitation too, Ichabod sounded just like him. Unfortunately, Trevor couldn't know that. The man had been dead for nearly a thousand years.

"Those who survived their encounter with Lucian," Ichabod began, "left him there and went back to build their homes as best they could. It proved to be a hard winter, for the dust from Lucian's fall continued to float above in rainless clouds and blocked the sun. As for Lucian, he was not seen or heard from for many years. Some believed that he had been misshapen by his fall and being a proud man, he feared ridicule. Others believed that he was only biding his time for another assault upon the Stair and the Watcher who guarded it.

"Then, after many years and lives of men, rumor came from

the Sundered Land, to the giant, Grandfather Rufus–"

"Was that the giant I saw?" Trevor said, without thinking. "I liked him, he was funny!"

Ichabod glared and his own voice came back. "Yes, it was the same giant. But giants aren't funny–especially since they're nearly gone. Now, do you want to hear the story or not?"

Trevor nodded.

"As I was saying, Grandfa–"

"Wait, you said many lives of men had passed. How could the same giant bring them the news?"

"Because giants live practically forever, unless they're killed in battle or fall off a cliff. Now hush, and listen to the tale!"

Trevor leaned forward and put his chin on his hands and covered his mouth. He wanted to ask why the giant was called "grandfather," but thought better of it and kept his mouth shut.

"Good. Where was I? Oh, yes–Grandfather Rufus heard news of dark stirrings from the Land of the Sundering Crash." (The ponderous voice was back.) "The rumors were of a deep digging in the lightless lands beneath the earth. Spurred on by his fears, Rufus entered Lucian's hole. Down, down into the dark he went, past the lands of cold to the deep lands of burning heat. Still down he went, and as he went, he saw many things both terrible and mighty–dark things that had been hidden since the making of the world. And still deeper he went, until at the last, he was set upon by strange, horrible creatures, who captured him. They dragged him before their prince, a tall, shadowy lord. But Rufus knew him, for when he spoke, a haughty contempt for all but himself hung about his speech. This Lord was none other than Lucian, the Greatest Illuminator of them all.

"The monsters who held him were bogeys, and they had come from another world. The door to it–along with many other doors to other worlds–had been discovered by Lucian as he quested for a new way to the Sacred Fire."

Trevor had to stifle himself. When he heard about doors to other worlds, it took every ounce of self-control to keep from asking if he could get home through one of them.

"By craft and deceit and the promise of a world of choice food, Lucian subdued the bogeys and made himself their master. But Rufus soon learned that the bogeys were not the worst of Lucian's discoveries. As he languished in a dungeon of terrible vastness, he learned there was a monster dwelling below—a monster of insatiable appetite. The bogeys whispered of it and the sacrifices they had to make to placate it; and as Rufus overheard them whisper, he learned that he was to be its next victim.

"None know how he managed it, for he never said, but Rufus escaped. Many credit his magical boots, but regardless of how it was done, Rufus returned from the depths. And he returned, not empty-handed, for with him he brought a book, a book both precious and singular, a book written in Lucian's own hand—*The Book of the Worlds*. And Rufus entrusted the book to the Illuminators, who in turn bent themselves to the task of understanding it."

A book! A book that shows the way home! Trevor looked around at the towers of books surrounding them. *Could it be here? Is that book somewhere in this mess?* Dismay quickly replaced momentary happiness. Ichabod droned on, oblivious.

"When he learned his book had been taken, Lucian unleashed his minions upon the world. They poured out of their holes like insects and the Wars of The Subjugation began. The tiny kingdoms that dared to resist them were swept away, for these were unprepared, and for the most part unschooled, in the arts of war. And amid the slaughter, nearly all called on the Illuminators for aid, but in their hearts, they blamed the

Illuminators for their troubles, saying, *If not for an Illuminator, the bogeys would not have come.*"

"That's not fair!" Trevor blurted out, then he winced expecting the old man's ire.

Instead, for the first time, Ichabod smiled. It seemed oddly out of place on his worn and wrinkled face. "I'm glad to hear you say so," he said. "Perhaps Epictetus is right about you, annoying curiosity notwithstanding."

What he meant by, *Perhaps Epictetus is right about you,* Trevor did not find out because, before he could ask, Ichabod had gone back to his tale. "It was in those days that divisions arose in the Guild, and some broke with the past and renounced the name of Illuminator. Indeed, the disagreements were so sharp that, if not for a common enemy, the Guild would have broken asunder. At first, there were the Alchemists and later came the Fishers. The Alchemists were founded to study the Troth–a power long venerated, but little understood. For, to the astonishment of all, at the end of the last great war when all seemed lost and the ragged remnants of the Guild had taken their final stand beneath its branches, it blazed forth and consumed a vast host of the enemy. Lucian himself barely escaped the conflagration. That bought them a little time– enough for Trothward to be raised. And those Illuminators who remained faithful and true, and whose lore had not yet been diminished, found a way to bend the light about it and hide it.

"Not long after, Lucian founded Superbia as a place of guardianship against the Guild, for news had come to him of the building of Trothward. An uneasy truce followed and many years came and went. In time, the Alchemists began selling useful goods in the markets, at first secretly and later openly. With the passing years both the people and the bogeys forgot the glory of the Guild, and with those same years, their glory truly faded."

Trevor's eyes were closed, vainly trying to imagine it all. The old man's words had been slowing and with "faded" they completely stopped. Trevor's eyes opened at the sound of a snore.

"No! Don't sleep now!"

He reached over and grabbed Ichabod's knee and started shaking it and shouting "Wake up!" at the top of his lungs. It was no use this time. There was no waking him up a second time.

Reluctantly he got up and slipped away, leaving Ichabod snoring among the towers of books.

When he stepped out of the library, he was momentarily blinded by the light. That's why he didn't see the man standing by the door. A soft, jewel-encrusted hand grabbed his arm.

"Finished so soon?" a soothing voice said to him. Trevor recognized it. He fumbled for his glasses and put them on. Master Paracelsus stood smiling at him.

"Uh, hi."

"Good to see you again, Trevor. I would like a word with you, if you please."

"Sure."

"Wonderful! You are a most helpful boy, I can see. Has our good Illuminator put you to work for him?"

"Yes sir, but not today. He fell asleep without telling me what to do."

"Well, don't concern yourself too much about your new master. He can be a bit difficult."

"I guess so."

"I know so," Paracelsus said, with an understanding smile. "Perhaps that will help you to see my little problem. Let me explain." He put his arm around Trevor's shoulder and began leading him toward the Alchemists' quarter.

After a pause, he said, "Trevor, do you like it here? In Trothward, I mean."

"Oh, yes sir. I like it a lot."

"Good. I hoped you'd say that. It is a much nicer place than the bogeys' Pantry or even Superbia, wouldn't you say?"

"Yes sir," Trevor said with conviction.

"Trevor, you left many children behind, didn't you?"

"Uh, sure."

"How do you feel about that? All those children sitting in the Pantry waiting to be eaten and the many others living in ignorance in Superbia—it's just horrible. Wouldn't you agree?"

Trevor suddenly felt guilty. He hadn't thought about any of that, with all the wonderful things to see and do in Trothward, and the new friends he'd made and all.

"Yes sir," he mumbled.

"I can't get those children off my mind," Paracelsus said, sadly. "Hundreds die nearly every day. Yet, here we are, safe and comfortable within these walls, doing so little. We're barely scratching the surface of the problem. It just doesn't seem right to me. Wouldn't you agree?"

"Uh, no, I guess. But what can I do?"

"I'm so glad to hear you ask because that is just the reason I came back to look for you. There is something you can do. But first you must tell me, can you keep a secret?"

Trevor became intensely interested in what the Alchemist had to say. "I think so."

"Good, good. What I am about to tell you, you must not share with anyone, not even good friends or even Epictetus. Can you do that?"

"Why not?"

They had come to the doors of the Alchemists' quarter. They swung in at their approach.

"Because, Trevor, some things are so important to keep secret, we must not even tell our friends. One slip of the tongue could ruin everything. You should know what I mean. Didn't Epictetus and Abigail keep their true identities secret from you when they were trying to help you? And they, after all, were on the same side of things as you. Sometimes the fewer who know the better."

That's right! Trevor thought. They *had* kept that secret from him. All the same, he hadn't liked it. It was miserable not knowing things other people did.

"Trevor, I want you to know that I believe they could have told you what they were up to because, from the moment I saw you, I knew you to be an exceptional boy–a special boy– someone I could trust and take into my confidence. Your bravery in the Pantry is proof of it."

A warm, happy feeling passed over Trevor from the hairs on his head to the tips of his toes.

"Uh, thanks!"

"No, don't thank me. I am just speaking the truth," the Alchemist said, looking at Trevor appreciatively. "But tell me, will you keep what I am about to tell you secret–just between the two of us?" There came an odd look into the Alchemist's eyes, a nervous look.

Part of Trevor felt uneasy about it. It didn't seem right to keep secrets from his friends. But that's just what bothered him– hadn't Maggie and Epictetus kept him in the dark? Didn't that show that they really hadn't trusted him? If Paracelsus could see that he was trustworthy, why didn't they? Then it occurred to him, in a very satisfying way, that if he did what Paracelsus wanted, that would prove that he really was better than they thought he was. And on top of that, he felt it would be nice to know something important that Maggie didn't for a change.

"Sure, I'll keep it secret."

"Wonderful!" Paracelsus said, smiling broadly as he gave

Trevor's shoulder a squeeze. "I knew I could count on you. What I want you to do won't be difficult to keep between us. Why, it's as simple as simple can be. All I need you to do is keep your eyes open for artifacts whenever you're working for Master Ichabod. Then, at the end of your time with him, just come to me and tell me what you've seen and where you've seen it. That's all there is to it."

It did sound pretty easy. It was so easy, it was a tad disappointing.

"What are you looking for?"

"Oh, just old things—the older the better. Most of the things in Ichabod's library are merely useless relics, but sometimes you can come across something useful. I am afraid our good Master Illuminator though, has lost something of his discernment at his advanced age—not that I think any less of him, mind you. I love the dear, old fellow."

"Why don't you just look for yourself?"

"Ah, I wish I could. I am afraid that our good Illuminator is a tad envious of we Alchemists. And that envy, I am sorry to say, makes me unwelcome in his library. He chased me out of it earlier today. I don't like putting him in a bad light, but you asked an honest question and you deserve an honest answer."

As they walked slowly along, Trevor recalled Ichabod's tone when the subject of the Alchemists came up. The old man didn't like them, that was for sure.

"What about Master Epictetus? Couldn't he look for you or get someone who could?"

A hardness passed quickly through the Alchemist's eyes, but was replaced just as quickly by a jovial regard. "Ah, I see I've chosen the right fellow for the job! You are a sharp one, Trevor Upjohn. I can see I can hold nothing back from you. What I am about to say in no way should be interpreted as a criticism of our wonderful Master Fisher. He is a brave and good man, and he does his best to serve the Guild and save as many children as he can. But sometimes even good men can be wrong in their methods. I am afraid that Master Epictetus is a bit conservative. He doesn't believe in trying new things. He feels that any departure from the old ways would be too risky."

"But don't the Fishers take risks?"

"Yes, yes, of course they do, Trevor—very noble risks. But they are such small risks with such small rewards: a child here, a child there. But tell me, Trevor, what is that in the face of hundreds lost daily? No, we must think bigger. We must try to save all of the children, and to do that, a much larger risk is necessary. Wouldn't you agree that saving the children of Superbia is worth almost any risk?"

They had stopped walking, and the Alchemist was now turned toward Trevor, holding him at arm's-length by both shoulders and looking him directly in the eyes. He was smiling broadly, but Trevor couldn't help thinking that his eyes weren't smiling. They were slightly red, and the lower eyelid of one of them was twitching slightly. What should he say? Paracelsus was right, saving all the children was about the best thing Trevor could imagine.

"I guess so."

"Good!" Paracelsus' eyes lit up, and the twitching stopped. "You'll help me then?"

"I'll try," Trevor said, feeling a little hesitant for some reason.

"Excellent!" the Alchemist said, squeezing both shoulders hard. "Have I told you that I knew you were a special boy from the first time I laid eyes on you?" he said, putting his arm around Trevor's shoulder once again and resuming their walk.

"Yes sir, you did," Trevor replied smiling, but he didn't mind hearing it again.

CHAPTER FOURTEEN

Trouble

Epictetus hadn't been himself since arriving for supper. "Abigail, you must go back to Superbia," he said stiffly.

There was a stunned silence. Finally, the Lady Rowena said, "Father, why must Abigail go? It is so soon since she has come home. I was hoping to have my daughter with me for a while." The Lady hadn't wanted Maggie to go the first time. Maggie, for her part, had an eager glint in her eye. "Why do you want me to go, Grandfather?" she asked.

"Something very odd is going on," said Epictetus. "In all my years in Superbia, I have never seen anything like it. Not long after you and Trevor disappeared, a rumor began to spread in your old hall that you had both gone home. And, as far as I can tell, Meno and his friends are behind it."

"Meno?!" exclaimed Trevor. "But why would he stir things up like that? He was always telling me to shut up whenever I said I wanted to go home."

"Yes," said Epictetus. "It is very curious. I wouldn't have believed it if I hadn't heard him myself. Just last night, he was arguing with a Guardian about you two."

"Really?" said Maggie.

"Yes. He yelled, *Stop lying to us! Trevor and Maggie got to go home! We want to go home, too! It's not fair!* There was more, but it just amounted to the same thing over and over. That's why you must go back, Abigail. Not only can you help me discover what is behind all this, you can help me put this rumor to rest.

I'll make up a story for you to explain where you've been, and I'll find a way to slip you back in to that hall."

"I don't get it," said Trevor. "Don't we want the children to remember their homes? Isn't this a good thing?"

"Yes, that's true," Epictetus said slowly. "But Trevor, you must understand, our work is balanced on a tightrope. We can only save children if we remain hidden. And we only take those who will not be missed–the ones who fall between the cracks, so to speak. That's why I'm concerned. These children are so brazen. They go unpunished. I thought Meno would have gone missing in the night days ago, but nothing's happened to him. It can only lead to trouble for us all."

Trevor remembered what Paracelsus had said about Epictetus. "*I am afraid that Master Epictetus is a bit conservative,*" were his words. He'd not understood what that meant before; now he thought he did. A tiny feeling of contempt stirred inside Trevor's heart, and suddenly Epictetus seemed different–smaller somehow.

"But Master," Trevor ventured. "What if we could get all the kids to want to go home? There are thousands of them! If they all tried to escape at the same time, the Guardians couldn't stop them! Not even the bogeys could! We could save thousands of kids–not just a few here and there!"

The Master Fisher leaned back in his chair and looked appraisingly at Trevor. His hand went to his beard, and he began stroking it. Trevor looked around the table and saw both Maggie and the Lady Rowena looking back at him in surprise. Maggie's eyes had the unmistakable message of, *Are you crazy?!*

Finally Epictetus spoke. "That's a very bold and desperate idea, Trevor. It reminds me of others I've heard in recent days. I'm glad to see you care about those you've left behind, but we must think these things through. We must make our plans carefully. How do you propose we spread the word, so that the children in the other halls would join in this revolt?"

Trevor's mind went blank. "I, uh, I–maybe we could, uh..."

"And let us suppose we managed to overcome the fear and disbelief of the majority of those children, how could we prevent the ones we couldn't from informing the authorities of our plan?"

"Uh–"

"Then, let us suppose we did that, as unlikely as that is–how would we lead all the children out of Superbia? Certainly we couldn't just let them run amuck. They'd be easily captured, one by one and in small groups, and taken back to their halls. And once there, they'd be soundly punished and questioned until not a few would confess what they knew and the Guild would be found out in the end."

Trevor's hopes sunk with every word. "I guess, umm–"

"But let us just imagine, for the sake of argument, that all these difficulties were overcome by some miracle–what then? Where would we put all those children? Surely the Ward couldn't hold them. And the people of Olton already resent the Guild. Most wouldn't help, and those who did would be quickly found out and punished by the bogeys. No, Trevor," Epictetus said, with a sigh, "it is impractical."

Now, not only were Trevor's hopes completely sunk, he felt sort of stupid. But still he couldn't stop believing that Paracelsus was right–there *had* to be a way of saving *all* the children.

"Father, you don't think it is a ruse, do you? I will not allow Abigail to be led into a trap!"

"Daughter, I understand your fear. But I do not believe that is the case. I fear it is what we have been adding to the food. I was unsure about it, but Paracelsus insisted we try it. I thought we could risk it for the sakes of a few more children–but this development is something completely unforeseen. I will send word out immediately to stop it. But, as for Meno and his friends, we must act quickly before things get out of hand, and I'm afraid Abigail is our best hope."

Trevor looked over at Maggie. She was sitting up in her chair looking immensely pleased. He didn't know why that should bother him, but it did. Then an unlooked-for thought came into his head. He could hardly believe what he was about to say, but before he could stop himself, it came out. "But what if they really do want to go home? Shouldn't we help them?"

The old Fisher smiled at him. "My, you are full of surprises today! Considering what Meno put you through, I'm pleased you could even entertain that thought. I know it's hard to believe, but even Meno had a home, and I'm sure he is missed by someone who loved him. Not to worry, I promise you, if he is sincere, we'll do what we can to bring him back with us, and the others, too."

Trevor wasn't sure he ever wanted to see Meno again, sincere or not.

"You know how I feel about Abigail's part in this," said Maggie's mother.

"Yes, I know daughter," said Epictetus with a sigh. "If there were any other way, I would take it. But I will be with her. I promise you, I will protect her."

For Maggie there had never been a question about whether she would go back or not. "Well, now that we've settled that, when do I leave?"

"Tonight."

"Yippie!" she shouted and rushed to her room.

The Lady Rowena looked at her father with a pained expression, got up without speaking, and left the room.

An awkward silence followed in which Epictetus looked down at his food thoughtfully, and Trevor shifted uncomfortably in his chair. An argument was being waged in his brain. Part of him wanted to stay out of it; he'd not been asked to do anything, after all. But another part was saying he should do something–it just wasn't right to sit around while other people were trying to make a difference. It was close, but in the end, the side that wanted to help won–barely.

"Master," he said quietly. "Can I come, too?"

"Ah, Trevor, that's a brave thing to ask–but no. Perhaps someday. You see, I've spent considerable time with Abigail, teaching her the passwords and our ways of getting in and out of Superbia unawares. Besides, all the Guildsmen in Superbia know she is my granddaughter and would give their lives to save her if she got into trouble."

At that moment, Maggie returned wearing the drab gray robe Trevor remembered her wearing during their days in their old hall. "Well, I'm back. I tried to say goodbye to Mother, but she's locked herself in her room and wouldn't answer me when I called."

Epictetus gave another sigh. "Understandable. Well, let's go Abigail."

It was time to say goodbye, and Trevor felt a sudden awkwardness. He stood up but he wasn't sure what he should do. He was plunged into a foggy soup of conflicting emotions. There was concern, envy, irritation, but most of all, worry. He was afraid Maggie might not come back–but he didn't want to show it. So, he just cleared his throat and said, "See ya."

Maggie pursed her lips, and an angry look came into her eyes. It even looked like she might say something nasty, but all of a sudden she ran up to him and gave him a hug, then turned away.

"Good night, Trevor," said Epictetus. As she went out the door, Maggie looked back with an expression Trevor didn't understand. Then he was alone with his supper.

CHAPTER FIFTEEN

Into the Dark

Maggie couldn't stop trembling. Partly it was the thrill of fishing. Even though this was more like anti-fishing, it was still thrilling. The other part was anger–that and disappointment. Her feelings were all jumbled up. It made her feel cold and all goose-bumpy. She reached up her sleeves and hugged herself. Her arms felt like sandpaper.

Her grandfather led the way; he had said something about getting something from his quarters. Maggie stalked behind him, looking downward. As she sifted through her murky thoughts, her mother's face appeared.

"She thinks I'm still a baby," she mumbled.

Epictetus looked over his shoulder, "Eh? What was that, Abigail?"

"Nothing," she answered, not looking up.

The old man was wise enough to leave her alone. He just looked down sympathetically and strode on.

She probably wants me to waste my life making dresses, Maggie thought to herself. *Not me. I'm not going to hide inside and make doilies while other people do important things.* She knew there was more to it than that. Her mother was afraid of losing her just like she had lost her husband; but, she wasn't in the mood to be understanding. Being angry was just too satisfying. But the unguarded moment of reason brought her father's face to mind. A different feeling accompanied it. She remembered how he used to throw her over one of his giant shoulders and carry her around. How long had he been gone now? Two years? It seemed like forever. He'd understand; he never treated her like a baby. He'd be proud. If only he could know she was the youngest Fisher ever! Another emotion came up and she felt like she might let out a sob. *No!* She swallowed it down.

Now she saw a third face. It was a handsome face, and it was all the more endearing because the person to whom it belonged didn't know he was handsome. A new sort of thrill went through her at the thought of Trevor Upjohn. But she was mad at him! *What sort of goodbye was that? "See ya"? Didn't he realize that she was going into danger; that they might not see each other again? He could have said that to Tubby! Was that all he thought of her?* If she got back alive, the first thing she was going to do was walk right up to him and punch him in the stomach.

Then a very pleasant notion occurred to her—what if she were carried away by bogeys while *he* watched? She could see his face, twisted with remorse. *"I'm sorry, Maggie!"* she could hear him saying. *"I'm sorry I never told you how wonderful you are. You're the bravest girl who ever lived! Maggie, forgive me!"* She smiled. *Serve him right. Then he'd appreciate me. But it would be too late and he'd have to live with the guilt of it for the rest of his life.* The goosebumps were gone now and her blood was running hot.

When she finally looked up, they were in front of the hedge surrounding her grandfather's house. The entire walk had gone by, and she couldn't remember any of it. They'd passed out of a corner of the quadrangle and into the twilight of early evening. They weren't in the Great Garden but in one of the lesser gardens that surrounded each Master's house. She'd been to them all, and each reflected the master who lived in it. Ichabod's was overgrown and weedy but, whenever anyone tried to tend it, he shooed them away. Brendleback's was a big yard of closely cropped grass that he used to practice sword-craft with his men and charges. Paracelsus' was opulent, like everything else about the man, with big, smelly flowers imported from the southlands and droopy vines everywhere.

But her grandfather's garden had a hedge and that hedge formed a maze. It was far too tall to look over, and it came to dozens of dead ends. There was only one way through and naturally, he led her along without any hesitation. She'd gotten lost in it once, years before, when she had tried to visit when her grandmother was dying. Epictetus had found her crying and sitting on the ground. After wiping away her tears, he'd spent the whole afternoon leading her through it again and again and making her memorize the way. That's the day he first took a real interest in her. "Two left, one right, skip an opening, another right..." she said to herself, as she walked behind him. The hedge was thick, no seeing through it, and it seemed like they were walking between fuzzy walls by the dim light of dusk.

When they finally got to the house, there was a red glow coming from the windows. When they stepped inside, she saw the dying embers of a fire in the hearth.

"Sit down, Abigail. We must talk before we go. I have things to say that I couldn't say at dinner. First though, let me stoke these coals and stir up some light."

Maggie took a chair across from her grandfather's big leather one. She loved it here. The walls were paneled in a dark wood that gave the room a cozy feel. Even during the daytime, it always seemed like night. There were swords and walking sticks in the corners, and big chests strewn about. And there were books, some on shelves, but more in stacks on the floor. A brilliant sword hung over the mantel. She'd seen her grandfather polish it, but she'd never seen him use it. He never spoke of it, but according to Uncle Max, he was a master swordsman. He'd been a hero, he said, in the wars down south. That's how he'd lost his eye. He never talked about that either, and she never asked. Somehow she just knew the subject was off limits.

She watched him stir the embers into a flame and retrieve his lamp from a desk and wind it. He set it on a table between them. Its light shone blue. She'd always wondered why it was shaped like a mountain with a cave. It didn't seem like a very good design for lighting up a room. It just sent a beam wherever you pointed it. She'd wanted to ask about that but, whenever she remembered to, it was always a bad moment.

"Granddaughter," he said, as he sat. He was using the tone he always used when trying to say something important. "Things have changed since you were last in Superbia, and I'm not referring to your old classmates. It's the city itself that's different. I won't be able to take you in any of the regular ways. They're being watched more closely than I can ever remember. All the guards at the gates have been replaced by bogeys. We lost two Fishers just yesterday when they tried to get in using the standard bribe. All the other ways are being watched, too."

Maggie leaned forward; this was exciting! "Then how can I get in, Grandfather?"

Epictetus shifted in his chair. Maggie could tell he was having difficulty bringing himself to say what he needed to say.

"What is it, Grandfather?"

"Child, you will have to go by a dark, forgotten way. As you know, the bogeys have tunnels under Superbia. But there are other tunnels that the bogeys don't know about. They were made by the Guild in the bad times, before we could move about unmolested. Most are for passing in and out of Olton unseen, but one goes into Superbia. You must go that way."

"Aren't you coming with me?" Maggie said, the slightest quiver in her voice.

"Partway, child. I am expected in the city shortly, and it will look suspicious if I do not pass in by way of the gate. I am a known Guildsman, after all."

Maggie felt a chill and began hugging herself again.

"I won't send you into the dark without some light; and as long as you obey my words, you should pass through the tunnels without incident. The primary danger is getting lost. But, I seem to recall that your memory is good. Before we part, you must be able to recite to me the directions I will give you. If you follow them exactly, you will find me waiting at the other end."

In the red glow of the fire and the blue glow of the electric torch, her grandfather's beard shone like a glistening waterfall, all red and blue and purple, pouring over his chest. Shadows danced behind him as he sat motionless in his chair. His good eye sparkled moist and sharp as it rested on her.

"Are you afraid my granddaughter?"

She desperately wanted to say no; but she couldn't lie to him—to Giles or Max or even her mother, sure: but not him. She knew he could tell anyway.

"Yes," she admitted.

"Good. I hoped you'd be afraid. Indeed, if you'd not been, I'd forbid you from going. Only a fool wouldn't be afraid, and I'd be ashamed to have a fool for a granddaughter."

Maggie smiled reluctantly and looked at the floor.

Epictetus leaned over and took both of her hands in one of his large ones. Then, with one of his giant thumbs, he pushed open her hands and placed his lamp on her upturned palms.

"Crank this while I recite the way to you. We will need the light where we are going."

Then as she turned the lamp's dragon tail handle, her grandfather began to softly chant.

"Right and right and right again;
skip two ways, and right once more—"

When he finished a refrain, he had her repeat it. It wasn't hard to do, with the rhythm of his words and the whirling of the inner workings of the lamp helping her remember. It grew brighter and whiter the longer she turned.

The directions became a monotony–left, right and skip. But her memory was good and before long, she was able to repeat them back without a mistake. It helped that in the middle there was a surprise.

"When one comes to the meet-some ways,
    where the Sentinel Stone with help parlays;
        there, right is wrong and wrong is right;
            and one's choice is made, with no trust to sight."

It puzzled her and she tried to ask about it, but Epictetus simply drowned her out when she attempted it. So she cranked faster in frustration and repeated her lines faster to shorten the whole tedious exercise.

Finally, only after reciting the whole of it without mistake three times, did he permit her to ask.

"That, Granddaughter, you must see to understand," he answered.

It was the sort of answer she had come to expect from him.

"Speaking of seeing, I think you've cranked that enough," he said, nodding to the lamp.

She stopped, and her arm fell limply to her side. It was numb.

"Come, it is time to be going," he said, standing up. He took the lamp and led her back outside. It was night now.

Once out of the maze, Maggie was surprised to see that they were going away from the front door. Instead, they entered the Great Garden. The swaying of the Troth's fruit sent patches of light dancing all around. No one was in sight, which was odd, since early evening was a favorite time for young couples to walk the garden hand in hand. They went to a particularly high and thick hedge standing against an outer wall. For some reason, in all of her games of hide and seek, she had never thought to look behind it. They squeezed between it and the wall, catching their clothes on twigs as they did. Soon they came to a door.

It stood dark and impassive. It was oversized, and when Maggie touched it, it felt cold, like it was made of iron. Her grandfather produced a thick key from a pocket.

"This door," he said, putting the key into a hole, "is never used. It was put here as a way of escape should the Ward ever be taken."

He turned the key with a muscled hand. Even with his great strength, his hand went white and red with the strain. Eventually, something gave and there was a metallic clunk. He put his shoulder against the door and leaned hard into it. Initially it gave with a rusty screech, but after that, it swung smoothly and noiselessly. The light of his lamp went down a set of stone steps.

"Come, Granddaughter," he said.

When their feet crossed the threshold, puffs of dust rose wherever they stepped. Epictetus pushed the door shut behind them, but he did not relock it. At the end of a short descent, a long, straight tunnel opened before them. The floor and walls were made of smooth, tightly fitted stone. But the ceiling was made of rough, native rock pocketed with chisel marks. The tunnel disappeared beyond the fading reach of the lamp.

"The way runs straight for some time," Epictetus said quietly. His voice was very soft, but it sounded loud in that place–the air was so still and silent.

They began to walk. The walls ran in perfect parallel, never getting closer together or further apart. It was hard to believe the tunnel had always been there. It made Maggie wonder about other things she didn't know. The world of home that had seemed so ordinary just a few hours ago suddenly seemed mysterious. She began to wonder whether she wanted to go on an adventure after all. Home looked better than it had in a long time. Eventually, the lamp revealed a fork in the way.

It presented them with the choice of going either left or right. The left way descended steeply, and sounds of trickling water came from it. The right way, on the other hand, leveled out and no sounds came from it.

"Which way, Granddaughter?"

Maggie remembered her lesson. "Right."

"Right is right," the old man said with a smile.

After they turned, Maggie asked, "Since we're going part of the way together, why did you make me memorize the whole way?"

"Plans can go awry; if something happens to me, or if we are separated, you'll have to make it back to the Ward by yourself."

"But if I'm by myself, how can I know the way back?"

"By remembering the directions backwards, naturally."

He looked at her with an eyebrow raised over his good eye, like he was disappointed that she hadn't thought of that for herself. She decided to keep her mouth shut and began running the directions over and over again in her head, trying to remember them backwards.

The old man looked at her again and smiled. As they went along, he didn't ask her again where to turn, but simply led the way. He had them turn right and right again; they went straight and left, and before long, they were so far into the directions that if she'd not already memorized them, Maggie would have been hopelessly confused. They passed many dark openings to other tunnels. Those she walked past a little faster. She couldn't help feeling like something might reach out from one of them. On and on, the tunnels went. It felt like they would never end. Eventually, they came to a place where the ceiling rose and the walls flew away, and they entered a large circular chamber. It was lined with openings. Quickly, she counted them. There were nine. In the center of the cavern stood a tall and narrow stone, like a needle of rock, rising from the floor. They walked up to it.

"This is the Sentinel Stone. And here is where our paths part," Epictetus said.

A pang of fear shot through her. She tried to not let it show.

The stone, she now saw as she stood next to it, was set on a round, smooth medallion in the floor. On the medallion was a triangle that pointed like an arrow at one of the doorways. There was also an inscription on it in a strange alphabet she didn't know. But the stone itself was featureless and stared back at her blankly.

"What does it do?" she asked.

"What do my directions say?"

She recited them:

"When one comes to the meet-some ways,
      where the Sentinel Stone with help parlays;
          there, right is wrong and wrong is right;
              and one's choice is made, with no trust to sight."

"So–" her grandfather said, leadingly.

Maggie twisted her hair and thought. How could right be wrong and wrong be right? She had no idea. She shrugged.

The old man looked amused. "The stone serves two purposes– it gives direction, but it also keeps watch in its own dull way. The arrow points to a door. Because there are nine doors and none of them are marked, that means our hypothetical traveler has a one in nine chance of guessing the right one. Of course, even if he, or she should guess the right one, there are still dozens of turns in each of the tunnels where he could still go wrong. But for the builders of these tunnels, those odds were still too high. That is why they put the Sentinel Stone here."

"So, how does it help?"

"Why, you ask it, of course. That's what the inscription invites you to do."

"You mean, it can understand me?"

"That would be the correct inference," her grandfather said. "Go ahead, ask. Just say the name of the place you want to go."

"Uh, Trothward," she said blandly.

"My dear young lady, that won't do. You have to say it like you mean it."

If it had been anyone else telling her to talk to a stone, she would have refused. Still, she still felt a little silly, talking to a rock.

"Trothward," she said, with as much conviction as she could muster.

Slowly, the stone began to turn, the base in the floor rotated, and after a moment the triangle was pointing to a new passage. But it wasn't the one they had just come out of.

She looked at her grandfather quizzically.

"Remember, I said it serves two purposes—one to direct, but the other to protect. We can't have just anyone walking up willy-nilly into the Great Garden. What did that little rhyme say again?"

"You mean about wrong being right and right being wrong?"

"Yes."

"But if the arrow is pointing to the wrong door, then how are you supposed to know which one is right?"

"Abigail—think. What's the opposite of right?"

"Wrong, of course."

"And–?"

"Oh, left! It's the door to the left of the one the arrow is pointing at!"

The old man's face broke into a broad smile. "That's my girl. So, since we don't intend to go back to Trothward, at least not yet, let's find out the way we do want to go." After a pause, he said, "Superbia."

The stone turned again and when it had stopped, it was pointing to another opening. They went to the passage to the immediate left of it.

"As I said, Abigail, this is where we part. But I won't let you go without some light." He reached and removed part of the mechanism to his lantern. Half of the glowing element pulled away in his hand. He kept that half and gave her the part with the handle and the crank. Now they each had a light–but the light of each was less than half of what they had produced together.

"Go quickly, Granddaughter. I will meet you when you come to the end of your way. There will be a door, but do not knock! Don't make any noise, and don't try to open it. Just wait. When I arrive, I will open it from the other side." He looked directly into her eyes as he spoke, as though trying to read her thoughts. Now that it had come to actually separating, she felt like she might begin to cry.

"I'll be okay," she said.

"Good. I believe you will be," he said as he embraced her. "Now, go."

With an effort, she pushed away from him and went down the passage. It turned immediately to the right. Soon her grandfather was out of view. She wanted to call back to him, but in the stillness of that place, she didn't think it was a wise thing to do.

She heard his voice say, "Olton Market!" and then she heard the stone grind as it turned once more.

"Remember to take the left-hand way, Grandfather," she whispered as she walked alone by the flickering light. She wound the handle, and the lamp brightened a bit. The corridor continued to bend out of view, and the air began to feel cooler. She started running the directions over again in her mind, and it was with a sinking feeling that she realized that she still had more than half her journey ahead of her.

CHAPTER SIXTEEN

In Again

Her grandfather hadn't said how big the door would be. But it was short, only about half as tall as a normal door. Maggie saw that she'd have to bend over to get through it.

It didn't look like it had been opened in years; and considering the age of the tunnels and the little she knew of Guild history, perhaps hundreds of years. She held her flickering lantern up to examine it. It was dusty and cross-bucked by imposing slabs of dark wood. All the iron-wrought hardware, the hinges and such, were rusty. Her grandfather needn't have warned her about opening it. She doubted she could have budged it with a sledge hammer. There was nothing to do now but sit and wait.

There were half a dozen steps leading up to the door and those were flanked on either side by low, smooth, stonework. On the far sides of the stone work, there were small coves between the stairs and the outer walls of the tunnel.

She took a seat about midway down the stairs and put her head in her hands. It had been a largely uneventful journey. After saying goodbye to her grandfather, the ways she could go wrong grew fewer and fewer until the last third of her journey became pretty much a straight run to where she now sat.

It had taken her a couple of hours of steady walking to get there, and even though there never seemed to be a clear indication that she was going either up or down, her legs told the tale that her trek had been a steady ascent. Although geography was a subject she hated, it was a fact she observed every time she went outside–Superbia was uphill from Olton. So, even though she had traveled underground the whole way, it had been uphill all the same.

Now, time has a way of moving more slowly when you think about it. Whether it really does or not is hard to know. Regardless, Maggie felt like she had been waiting for an eternity when she finally heard something stirring behind her. It sounded like someone was sliding something along the ground on the other side of the door.

"At last!" she thought. Then a troubling idea popped into her head. What if it wasn't her grandfather? She knew it was absurd; how could someone just happen to open a door that hadn't been opened in a hundred years just when she was on the other side of it? The answer came in a flash; her grandfather may have been captured! That seemed just as crazy. He'd never tell. Still, she'd heard terrible things, just awful things, about what the bogeys did to people to get information out of them. She felt a pang of worry when she realized that that could be the reason it had taken so long. She jumped down the stairs and into one of the coves and shut off the lamp.

There was the sound of a key going into a lock and then a rusty latch clicking. The hinges strained, and dust fell on her head from above as the door opened. A dim light came through a widening crack. She caught a glimpse from below of what appeared to be the hem of a white robe. She got goose-bumpy again.

The door finished opening, and a silhouette of a beardless person stooped and came in against a gray light. Even in the darkness, Maggie knew she was looking at a Guardian. *What should I do? Run?* she wondered. Coiled, she got ready to spring.

"Abigail, are you here?" a woman's voice said softly.

She knows my name! She could hardly believe it! Grandfather had talked!

"Abigail, come out. Your grandfather sent me for you. I'm a Guildsman, too. I'm here to take you to him."

A wave of relief washed over her, then she stiffened. It could be a trick. It could be made up. How could she know?

The woman anticipated that. "Abigail, you can trust me. Your mother is named Rowena and your father is Marcus. Now, if I weren't a Guildsman, would I know their names?"

Maggie risked coming out.

"There you are! Come along. It's taken too long for me to find this door, and I'm running a terrible risk being away from the Great Hall. There are bound to be questions waiting for me when I get back."

"Where's Grandfather?" Maggie said, expressing the only thing she cared about at that moment.

"He's fine. He couldn't get away. There's trouble in your hall, but I've been told you know that already. He discovered this evening that there's now a special watch dedicated to it. Originally, our plan had been for me to stay behind and keep the evening watch in your hall while he looked for you. But if he had tried to get away, it would have triggered suspicion. So, we switched. I came and he stayed."

By this point, they had squeezed through the door and entered a huge semi-empty room. Dusty, many-paned windows shone dully high above. Streams of dull, evening light came down and streaked the air. Maggie barely made out a latticework of metal beams holding up the roof. She was informed by the Guardian that they were in an old abandoned warehouse.

"What's your name?" Maggie asked.

"That is better left unknown. Come," said the woman.

Before leaving, Maggie helped slide a wooden packing crate back over the door.

Maggie had never seen Superbia at night. It was bad enough in the daytime, with its long, square buildings and its vacant windows. But it was worse after dark, particularly in this part of town. There were no lights coming from any of the buildings. The only lights were those at the intersections of the larger roads. These sent shafts of illumination down the streets, creating elongated shadows wherever they struck a barrel or a pile of debris. The alleys off the streets remained completely black and reminded Maggie of all the dark passages she had skipped past underground. That thought made her wish for her grandfather's lamp. *Oh, no. I left it beside the stairs!*, she realized with a sinking feeling.

She kept close behind her guide. Maggie didn't know what to think of her. At one moment, she thought of her as a Fisher, then the sight of those robes in a street light would shout, "Guardian!" and her mind would flood with apprehension. Had she done the right thing by revealing herself? Maybe it was all a ruse after all? If they had wrung the hidden location of the door from her grandfather, they could have learned her parents' names too. When she thought of that, she was mortified. *How could I have been so gullible?* Still, she followed on; what else could she do? If her grandfather had been captured, he needed her help. And even if this were a trap, it was also the quickest way of finding him. She didn't doubt that they would be reunited either way. And if they had done anything to her grandfather, well, they would have Maggie Blaise to reckon with! She gritted her teeth and tried to remember all the lessons she'd learned from Brendleback in the art of hand to hand combat.

As they approached an inhabited part of Superbia, Maggie's guide thrust a hand back and waved for her to get out of sight.

"What is it?" Maggie whispered.

"Shh! Get down."

Maggie spotted a collection of barrels against a building and ducked for cover. They were full of garbage, and there she met her first rat of the night. She swallowed the scream that wanted to come out. Luckily, it was fat and drowsy from a night of overeating, and it just looked up at her with mild annoyance and waddled away.

"Well, at least somebody eats well around here," Maggie mumbled to herself.

"Shh!, I said. Someone's coming."

Her guide stood against the other side of the garbage cans, but she didn't look back at Maggie. Instead, she looked around a corner as if waiting. It was at that moment that Maggie noticed the smell of the garbage. It was putrid. She felt as though she might retch.

That's when she heard voices.

They were loud, unpleasant, masculine voices, and they were getting louder. There were also sounds of clangs and shuffling, as though someone was kicking what Maggie imagined were more garbage cans around the corner. That was an accurate impression because that was exactly what was happening.

Maggie could tell that her guide was frightened by the way she stiffened at the sound of the voices. In a way, it was reassuring. If she wasn't scared, that would be something to worry about.

"Saayy, what's thish?" a deep voice slurred, as two tall shadowy forms came into view. They dwarfed Maggie's guide.

"Looks like food to me; hee, hee!" said the other.

They were bogeys! Worse, even through the stink of the

garbage Maggie could smell alcohol. They were drunk!

"I am Guardian Helen," her guide said nervously. "I am on my way to the Great Hall. If I do not report, First Guardian Glaucon will know of it."

"Glaucon! Ha! There's a joke," said the first bogey, putting a set of over-sized and very crooked teeth on display. "From what I hear, he's nearly in the Pantry his-self!"

"Ha! Ha! That's right," said the second, slapping the back of the first. "But he's too old and stringy for my liking. Now you, on the other hand, you're young and tender. You're the way I like 'em." With that he grabbed one of Helen's arms.

"Here, let me see," said the first, grabbing the other arm.

Maggie could see Helen recoil from their hands, but she didn't run. Maggie noticed for the first time that she was a beautiful woman. She was brave, too.

The last of Maggie's reservations evaporated. If Helen really were a Guardian, then the surest way to save herself would be to betray the girl cowering behind the garbage cans. But she didn't.

Maggie began racking her brain for a way to help. The bogeys were now sniffing Helen's hair and licking their lips. Helen was shaking and shrinking away. Maggie spotted a loose piece of lumber and hefted it in her hands. It would do for a club in a pinch, and this was certainly that. Unexpectedly a voice cried out–

"Hey! What's going on there?"

It was a powerful voice. Maggie felt a need to jump up when she heard it. The bogeys stiffened, and one of them cursed beneath his breath. They let Helen go and slowly turned to greet someone approaching.

The sound of several feet walking quickly came around the corner, then a small troop came into view. From Maggie's vantage point, they looked like armed men. But she knew they were really bogeys by the way the others reacted to them.

"What are you two doing? And out of uniform, too?" said a tall, incredibly broad bogey with an air of authority.

"Uh, nothing Azrazel. We're just on leave," said one of the bogeys with Helen.

"Leave, eh? The last I heard, all leave was to be taken below. What's that smell?"

Azrazel grabbed each of the bogeys quickly in turn and smelled their mouths.

"You're drunk, each of you! That's two violations! And what about this morsel here?" he said, with a nod toward Helen. You weren't planning to have an unauthorized snack, were you? You know the court has the first choice of all fresh meat. It looks to me like you boys have been slumming. What do you think, men?" Azrazel finished over his shoulder to his companions.

There was a chorus of unhappy grunts. Maggie looked at the others; they had the typical bogey look–yellow slits for eyes and wide, unsympathetic mouths. A chill went up Maggie's spine. She nestled down a little lower out of view.

"No, Azrazel, it wasn't that way. You don't understand," one of the original bogeys said nervously. "We'd never do that. We ain't poachers! We know what happens to poachers!"

"Good," said Azrazel, with a grin spreading across his face that made Maggie almost sorry for the two culprits. "We won't have to show you then. Come on boys, let's take 'em in."

Helen stepped back just in time before a horrible scuffle broke out. There was a lot of cursing and wrestling and fortunately, it veered away from Maggie and her trash bins and out into the street. It wasn't long before the drunken bogeys were dragged off by the others.

It was with a trembling hand that Helen reached for Maggie's when the bogeys were finally out of view. Maggie felt odd–she was relieved to know that she was with someone who could be trusted. No doubt remained as to whose side Helen was on. But it seemed more like dumb luck had saved her. The robes of a Guardian had been no protection at all.

Now that she knew her name, Helen wasn't just another Guildsman or even a Guardian; she was a person. Maggie looked up at the woman's pretty face under the rays of the passing street lamps. Maggie wasn't sure, but it looked like she was crying.

"Hey, thanks for helping me back there."

After a pause that looked like she was trying to speak without emotion, Helen replied, "You're Epictetus's granddaughter. I couldn't have lived with myself if they'd found you."

There it was again!—someone treating her like she was just a kid! She almost said, "I'm no baby, I can take care of myself!" but fortunately, another part of her kept her clammed up. It took a few minutes before she could talk without an edge to her voice.

"I think you were really brave back there. The bogeys almost got you."

"They've always been bad, but they're getting worse," Helen said, having by now composed herself. "The Guardians I've talked to don't know why, but poaching is a growing problem; and what's more, they don't even pretend to respect the Guardians like they once did. You heard what they said about the First Guardian."

The thought of more poachers made Maggie want to get out of the night air even more than she had. Helen apparently felt the same and the two of them picked up their pace.

Eventually, they came to a broad open space. Maggie recognized it as the marching grounds, where children from the halls were forced to exercise by marching in formations. She remembered the shouting matches between halls as they competed for best formation. She also recalled a fight that had broken out between halls that led to a huge melee and had resulted in a loss of marching privileges for her old hall. Like most kids, she had felt no loss.

The glow of the Great Hall overlooking Superbia in the distance shone through the smoke stacks and sent long shadows across the grounds. Dimly, Maggie could make out the huge numbers painted on the buildings that lined the space. They were back in an inhabited part of Superbia at last. In those boxy hulks lining the area, thousands of children were bedded down for the night. The kids in them were totally ignorant of the fate that awaited them in the Pantry below if they weren't lucky enough to become Guardians. It was an awful thought, and a worse place to be hardly seemed possible, but at that moment Maggie desperately wanted to join them.

By the time they reached hall number 37, Helen had regained full possession of herself. It was a good thing, too. A cluster of Guardians was by the front door. Her grip on Maggie's hand tightened. When they got to the steps, she nodded curtly to the others and walked officiously through them. No one stopped them to ask why a girl was outside after hours. It was simply assumed that the office of Incorrigible Children was open late again. The Inspector had more work than usual with all the recent trouble, it was believed.

Even though Maggie had only been gone a short time, it seemed like years since she had been there last. As she climbed the stairs to the sleeping chamber, she recalled watching her grandfather reading by the light of his lamp as she fell asleep each evening. The long climb through those broad, depressing, industrial corridors strangely awakened feelings of excitement for adventure. Just as strangely, they also brought back the warm feelings of security she felt whenever she was with the man who always knew what to do and how to do it. She adored him. He was so wise and kind and strong. Her earlier fears for her grandfather suddenly came back. What if he wasn't there? What would she do without him? They had come to the landing before the door to where the children slept in ordered rows.

A large hand fell on her shoulder from behind.

"Abigail."

She jumped and turned around in a single motion. Standing in the shadows was her grandfather.

She rushed to him and threw her arms around his middle.

"Grandfather!"

Epictetus smiled, but that was wiped away in a blink.

"Abigail," he said, in a harsh whisper. "Remember your discipline. It's a good thing it's Helen with us and not someone else." After a quick word with Helen about the bogeys, during which Epictetus looked deeply troubled, he turned to Maggie and commanded she get to bed.

She went to hug Helen goodbye, but her grandfather pulled her back by an arm. In the dimness, she could see Helen was in full character. She looked disdainfully down on her. She was all Guardian now.

"Get to bed, you little scamp," she said with a sniff, and turned to descend the stairs.

Maggie felt like she'd been slapped. In a way, she had and it was for the good. It woke her up and sent her into character. She was just another morsel from Hall 37. The old slave she knew and loved opened the door.

"Find a bed, child. Your old one has been taken."

As she slipped down a narrow aisle, she saw that indeed it had been. None other than that idiot Willis was in her old bed. Worse, Trevor's was now occupied by the corpulent mound commonly known as Meno. She wondered how Drake could stand being near them.

She looked back to her grandfather, but his head was already in his book. No help from that direction. Eventually she found a rickety cot at the back of the hall. There were other beds, but they were worse. This was where new kids went when they first arrived. The best beds were at the other end—nearest to the dining hall. She'd have to fight her way back into the pecking order.

It didn't matter though that the bed's legs were uneven, or that it rocked back and forth at her slightest movement. She was so tired she fell to sleep almost instantly.

CHAPTER SEVENTEEN

Out Again

The curtains flew back with a swish, and pallid beams of milky light poured into the vast room. Maggie opened an eye and groaned, then put a pillow over her head. Many voices began talking all at once. They rose and fell like waves and washed over her. She couldn't make out what anyone was saying, and she didn't want to. It felt like she had just gotten to sleep. She could have dozed off again, even with the noise, if it hadn't been for the bony hand that began shaking her with remarkable vigor.

"Just what do you mean by sleeping in, you lazy imp?! The day has begun!"

Maggie squinted up at a blurry face. It moved back and forth across her line of vision until she realized that she was the one moving and not the face. With reluctance, she sat up and swung her feet over the bed. The face said something and walked off. Maggie's mind was too foggy to hear. It was a good thing; it would have only made her grumpier.

When she looked around, she saw that morning had come to Superbia. Kids were finishing up their beds and moving toward the breakfast lines. Already, just about everyone had moved to the far end of the hall. With a sigh, she noted that her grandfather was gone. His chair and little desk were empty. She'd expected it, but still it's never nice to realize you're on your own. And she would have felt alone, too, if not for one thing. Meno, Willis and Drake were staring at her across a wide space. And it looked like they were talking about her.

That woke her up. She began making her bed with the awareness of being watched. Thinking about what you're doing makes you prone to forget how to do things you normally do without thinking. Being tired makes it worse. But thinking about other people thinking about you is worst of all–not twice as bad, more like ten times as bad. She flubbed at every point, and the more she flubbed, the angrier it made her, and that made her flub even more. What finally topped it was Willis's insufferable laughter carrying across the room. She knew he was laughing at her. It was the mindlessness of it that was so galling. When she looked up, she saw three wicked grins in her direction.

"Oh, forget it," she said, throwing a pillow in the vicinity of the head of the bed. She would get demerits for that, but she didn't care. She stalked toward the serving tables. As she did, the boys began pushing their ways between the beds in her direction. When she reached the tables, she picked up a bowl. They soon arrived and fell in behind her.

"Well, well, well, if it isn't Maggie Blaise," Meno said, with his best imitation of a smile. The mound of meat seemed even bigger than ever, if that were possible.

"Yeah, if it isn't Maggie Blaise!" Willis repeated like a human echo chamber.

"What do you morons want?" Maggie said, sounding just as cranky as she felt.

"Aw, come on Maggie," said Meno, like his feelings were actually hurt. "I know we've had our little disagreements, but we just want to talk to you. Right, guys?"

"Yeah, right; we just want to talk," Willis added needlessly.

Maggie leaned forward and looked down at Drake. "What are you doing with these clowns?"

"I know what you're thinking, Maggie," he said. "But things

have changed since you left. We're all on your side now."

"Yeah, your side," Willis chimed in.

Maggie had a bad feeling about where this conversation could be heading. She had expected something like this, but not so soon—and not in the serving line of all places! They were nearly to the ladlers. She instinctively lowered her head and tried to pretend none of this was happening.

"Maggie, we know where you've been," Meno said.

There was only one kid between her and the ladlers.

"I don't know what you're talking about," she mumbled beneath her breath.

"Come on. Fess up. You know what I'm talking about."

She held out a bowl to a double-chinned Guardian. She couldn't tell if it was a man or a woman. It sometimes seemed that was the way they wanted it.

"I was in Hall 98. What's so special about that? It got crowded over there, so they sent me back."

The Guardian slopped some flesh-colored stuff into her bowl.

"You're lying," Meno said, sounding more like his old self. "You've been *home*—you and that twit, Trevor Upjohn!"

To Maggie's shock, the Guardian didn't react. Not even a blink.

"You're crazy!" she spat out. Then she wheeled on her heels and walked as fast as she could to a table.

She found a crowded one with one empty chair, hoping her tormentors would have to sit someplace else. She needed time to think. She didn't know why she had assumed they would just believe her when she said she hadn't been home, but she had. Being called a liar is disturbing, but it is even worse when you are lying. She saw that her hand was trembling as she raised her spoon to her lips. *Come on. Get a grip!* she told herself. She was so engrossed in her own thoughts that she didn't hear what the kids at the table were talking about until a single word pierced the curtains of her mind.

"Yeah, I dreamed about my *brother* again last night," a skinny girl was saying.

Her brother? Maggie thought. During her last stay in Superbia that would have been an encouraging sign—something she would have reported to her grandfather with a flurry of enthusiasm. But as it was, it was a bad omen. Things truly were out of hand. As she was wondering about this, a shadow fell over her. She looked up and saw Meno looking down.

"Mind if we have a little talk with you?" the human lump asked.

"Yes, I mind," she answered.

"Good," he said, apparently getting her meaning precisely backward. "All right, you twerps, get out-a-here," he said to the rest of the table.

"Yeah, out-a-here," You-know-who repeated.

Instantly, the other kids melted into the surrounding tables.

Willis and Drake plopped themselves on either side of her, and Meno took the chair directly across.

She decided she'd have to make her best case. It wasn't at all thought-out; she'd have to improvise.

"I don't know what you guys are talking about. I don't believe in home. I don't know what's going on around here, but I wish you'd stop saying I've been there. I don't want to get into any trouble."

A wide, slow grin spread across Meno's face. It was a knowing smile, and it made him look like a toad with a secret.

"Don't play dumb with me, girlie. I know all about playing dumb. I've had lots of practice," he said.

"That's right, we've had lots of practice," Willis added.

"Shut up, you idiot. You don't need any practice," said Meno.

"Gee, thanks!" said Willis.

Drake rolled his eyes, and Meno redirected his attention to Maggie. He leaned over the table and stuck his face right in front of hers. It was so wide and red and fat, Maggie had to draw back. That's when she noticed that Willis and Drake had put their arms around the back of her chair. They drew her back in.

"We know what you're up to," said Meno in a hoarse whisper. Maggie was in a perfect spot to see that he seldom brushed his teeth after meals. "You're here to help kids get home. You're looking for kids who are ready so you can sneak them out."

The accuracy of his words disarmed her like nothing else could have. Her face got nearly as red as his, and her eyes grew wide. Perspiration appeared on her forehead even though the room was chilly. She tried to push away, but she couldn't budge.

"Sneak out?" she said, with a nervous laugh. "Why would I do that?"

The boys looked at each other, and Meno nodded toward Drake.

"How about the food, for one thing," said Drake. "You told us you hated it here."

"And I remember you said your *mother* used to make you— what was it?" Meno added.

"Eggs," Drake helped.

"Yeah, eggs," Meno said triumphantly.

"I made it all up," Maggie blurted, thinking as fast as she could.

"Okay, I'll buy that you made part of it up," Meno conceded unexpectedly. "Eggs were a pretty stupid idea. But the mother part, that was real. And then there was that punk, Trevor. He was always blabbing about home, and you two were always together. Just a couple of lovey-doveys. Right guys?"

"Right," said Willis, making a kissy face. "Lovey-doveys."

Maggie felt heat rising up her face, "No way!" she protested. "I don't even like him; he's a jerk." There was enough venom in her remark that it made the boys pause, but not for long.

"If that twit didn't go home, where is he?" said Meno.

"How should I know?" Maggie said, trying to look incredulous. "The Behavior Modifiers separated us."

"A likely story," Meno said, sneering.

Now Maggie saw her chance and instinctively, she pressed it. "Even if I had gone home, why would I be back, you moron?"

"Because," Meno said getting even closer. "You're here to try and shut us up. You're here to talk us out of wanting to go home. You want to keep *home* a precious secret between you and your chums. I know you don't like us. That's why you want to keep us out. But it's not going to work."

The truth stung. A riot of questions began shouting in her head. *How does he know? Who told him? What am I going to do?* But all she could say was, "I, uh ...I...uh,"

"We're on to you, Maggie Blaise. And we're going to keep our eyes on you. You're our ticket out of here, and we're not going to let you slip away."

Desperation gave her strength they didn't know she had, and she pushed hard enough to break the grip on her chair. She stood, shaking her head back and forth. *This isn't happening! It can't be happening!*

"Don't leave us, Maggie," Meno said, with a mock pout. "Take us home with you!"

"Yeah, take us home!" said Willis and Drake.

The eyes of the boys met and three mischievous smiles appeared. Together they said in unison, "Take us home." Then they pounded the table and made the dishware rattle. "Take us home!" they then shouted. They looked around, and others joined in. Again, pounding was followed by the shout, "Take us home!" Almost at once, the entire hall was shouting and pounding, "Take us home! Take us home! Take us home!" and every eye was on her–Maggie Blaise. The Guardians had disappeared. She desperately wanted to do the same. She covered her face and ran out of the room.

The whole rest of the day was like a nightmare. Throughout it, kids would spontaneously burst into applause when she entered a room. Someone, she was sure she knew who, had spread the rumor that she had come back to reunite them with their families. Whenever she denied it, kids just smiled or winked and said something like, "Sure, Maggie. We understand–whatever you say." But she could see they didn't understand, and when she said so, they'd invariably reply, "Good ol' Maggie. Trying to keep it all hush, hush. But don't worry; it's not like it used to be. The Guardians don't care anymore."

But she couldn't believe that, not with knowing what she did about the bogeys and the whole purpose for Superbia. It was very odd, though. She'd been told about the strange silence of the Guardians by her grandfather, but she'd only half believed it. They did seem to hang back, keeping their distance–not like before. When she was on her way to afternoon drills, she tried to approach one of them. But he just looked at her blankly when she tried to explain her predicament. "Please, you've got to help me tell them there's no such thing as home," she told him, whispering *home* and wincing as she did, expecting a slap, or at least a harsh reprimand. But it was like talking to a wall– absolutely no response. She kept at it, raising her voice and getting angry. "What's the matter with you, are you deaf?" she shouted. His impassive eyes slowly blinked as he gazed over her head. She stamped a foot and with a "Humph!" she spun around and rejoined the kids.

Along with this change, there were others that puzzled her

mightily. Before, during the course of a normal day, the kids of Hall 37 would see kids from other halls–on the parade grounds or on the way to classes. But on this day, they were nowhere to be seen. It was like they had been evacuated. Or worse, it occurred to her, Hall 37 had been quarantined. She also noticed more Guardians than usual, but always in the background, or on the edges of things, like a white-robed fence. She didn't make these observations all at once, it was more like an accumulation of facts, fact by fact, piling up and making something meaningful. But she couldn't figure it out.

At dinner that evening, she made her last desperate plea. She'd had enough knowing looks and eager smiles. The Guardians were on the edges, but by now her fear of them was largely gone. She got up and went to the serving tables. As she did, every eye followed her. Kids whispered as she went by, "Take me with you Maggie," or "Take me!" or "Remember me when you're ready to go, Maggie!" As she walked, she wondered if she was doing the right thing. Trevor's crazy idea about saving everybody popped into her head. "Don't get distracted," she scolded herself. "It's impossible; Grandfather said so." When she got to the front, she pulled back a chair and stepped on it. Instantly, Meno, Willis and Drake were on their feet.

"Hey, look everybody!" Meno shouted. "Maggie wants to say something! Listen up!" The room went completely still. She looked down on a sea of expectant faces.

"Hurray for Maggie!" a clique of girls Maggie had always despised shouted from a nearby table.

Cheers burst from around the room and her face got hot. What should she say? How could she explain it all? She'd been sent there to tell them all to give up their dreams of home–to stay put and go back to pretending everything was all right. But it wasn't all right. And Maggie had a need to be right. What's more, it would be a lie! And for what?–so that they could go on believing the lies of Superbia? It was crazy! Everything was backward! Her thoughts were interrupted by the sight of Meno and Drake exchanging looks. There was something in those looks that chilled her insides, and suddenly everything she saw looked different. The Guardians grew on the edge of sight, and the kids seemed to get smaller. Nothing had really changed; the change had happened inside of her. Before she could bring herself to say anything, Meno shouted.

"Come on Maggie–tell us how you're going to take us home!" There was something in his voice that said he didn't really mean what he was saying.

"Whahooo! Home, here we come!" crooned Willis as only Willis could.

As if on cue, one half of the room pounded on the tables and shouted, "Take us home!" Then the other half echoed their reply, "Take us now!" Then the first said again, "Take us home!" followed by "Take us now!"

Maggie stepped down from the chair and returned to her seat. No one was paying her any attention. They were too busy trying to shout each other down.

The rest of the evening was a waiting game, and since Maggie was very bad at waiting for things it made her absolutely miserable. She hadn't had many friends besides Trevor the last time she was in the hall, and she didn't want any phony ones now. When darkness finally fell and preparations were being made for bed, she kept as much to herself as she could manage. At first, kids plied her with questions about how she got kids out and what *home* was like. The word *candy* kept coming up. But her grumpiness and her refusal to answer even a single question eventually discouraged even the most single-minded pest.

It was impossible to relax with every eye on her, and the

huddled conversations all around. She so wanted the clock to speed up, and the lights to be put out and her grandfather to arrive. All these things did happen eventually, but they did with a slowness that only impatience can produce. She desperately wanted to talk with her grandfather, to tell him what had happened, to explain that it had all been a mistake.

When the last of the Guardians had finally doused the last of the lights and the only light was a long box of illumination coming from the crack left in the door, at last Epictetus stepped in. He shut the door behind him, and everything went dark. She wanted to jump up and run over to him right then. But it wouldn't do, not with everyone still whispering about her. She'd heard the prevailing theory. She would act after lights out. That's when so many kids had seemed to go missing in the past. It was a good theory, she had to admit. But besides being utterly wrong, it was most inconvenient. It meant that it would take longer than normal for everyone to doze off–probably a lot longer.

The whirling of a lamp being wound passed over the distance to her. Then a little light flashed. It was reddish and her grandfather's face shone above it. She remembered that she'd left the mechanism to his old lamp in the tunnel Helen had found her in. He must have borrowed this one from someone. She seemed to recall that Paracelsus had a lamp with a red filament. It made her grandfather look as though he were dipped in crimson.

Seeing him sitting there made time move even slower. A hum of conversation was rising from the sea of fidgety children between them. After hours of this with much restless tossing, a stillness finally settled upon the room. She jolted awake when she felt a heavy warmth on her shoulder. She'd fallen asleep. A tickle of whiskers and a low, soft voice in her ear brought her to full consciousness.

"All is clear, Granddaughter, come quickly. Time is short—you must leave tonight."

"Grandfa—" She couldn't finish. His hand had shot over her mouth. His lamp was in his other hand and was burning low. Even in the weak light, she could see the stern set of his face. She slipped on her robe and shoes and followed him to the doorway.

He cracked the door enough to glance out. A thin light leaked in, and Maggie saw a white robe through it. She caught her breath just as Epictetus caught her hand. They slipped out quickly, and he shut the door behind them.

Helen stood before them. Maggie exhaled.

"Grandfather, it's no good. I tried to tell them that I couldn't get them home, but no one believed me." Again, he cupped his hand over her mouth.

"It doesn't matter, Granddaughter. Helen has informed me that this very night, the bogeys are coming to take all the children away."

"All of them? To the Pantry?" Maggie said in shock.

"I am afraid so; but I think they'll have a little visit with the Inspector first. My guess is that they've been waiting for you, or someone like you, to show up. They'll want to speak with you, I'm sure."

Maggie had heard enough about the Inspector for a tremor to run through her at the thought of actually seeing him face to face.

"I am afraid, my Granddaughter, that I have brought you into a trap."

"No, Grandfather, I wanted to come."

"Hush, child. I need no consolation. I just want you out of here. Helen will lead you back. Come." He took her hand and led her down the stairs she had come up only the night before. Helen followed behind, soundlessly.

At the entrance to the hall, he took Paracelsus' lamp and pressed it into Helen's hands. Then he took half of the filament out for himself, leaving her with the handle, casing, and the remainder of the filament.

"Helen, thank you for your help. Please, take her quickly. Go, my Granddaughter. And remember directions and the secret of the Sentinel Stone."

There was no time for words. She quickly wrapped her arms around him, then pushed away. Helen simply nodded to the Master Fisher and took Maggie's hand. When they stepped out into the night air, Maggie saw that the landing which had been full of Guardians the night before was completely empty. Indeed, there was no one in sight.

⁎

Epictetus remained where he was after the door had closed behind them. "Go swiftly, Abigail," he said to himself. He made his way back up the stairs to his post slowly, wondering both about what would become of his precious granddaughter and when the bogeys would arrive. When he got back to the sleeping chamber, he saw that the door was ajar.

"That's odd, I would have sworn I shut this," he said, as he closed the door behind him.

He took out the portion of the lamp still in his possession. It occurred to him that he should check Maggie's bed for things she may have left behind. After seeing that she had left nothing that would provide a clue to her coming or going, he noticed an open spot to his right and went to investigate. What he came to were three unmade beds, empty of their usual occupants.

The old man cursed to himself. He knew who those beds had belonged to. He also knew that there were now five people to worry about in the night air—a woman, a girl and three boys.

CHAPTER EIGHTEEN

Pig

Trevor ran out of the Library and into the hall. He slipped on his glasses and noticed his stomach talking to him. He'd spent the entire day working without a thing to eat. "Things could use a bit of tidying up," Ichabod had said. Trevor thought "bit" was an understatement. The Master Illuminator had told him to: "Just sort things out. Categorize. Put things in order–boxes here, books there–use your *head*," he'd said, tapping his own impatiently. After that, the old man went to take a nap.

When he finally returned hours later, he said, "Hmmmm. Adequate. Now off you go and *tomorrow* bring a lunch." When Trevor went out the door, Ichabod was poking around the piles as though he was looking for something.

While he was wondering whether dinner would be ready when he got back to Maggie's, he remembered his promise to report to Paracelsus. As far as he could see, there was nothing to report, but he'd promised. He wasn't sure how he would find the Alchemist; but he needn't have worried, for as soon as he stepped out of the Illuminators' wing into the Alchemists' Quarter, a lean man stepped out of the shadows.

He had hunched shoulders and buck-teeth. When Trevor asked about Paracelsus, the buck-toothed man answered with a lisp, "Yes, he is expecting you. He sent me to look for a special boy named Trevor. I take it you're that boy?" he said, smiling and blinking.

"Uh, I guess so," Trevor responded, feeling a little awkward, but not at all displeased.

"Absolutely wonderful! Follow me."

He led Trevor through some of the workshops Trevor had only seen through doors before. Now he had an opportunity to see the work of the Alchemists at close range. It made no more sense to him than it had from the hallway.

Eventually, they came to the entrance of Paracelsus' garden. It was an archway in a vine-covered trellis. His nameless guide bowed with arms extended, and for the first time Trevor noticed a heavy, golden chain dangling from his neck. Trevor thanked the man and went in.

The vines on the trellis were filled with enormous white flowers that opened out with long, yellow antennae like tongues. Each flower was veined with pinkish lines and its odor was thick, sweet, and cloying. Trevor felt his throat constrict.

A cobblestone path wound before him through heavy undergrowth. On both sides of it, plants spilled out onto the stones. As he stepped gingerly between paddle-sized leaves and wispy stalks, he kept getting caught by a plant with long tendrils and little suckers. He had to stop several times to pull them off. Wherever they stuck to his clothes, they left behind a moist little pucker of cloth. But wherever they touched his unprotected skin they left a red mark. Those hurt.

When he finally got to the house, he saw that it was several stories tall, but it was being consumed by heaping mounds of vegetation that spilled from its eaves like a many-tiered waterfall. The greenery made it hard to see what the house was made of. It could have been a kind of brown stone. He stepped onto a porch full of potted plants. Fortunately there weren't any suckers but the surfeit abundance made the place stuffy. Gingerly, he stepped between them and managed to find his way to the door. It was green, and it had large splayed hinges across it with an enormous golden knocker to match.

He reached for the knocker but, before he could touch it, the door flew open to reveal a smiling Paracelsus. He was wearing a paisley-covered robe of green silk tied at the waist by a belt that accentuated his round belly. His beard and hair hung lank and loose, but his grin was broad and golden. He waved Trevor in.

"Come in, come in. So good of you to come! I take it you have finished your chores for the day for our fine Master Illuminator?"

"Uh, yes sir."

Trevor was a little dazzled by the surroundings. Every inch of floor was filled with thick, gaudy furniture or white ceramic statuary. On the walls, heavy tapestries hung in pregnant swags. The ceiling was twice the normal height, and at the far end of the room stood a tall mantel bounded by fluted pillars and crowned with carved flowers and little figures. Above it stood a polished mirror of special brilliance which, unfortunately, doubled the room and its contents.

"Come child, have a chair and tell me of your day," Paracelsus said.

He directed Trevor to a silver chair with twisted legs and tasseled cushions. As he did, he walked to another even more ornate chair, this one all gold. Trevor couldn't help but notice the flash of his open-toed slippers as they peeked out from beneath his robes. His feet were unusually small for a man so large and round.

When they were both seated, Trevor saw that the Alchemist's toenails were long and shiny–like they had been polished. Paracelsus clapped his hands twice and a pale-faced girl with mousy hair stepped in from another room. Trevor recognized her as one of the gigglers from the banquet.

"Sardena, fetch something cool to drink for our good friend Trevor Upjohn would you?"

"Yes, Uncle," she said with a furtive glance at Trevor. Then she stepped back out.

"Well, well, how was your first day on the job?" the Alchemist asked, lacing his hands over his broad middle and putting his fingered adornment on full display.

"Fine, sir."

"Any outbursts of grumpiness from the good Master Ichabod?" he asked, with an understanding smile.

"No, sir. He slept most of the day."

"Ahh, very good." Paracelsus said, sounding especially pleased. "Let us hope he sleeps long and well every day you're with him."

Sardena walked in at that point, carrying a tray. Two tall glasses were perched on it along with a pitcher made to resemble a long-necked swan. But as she drew near, she caught a foot on a table leg and pitched forward. The tray tipped, and everything on it crashed to the floor. The pitcher stuck with particular force, and a dark drink splattered everywhere speckling Trevor and Paracelsus.

"Why, you clumsy fool!" Paracelsus shouted, jumping up.

"I'm sorry, Uncle!" Sardena said, eyes wide. She quickly fell to her hands and knees and began trying to mop up the spill with the hem of her robe.

Trevor got down to help and their eyes met briefly, but she lowered her head in embarrassment. Trevor retrieved the pitcher and glasses which, miraculously, hadn't broken. She made fast work of the spill.

"Look at me!" Paracelsus said in disgust, holding up his garment. There appeared to be a few small, dark spots. "It's ruined, I tell you! I shall have to get another, and all the way from Ophir too! I knew I should have never taken you into my service, you little oaf! When you're done with that, go back to your mother and tell her I'm through with you."

Sardena quickly took the proffered tray from Trevor's hands without looking up and said weakly, "Yes, Uncle." Then she shot out of the room. What sounded like a sob followed after her.

Paracelsus dabbed himself with an oversized silk kerchief and said, "Look at me. Just look at me. Ruined. The finest smoking jacket money can buy, just ruined."

"I'm sorry, sir," Trevor said, sounding more sympathetic than he felt.

"Wha? Oh, it's you. Yes, yes, I am afraid our little interview is over for the day. I'm so upset."

"But sir, what about my report?"

"Oh, yes, of course. Did you see anything in that old fool's library?"

Trevor shook his head.

"No? I thought not. Well, off with you. Come back tomorrow. Perhaps by then I'll be over the trauma of this, though I doubt it."

With a back-handed wave, he shooed Trevor to the door.

When Trevor got outside, he wandered slowly back to Maggie's. Yes, getting your best smoking jacket a little wet was sad, but Sardena didn't mean to do it. He wondered where she had gone to, and when he'd see her again, and what he should say to her when he did see her.

✻

When he got to Maggie's, he expected to find the Lady Rowena, but instead he was met at the door by Janet. "The Lady has retired for the evening," she said. She hinted that the Lady was very worried about Maggie and probably wouldn't get out much while she was gone. But Janet had prepared supper for them. As they ate together, they reminisced about old times back in Superbia. They laughed late into the night, remembering the pranks they'd played. Once they had put Guardian Medea's podium on blocks. She was so short, she had to stand on tiptoes for the entire class period just to see over it. That's when she started wearing the boots with the extra thick soles. Trevor realized his days there hadn't been all bad; friendship and fun had managed to survive in the nooks and the crannies.

That night he had a dream; actually, more like a nightmare. He found himself in familiar surroundings. There was a night light and toy-lined shelves. Along with it all, he heard the unsettling sound of someone sniffing. He couldn't move–icy pangs of fear shot through his sweaty body, freezing him in place. Then he saw it–a hideous nose-filled face hungrily staring down at him.

"The door, the door, the door..." cackled the bogeyman... he forgot to lock the door! Always remember to lock the door behind you! Someone might come in after you. Hee, hee! You thought you could slip away, did you, my sweet little morsel? Not so fast. I've a hole for you to fill–oh, I do, I do, my tasty treat! Come now, come. It's time for you to go where you belong." The mouth of a burlap bag began descending upon him, and everything went dark. "No!" Trevor shouted and awoke with a start. It was hard to sleep after that.

Something pleasant happened to him the next day that helped him to make up for the lost sleep. That afternoon, while he was in the Illuminators' library, as he was breaking down yet another pile of stuff–books, boxes, and so forth–he heard the sound of something scurry behind him. He looked back to see what it was and, as if out of nowhere, there sat an oddly-shaped box right at his feet.

"Where'd this come from?" he said, looking around. He was alone, as usual.

It was a little pyramid made of wood, with carefully dove-tailed corners. The box was small enough to hold with one hand, and it had a hinge about midway up that allowed him to open it. Fortunately, the latch wasn't locked, and he was able to look inside. The interior was lined with a soft, light blue felt, and there—in the center—in a place especially designed to hold it, sat a perfectly round golden ball. He lifted it out. It fit right in the palm of his hand, and it felt good to hold. Although it was made of metal, it wasn't heavy at all—quite the opposite. He hefted it a few times and tossed it up in the air. Then he noticed a small hole in it, about the width of his pinky finger. He stuck it in and fished around. Nothing. Apparently, it was hollow. He raised it to his eye and looked inside. Nothing again. It was completely dark.

"You've found Pig!" boomed a voice behind him. Trevor jumped and turned around. It was Ichabod with a strange, hungry look. "Isn't she a beauty? Toss her here." Realizing he meant the ball, Trevor gently underhanded it to the old man. He managed to grab it awkwardly with his two wrinkled hands. "Well, I am not the boy I once was," he said, sounding a little embarrassed. Then he threw it to the floor, and to Trevor's surprise and delight, it bounced right back up. He bounced it several more times.

Something had come over the old fellow; he didn't seem his normal irritable self. Trevor thought he could even see a hint of boyishness beneath the beard and wrinkles.

"My, my, this takes me back," he said, longingly. "When I was your age, I had such fun playing *mallow toss* and *slap the pig* with this."

"Excuse me, sir. Why did you call that ball *pig*?"

"Oh, just an old nickname. A term of endearment. When we played as children, we boys used balls of string wrapped with pig skin. We called them pigs. Years ago, when I found this ball at the bottom of a chest in this very room, I thought it was just the right size. And when I discovered that it was unbreakable, well, that settled it. It became my pig.

"At first my father, who was Master Illuminator before me, wouldn't allow it. He was certain it was an important artifact with hidden powers. But he never discovered any. I was sure it was just a fancy pig, and I stole it from his study," he said with a smile. "When he found out he was very angry, but I showed him that I couldn't harm it. When he saw that, he relented and gave it to me.

"But that was ages ago," sighed the old man. "Here," he said, tossing it to Trevor. "You can have it. I'm sure those friends I've seen you with can show you how to play *slap the pig*."

Trevor smiled and bounced the ball a few times before putting it in his pocket. After all the work he had put into cleaning the library, he finally had something to show for it. He could hardly wait to tell Tubby.

Ichabod began a search through the items Trevor had uncovered.

Trevor's curiosity prompted him to ask, "Excuse me, sir. What are you looking for?"

"Yes, what am I looking for?" Ichabod said, as if trying to remind himself. "Oh, yes...I'm looking for something that will help me read that book you saw the other day. It's called an *Augo*. Very rare, very ancient."

"What does it look like?"

"I wish I knew," Ichabod mumbled into his beard. "All I have is a name and some incredible stories about it. My great-great-grandfather's journals say it's in this library–somewhere. If the stories are true though, well, it would be useful for all sorts of things, like finding out what Paracelsus is up to," he finished, under his breath.

Trevor swallowed. "Paracelsus, sir?"

"What? Paracelsus? Where?" Ichabod looked lost for a moment. "Oh yes, Paracelsus! He's up to something. Can feel it in my bones. Those dratted Alchemists–always up to things!"

Trevor began feeling uncomfortable. "Umm, pardon me sir, will you need me anymore today?"

"Humph, what was that? Need you? Well, no. I have plenty to look through here." He smiled. "Why not take Pig and find those friends of yours?"

"Thanks!" Trevor said and ran out the door.

Part of him wanted to find Tubby, but another part just wanted to get away from Ichabod. Once he was in the hall with his glasses on, he wondered if he should go tell Paracelsus what he had found. He pulled Pig out of his pocket and hefted it in his palm again. It was pretty. Suddenly the thought of telling the Alchemist about it seemed, well, unnecessary. *It's just an old pig*, Trevor thought. *Ichabod said so.* Then the memory of Sardena's tears came to mind, and Trevor felt afraid. *Besides*, he told himself, *Master Paracelsus is a busy man, I shouldn't waste his time on toys.* So, with that, he shoved the ball back into his pocket and ran for the Great Garden hoping to find somebody to teach him how to play *slap the pig*.

CHAPTER NINETEEN

Together Again

"Trevor, I'm back!" rang a voice from outside the room. Trevor sat up quickly, sending Pig to the floor where it bounced to the foot of the door.

Whoever it was began rapping hard, "Trevor, wake up! It's me, Maggie! I'm back!"

"Whaa?" he said groggily. "Come in."

"I can't, silly, the door's locked."

"Oh, yeah." Trevor swung out of bed and stumbled to open it.

Maggie burst into the room and threw her arms around him. "I'm so glad to see you! Oh, how have you been? Mother's feeling better since I got back. She's making breakfast. Oooo, I've got so much to tell you. Wait, I've got to do something." She pushed away; then, in one smooth practiced motion, she balled up a fist and punched him in the stomach.

The air that had formerly been in his lungs escaped through an opening in his head as he folded in two and fell back on the bed.

"Whaa, what'd you do that for?!" he said, between gasps.

"Oh, I'm sorry!" she said, lunging at him with her arms outstretched.

Trevor recoiled, uncomprehending.

"What, aren't you happy to see me?"

She sat down next to him trying to embrace him. Trevor pulled back, wild eyed.

"Don't look at me like that! You deserved it, and you know it!"

Trevor had no idea what she was talking about, but her eyes were so confident and accusing that he couldn't help looking away and feeling vaguely guilty. But his stomach cramps fortified his sense of outrage. "What are you talking about?" he shot back.

"Oh, forget it, dimwit, and get dressed. I've got so much to tell you. Mother is making breakfast, I'll tell you while we eat." Her mood had changed from vindictiveness to hyperventilating enthusiasm in an instant. She hugged him before he could pull away and was up and out of the room before he could speak.

Trevor sat there for a moment not knowing what to think. That much enthusiasm at that hour of the morning was a little overwhelming, not to mention he'd just been punched in the stomach. With a groan, he began to get dressed. As he was finishing, he heard a voice he hadn't heard in days, "Children, time to eat!"

Maggie was waiting for him at the table, wearing a sheepish smile. Trevor thought her mother looked careworn, but she welcomed him warmly. "Let's celebrate our little reunion. Abigail, I've made your favorite."

As soon as he had sat down Maggie began talking about her adventure in Superbia, but her mother cut her off. "Abigail, please! Let's talk about pleasant things, shall we?"

"But Mother! This is important! Don't you want to know what happened to me?"

"No, I do not! It will only encourage you in your wild nonsense. Before you know it, you'll be just like your father, running off and leaving people to worry themselves sick over you!"

An awkward silence followed. Maggie stared down at her empty plate, and her mother's eyes burrowed into the side of her head. Trevor wanted to leave, but the breakfast did look awfully good, and the only cramps he felt now were hunger pangs. He reached for the bread. "Please pass the butter," he murmured, a little louder than he had wanted to. Maggie pushed a plate of it across the table sulkily.

Maggie's mother spoke. "We will only talk of nice things at this table from now on. No more fishing, and no more having your grandfather over." Maggie looked up and was about to protest, but she wasn't able to get a word out. "And, that's final," her mother said with particular force. "Now, I've made you some dresses while you were gone, and right after we're done eating you're going to put them on for me. I can't do all my work from memory, you know." The last part sounded like an accusation. "After that, we'll go to the Garden and do our share of the weeding. And as for you, Trevor, I have already sent word to Ichabod to let him know I'll be needing you today, so you can help."

✧

"Oooo, I wish Mother would let me grow up!" Maggie said, when they were finally free. "She never wants to hear about my adventures or anything to do with fishing!" It had taken all morning and a good chunk of the afternoon just to get away.

They wandered aimlessly through the Fishers' Quarter while Maggie fumed. She seemed more interested in complaining about what she had not been allowed to say than actually saying it now that she had the chance. Dying with curiosity himself, Trevor was about to bring that very fact up when Tubby rushed through a doorway up ahead and ran over.

"Did you hear the news?! Some new kids just got here from Superbia."

"So what? It happens all the time," grumbled Maggie.

"They didn't come the usual way–they just appeared in the Great Garden a little while ago like they had just popped out of the ground. Your Uncle Max found them. Boy, was he surprised!"

199

"The Garden?" Maggie said, sitting down unexpectedly, like her legs had given out.

"Yeah, there were three of them, I think."

"Three of them," she said, looking pale. "What did they look like?"

"I didn't see them up close, but one of them was a really big kid."

"Meno," Maggie said, staring into space.

"Meno? How?" said Trevor, feeling a chill in the air he hadn't noticed before.

"It can't be," she said to herself. "I didn't use the Stone. I just went to the left door and followed the way Grandfather went to the market. But–" her voice died away and her head fell into her hands.

"What are you talking about?" said Trevor.

"That's it!" she said, standing up and looking back and forth between Trevor and Tubby. "The arrow must have pointed at the door to Trothward!"

Trevor looked at her blankly.

"Ooo, I wish Mother had let me tell you everything. Anyway, I got to Superbia in a secret tunnel that Grandfather showed me. When I was coming back, I heard someone following me. So, when I got to the Sentinel Stone I took the wrong way, but it was really the right way, but the wrong way must have been the right way! See what I mean? Oh, it's so complicated! Don't look at me that way! The passage I took went to Olton Market, but the arrow must have been pointing here! They were the ones following me! But there were so many ways they could have gone wrong! It was a million-to-one chance! Someone must have shown them the rest of the way!"

"Well, don't look at me," said Tubby. "You're the one who led them here."

"No I didn't! You take that back!" Maggie said, balling up a fist.

The unmistakable voice of Max then came booming through the doorway.

"That must be them," said Tubby. "I heard your uncle say he would give them a walk around the place before taking them to their room."

Four bodies emerged, and Trevor's heart leapt into his throat. There was the large form of Max followed by three others. First came the lumpen shape of Meno, then Willis, looking as dull-witted as ever, and finally Drake, trying hard to not be impressed by everything. Each had the standard-issue book bag over his shoulder, which was really weird since Trevor had never seen Meno or Willis holding a book. He wasn't sure they even knew how to read.

"Here are some new friends!" said Max cheerfully. "Hello, Maggie! Thank heaven you made it back in one piece!" He gave her a bear hug. "I'm showing these fresh catches around. It was the darnedest thing. They actually came through that old door in the Garden! And I thought it was locked, too. Say they just escaped from Superbia through a hidden door there and going down a tunnel got them here! Why, I can't wait for the next banquet so I can see it with my own eyes. I don't imagine you know them."

"Actually, I do." said Maggie. "Uh, hi, guys."

"Well, how about that! Now don't you be modest, Darling. You had something to do with getting them here, didn't you?" Maggie turned red, but didn't say a thing. Her uncle looked at her quizzically. "Now, what about you then, Trevor? You must recognize these fellows, seeing that they're from your old hall?"

"Uhhh, hi," Trevor said nervously.

For their part, Willis and Drake seemed nearly as

uncomfortable as Trevor and Maggie. "Hi," they said lamely. Meno was different. He actually looked pleased, triumphant even–like a wolf looks when he catches a rabbit.

"Come now," remarked Max, "won't it be nice to be together again?"

"Sure," said Trevor without conviction.

Max eyed both Maggie and Trevor. He seemed to be trying to work out a solution for their odd behavior. After a moment, he said, "Well, we've got to get going boys. You'll be able to renew acquaintances later." With that, he started off. Meno lingered just long enough to lean over to Trevor and say in a low voice, "Hey, kid, been home yet?" He didn't wait for an answer, which was just as well since Trevor was speechless.

"That was really strange," said Tubby. "What's the matter with you guys? You act like you've just seen a bunch of bogeys."

"Maybe we have," said Maggie. "Come on, Trevor. Let's go see Grandfather."

They left a flummoxed Tubby and went into a section of the Ward Trevor hadn't been to before.

"If we're lucky, we'll get to him before he gets busy."

"What do you think is going on?" said Trevor.

"I don't know, but I sure don't feel good about it, whatever it is," she said.

Trevor didn't feel good just then either. He found himself thinking of home for the first time in a long time.

They sped through the Fishers' quarter until they went through a door leading outside. They stopped at a hedge which had an opening. Trevor looked at Maggie. Without a glance, she grabbed his hand and pulled him through after her. He felt a twinge of annoyance as she led the way.

"It's a maze," she said. "Grandfather's house is on the other side."

There were so many twists and turns, Trevor was lost immediately. Maggie proceeded confidently while talking to herself. "Two right, one left; two right, two left..." and so forth until she finally said, "Here we are!" They stepped into a cobblestone courtyard. Before them, under an arch, stood a door—much like the one to the Illuminator's quarter—but instead of glass, this one was made of oak. On its posts were fish, mouth to tail, all swimming without going anywhere. They looked wet and glossy in the dancing light of the lamp that hung nearby. Trevor reached out to touch one, certain that it was just a trick; to his surprise he pulled back a damp hand.

"Pretty neat, huh?" said Maggie.

A testy, tremulous voice came from beneath the door just then. "Paracelsus, how can you say that?"

"Ichabod," said Trevor.

"Shhh!" said Maggie, with a finger to her lips. She waved to him to follow her, and they stepped away from the door. Another voice began to speak. It faded for a moment, then grew louder when they came to an open window. Crouching behind a bush, they listened to what sounded like an argument.

"What do you think about our recent arrivals, Brend?" said Epictetus.

"Master," said the gravelly voice of the captain, "they've not come in the time-tested way. I'm told they do not even know our sign. I sense the craft of the enemy in this. Turn them out before they learn any more than they have already. That's the safest policy. They're not our responsibility."

"What difference does it make how they came to be here, Captain?" asked the Alchemist, sounding exasperated. "They are here now, and the policy of this house has always been to give amnesty to children in need!"

Silence followed. Maggie and Trevor exchanged worried

looks. Finally, they heard Epictetus's voice through the window. It sounded strained. "True, my friend. That has always been our policy, but we've never had children arrive in this manner before. Brendleback is likely right about the craft of the enemy in this."

"They are *children*. What *harm* could they possibly perform?" said Paracelsus.

"What do you say, Ichabod?" asked Epictetus.

"What do I say? What do I say?! They're spies sent by Lucian! That's what I say!"

"Spies?" Paracelsus said with amusement. "They are innocents caught up in matters far too large for them. Come now," he said, changing his tone. "What of compassion, old friend? What does it say if we turn the needy away?"

"I don't care what it says—I care what it is! Turn them out!"

After a tense silence, Epictetus spoke again. "Brothers, let us not tax the cords of friendship like this." After another pause, he spoke again. "I have made my decision. They are here now, whether they are meant for harm or not. If they are not, then turning them out is certain death for them. No one in Olton will harbor them, and sooner or later they would be sent to the Sewers. If they are a trap then turning them out would mean they had failed, and again they would be sent to the Sewers. Either way, I cannot live with that outcome. My heart speaks clearly. We must keep them and hope for the best."

"Master," said Brendleback, with some heat, "you are head of the Guild. All must live with your decision. Should conscience be your only guide? Shouldn't you consider the outcomes? Sometimes we must live with the lesser of two evils."

"That is true, my friend, but only partly," said Epictetus. "If we could see all outcomes, then we could choose the way that seems best. Tell me, Brend, can you see all the possible outcomes?" There was a silence. "I thought not. Our knowledge is limited. I tell you, there are more powers at work in the world than we know. Who can say what they will do? No, we must do what is right and hope for the best. I have decided. The children will stay."

CHAPTER TWENTY

A Gift is Opened

T he conversation inside had died out. Maggie looked troubled, even a little scared. She mouthed, *We need to talk,* and pointed to the hedges. Trevor followed her in.

Finding a private spot in the maze would be easy; finding a way out again wouldn't be. Maggie thought of that, so when they came to the first turn she broke a twig and let it hang. Each twist or turn she broke another. Finally, when she was sure they were far enough away from her grandfather's door to talk unheard, she stopped and sat down. With the hedges towering over them and closing in around, the only sound Trevor heard was their breathing.

"How can Grandfather be so dumb?" she said in a voice that couldn't make up its mind whether it was a whisper or a shout.

"I want to know what those guys are up to," said Trevor.

"And what I want to know is how they found their way here. There were so many ways they could have gone wrong–and in the dark, too. How did they see where they were going? I had the lamp Grandfather had given me."

"Do you think they had help?" Trevor asked.

"They must have," said Maggie.

"What are you confounded youngsters babbling about?" said a voice.

They jumped up onto their feet. The spidery form of Master Ichabod came out from behind a hedge.

"Wondering what I've heard, eh? Well, I've heard enough to know I'm not the first to eavesdrop today."

"We didn't mean to, Master. We just wanted to talk to Grandfather; but you, Master Paracelsus, and Captain Brendleback were already with him."

"Sooo, rather than knock and interrupt us, you politely listened to a conversation not intended for your little ears," he said, shaking his walking stick at her.

"I'm sorry, Master Ichabod," Maggie said, bowing her head.

"Master," put in Trevor, "we came to see Master Epictetus because we think the new kids are spies."

"Why, of course they're spies," said Ichabod, getting agitated. "Plainest thing in the world. Anyone can see that."

"Then why doesn't Grandfather think so?"

"Oh, he thinks so–he knows so," said Ichabod.

"So, how come he doesn't kick them out?"

"His heart is too blasted soft, that's why! It's made his head soft!"

"You mean that stuff about not wanting them to get hurt?"

"That's right. Your grandfather is a good man, Abigail. Too good for this world, I think sometimes."

"What can we do?" asked Trevor.

"Yeah, what?" agreed Maggie.

Both looked at the old man, and he looked back at them with sharp eyes, "Yes, what to do, what to do?" he said. Then, suddenly, his eyes went vacant. "Beg your pardon, what are we talking about?"

"Uh, the spies, sir," said Trevor, feeling a little embarrassed for the old fellow.

"Spies? Where?" said the aged Illuminator, looking around quickly.

"The new kids," said Maggie, getting frustrated.

"Oh, yes! They're spies! Of course they're spies! Don't argue with me!"

"But what should we *do* about them?" said Trevor desperately.

"Why, spy back on them, of course! Fight fire with fire, as they say." Ichabod said, poking the hedge with his walking stick. The old man looked like he was feeling feisty now. "But who will do the spying?"

Maggie got excited, "Why not us, Master?!"

"Whaaa, you? We can't have you!"

"Why not?" Maggie said, sounding feisty herself.

"Well, I uh, I don't know. I suppose you could do it," he said, with a new expression on his wrinkled face.

"Good!" said Maggie, with a big smile.

"But what are we trying to do?" asked Trevor.

"But what are we trying to do?" Ichabod mimicked. "Why, discover their plan, of course! Even Epictetus can't object to that. Well, then," he said, looking back and forth between them with a squinty expression, "You two are apparently good at eavesdropping: I hereby authorize you to eavesdrop on these boys. Can you do it?"

"Oh, sure," Maggie said. Then she added truthfully, "I do it all the time."

"And how about you?" he asked, turning to Trevor. "I'll need you to give me regular updates on the activities of these boys."

"No problem," Trevor fibbed. Then it suddenly struck him that he had managed to get roped into spying for two masters in the same week.

"Good!" said Ichabod, his eyebrows rising with pleasure. "Information will help. Now get to it! Be careful though, and make sure you cover your tracks a little better in the future. I was on my way back to my quarters for my mid-day nap when

I came upon one broken twig and then another until I stumbled on you two," he explained. After a final glance, he hobbled away mumbling to himself and poking the bushes.

"Come on, there's not a moment to lose," said Maggie. She took Trevor's hand, again, and began leading them out of the maze.

"Let go, I don't need to be led like a baby," he said, shaking himself free.

She looked back with a wounded expression that quickly flashed to anger. "Fine, then, but stay close."

When they were out, he asked moodily, "Where do we start?"

"The place all Fresh Fish go when they get here. I'm sure that's where Uncle Max put them," she answered testily.

"Where's that?"

"In one of the rooms surrounding the Garden, of course," she said in her most irritating, I-know-more-than-you, voice. "Fresh Fish always go to the Tree after coming to the Ward. We have a saying that goes—*The Troth's roots reach deeply into body and soul to renew the fresh catch and make him whole.* "Let's go!"

Once out of the maze they rushed through the corridors of the Ward, passing members of the great house without returning greetings. They came on Giles, who blocked nearly an entire passage with his tremendous girth.

"Good day, young ones! Now, where would you be going in such a rush?"

"No time, Giles. Gotta run!" said Maggie as they squeezed by him.

"Yeah, gotta run!" added Trevor.

The Master Cook watched them scurry down the corridor and around a corner. "Now, what is that girl up to this time?" he wondered aloud.

Finally, they came to the chambers that surrounded the Tree. Since there were dozens of rooms on each side, Maggie decided they should split up.

"You go that way, and I'll go this," she said pointing in both directions. "Look through the keyholes. If you see them, wait for me."

"And if you find them, wait for me," Trevor said.

"Of course."

Off she ran moving quickly from one door to the next. Trevor set off in the opposite direction. Each room he peered into was completely dark. "This could take a while," he said to himself. He looked back toward Maggie and saw that she had already turned a corner and was out of sight.

What should I do if I find those guys first? he wondered. Generally things were done to him; as he drifted from keyhole to keyhole, he found it very pleasant to consider the possibility of doing something to somebody else for a change. First, Trevor thought it would be nice to whip Meno, Willis, and Drake with his bare hands before Maggie or anyone else could show up. That made him smile. Then, he decided it would be very pleasant to bring them to Epictetus on a rope and make them tearfully confess their crimes. That made him chuckle. Finally, he decided, he would he would really enjoy recounting his exploits at the next banquet to the wonder and admiration of all–especially Maggie. Now that made him so giddy he started to hiccup.

After absently looking into countless dark rooms, he finally came to a keyhole with light coming out of it. Stooping down, he peeped in and, there, peeking back at him, was an eye. He hiccupped. A voice on the other side of the door said, "Hey, someone's out there! Put it away, quick!"

Before he could pull away the door swung open, and he fell face first into the room.

Looking up from the floor, he saw three very unwelcome faces looking down at him. Suddenly his plans vanished like a mist before his eyes. The old feelings came rushing back: the dull pit in the stomach, the mind freeze, the urge to beg for mercy, the cold sweat. At least his hiccups were gone.

"Uh...hi, guys," he said, with a weak smile.

"Well, if it isn't our homesick little friend, Trevor," Meno said with a sneer. "How about it punk, still looking for Mommy and Daddy? They're not here, unless Willis is your mommy. What do ya say, Willis, are you Trevor's mommy?" The others laughed.

Trevor jumped up and mysteriously, from somewhere deep inside, he felt something hard. "What are you doing here, Meno? You guys don't belong in Trothward," he said.

"Haven't you heard, twerp? We want to go home, too. We miss our mommies and daddies."

Trevor's neck stiffened. It seemed like he was looking at Meno down a long tunnel.

"Punk, you're so stupid," Meno went on. "You should have stayed back in Superbia. *Home* is just a bunch of slave nonsense. And this *trooth* place, or whatever you call it, won't be here long, you'll see."

Whether it was wise or not, whether it was right or not, Trevor did something out of the blue, something neither he nor anyone else in the room expected. He reared back and swung as hard as he could. His fist landed smack! on Meno's nose, and the bully's big body fell straight back and hit the floor hard. Drake and Willis stepped back in shock. Meno looked up from the floor in disbelief. This wasn't the way things happened to him. Tears were forming in his eyes and, strange as it may sound, Trevor kind of felt bad for hitting him. But he felt good, too; exhilarated in fact. His feelings were a bit mixed up at the moment.

Meno staggered to his feet, choked back a sob, and wiped the blood coming from his nose on his sleeve. "Kid, you shouldn't have done that," he said. "You're gonna pay. You and all your stupid friends are gonna pay."

Someone gasped. Trevor looked back and saw Maggie standing wide-eyed in the doorway. Then, Max stepped in front of her.

"Well, isn't this nice? Catching up on old times, eh?" Max said, casting an eye toward Trevor. "No time for that now. Master Epictetus wants you and Abigail. Told me I'd find you both down here, he did. How he knew baffles me. Well, that's why he's a Master and I'm not, I suppose. Come along." He looked at the others and said, "You boys sit tight. Your suppers will be along presently."

Trevor backed out of the room, stiff-legged, and into the hall. As he joined Max and Maggie, he was shaking all over, partly from left-over fear, but mostly from the thrill of actually punching Meno in the nose.

Once they were down the hall, Max turned to Trevor. "You don't like that big fellow, do you?" Trevor looked surprised. "I'm not blind, you know. I could tell you just laid him out by the tears he was holding back. Besides, I heard some hard words as I was coming up."

"No, I don't," Trevor said. He looked back at Maggie, hoping she'd heard Max say he'd laid Meno out. But it didn't look like she had; instead her face was pale, and it had a haunted look. Her mouth was moving over something, but no words were coming out.

He dropped back. "What's the matter?"

"The lantern," she said hoarsely. "Didn't you see it? They had the lantern Grandfather gave to Helen! That's how they could see in the tunnels. If they did anything to her, I'll kill 'em."

"Who's Helen?" Trevor asked.

"Not now. I'll tell you later."

Trevor's feelings of elation came crashing down. She hadn't even noticed that he'd beaten up Meno, and now he wasn't even important enough to know who this Helen person was.

"Uncle Max," Maggie said. "We've got to do something–those kids are spies."

"Now, now, I admit they're not the pleasant sort, but I wouldn't go calling them spies," he responded. "They wouldn't have made it here if they were. Do you really think the Masters would let them stay if they thought they were spies?"

"But they do think so!" exclaimed Maggie. "At least Master Ichabod does and even Grandfather!"

"Posh, girl. How do you know that? I think you're letting your recent success go to your head. Some things are better left to your elders. Now, come along. Your grandfather says he will meet you at your mother's apartment."

✳

When they got there, Lady Rowena was absent and Epictetus hadn't arrived yet.

"You're to stay here–'til your grandfather gets here."

"But..." blurted Maggie.

"None of your sass, now. And don't you be a-running off. These are difficult days, and your grandfather has more important things to worry about than a couple of ornery kids. I've got a few things to see about, but I'll be back."

After the door had shut, they wandered into Trevor's room, and he threw himself down on his bed. He reached over to his nightstand and picked up his golden ball. He liked the feel of it in his hand, and he fingered it absentmindedly as he tried to sort his feelings out.

"Babies!" said Maggie. "That's what they think we are, just babies!"

"Who cares?" Trevor said at the ceiling. "Meno's not pretending he wants to go home anymore."

"What do you mean?"

Getting up on one elbow, Trevor leaned toward her. *Well, before I beat him up, if you hadn't noticed,* he told me that home was just a bunch of slave talk."

"That changes everything! Let's go tell Ichabod what you heard," Maggie said, still not noticing Trevor's heroics.

"We can't. You heard your uncle," Trevor said, falling back on his bed. "Besides, what do we tell him? We don't know anything. I just wish I could see what those guys are doing," he said absentmindedly, holding up his golden ball.

Suddenly, a little light shot out of the hole in the orb and landed on his face.

"Whoa," he said. He'd looked into that hole several times, even sticking a finger in as far as he could. He'd thought it was just an empty ball. Now a bluish light flickered out of it. Maggie looked at the orb, then at him.

"What is that thing?" she asked.

"Ichabod said it was just his old pig," he said, with a shrug. "He gave it to me after I found it in the Library." He brought the ball to his eye and looked inside.

"Amazing," he said, and pulled it away to rub his eye in disbelief.

"What? What is it?" asked Maggie, edging nearer.

"I thought I saw Meno!"

"No way!"

"No, really," he said, putting it back to his eye. "Yes, yes I do! It's like I'm a fly on the ceiling–I'm looking down at them! What is this thing?" he said, pulling it away from his eye again.

"Since you got it from the Illuminators' Library, it could be anything. It must be really old," said Maggie.

"Ichabod told me his father thought so, but he couldn't figure it out, so he let Ichabod use it for a pig! Can you believe it?" said Trevor. He put it up to his eye again. "Yeah, it's definitely them. Meno's walking back and forth, and he's holding some kind of box. The others are eating, and it looks like Meno's talking to them."

"Here, let me try!" Maggie said. She reached over and snatched it from his hand, but as soon as she touched it the light went out. "Hey, what happened?" she said, looking inside. "I don't see anything."

"You broke it. Figures a girl would break a magic ball," Trevor said, feeling an odd mixture of pleasure and concern. "Here, give it back."

"All I did was touch it!"

"Say—*I want to see Meno.*"

"I want to see Meno."

Nothing happened.

"Come on, give it back. Let me try."

She reluctantly offered it back. As soon as it touched his hand, the light went back on.

"Hey, no fair!" Maggie crossed her arms and slumped in her chair. "It's probably not real anyway. That old stuff is tricky. Grandfather always says so."

"It must be real," Trevor said, feeling immensely satisfied. "You're just mad because it won't work for you. I just wish I could hear what they're saying." As if on command, the orb obliged and Meno's voice began coming from the ball.

"How can you eat that slave stuff?" the voice said, sounding far away and tinny.

"You should try it. It ain't so bad," said a voice that sounded like Willis. "How long do we have to stay here? This place gives me the creeps. That thing out there with the lights, I don't like it."

"Don't you remember, dummy, that's why we're here. Santa told us about it. What did he call it?"

"A tree–a magic tree," chimed in Drake.

"Yeah, that's it. He said it was wild magic, and whatever is in this box would kill it."

"Well open it then," said Willis. "Let's get this over with and get back to our hall. Those jerks from Hall 57 may move in on our territory if they see we're not there."

"Don't you remember, moron? Gourmand told us to wait 'til dark before we open the box."

"Why do we have to wait 'til then?"

"Because, stupid, that's when the Behavior Modifiers are coming. We'll be back in Superbia soon enough once these uppity slaves are put in their place. I can't wait to see that Trevor punk get it."

Maggie blurted out, "We've got to stop them!"

"What was that?" said the voice of Drake.

"It sounded like that dumb Maggie girl," said Willis.

"Shut up, you two," said Meno. "They're probably outside. Check the door."

Trevor pulled the orb away, and the light and sounds abruptly stopped.

"They heard you!" said Trevor.

"Shhh!" said Maggie. "Maybe they still can."

He looked at the ball closely. "I don't think so. It seems to have shut off."

"Now, we have to tell Ichabod what we heard. It's nearly dark," Maggie said.

"If it's nearly dark that means they're going to let whatever's in that box out. We have to stop them!" said Trevor.

"But bogeymen are coming—we've got to warn people."

"It won't matter if the Tree's dead. Your grandfather told me it's the only reason the bogeys haven't attacked before now. They're afraid of it."

"Ohhh, what should we do? If only Mother hadn't made me try on all those stupid dresses, we could have known hours ago!" Maggie said pitifully.

"We've got to split up," said Trevor. "You go look for Ichabod and I'll try to stop them."

Maggie looked like she wanted to say something smart-alecky but nothing came out.

"You got a better idea?" Trevor said getting up.

"No."

"Well, let's go already then."

CHAPTER TWENTY-ONE

Another Gift is Opened

Trevor and Maggie burst out of the entry that led to her mother's apartment and into a short corridor. Who should enter the other end at that very moment, but Max?

"Hey, get back inside!" he roared.

The kids glanced at each other, then ran right at him. The hallway was just wide enough to squeeze by on either side, but he stretched his arms to block their way. They bent low and made for the walls. Max shifted his hips toward Maggie's side and tried to block her.

"Oh, no you don't!"

Trevor's side was open. He slipped by and glanced back just in time to see Maggie kick her uncle in the shin.

"Sorry, Uncle Max!" she shouted, as she ran by him.

The last thing Trevor saw before running for the Troth was Max hobbling after Maggie as she raced to find Ichabod.

It wasn't long before Trevor was standing in the grand archway to the Garden. The gardeners had gone and no one was in sight. Night had already fallen; the sky was black as pitch, and the Tree provided the only illumination. Light and shadow jostled with each other as the glowing fruit bobbed and swayed in a cool evening breeze. The conditions were perfect for hide-and-seek.

Trevor dove into a dark patch. He didn't want to be seen if he could help it. It was three against one. All he really wanted was the box. He thought that maybe, if he were fast and quick, he could grab it and run. He scanned the terrain.

Something moved at the far end of the quadrangle. Three stooped figures were creeping toward the Tree. They were much closer to it than he was. Forget surprise. Realizing it was his only hope, he leapt into the open and ran at them shouting for help as loud as he could.

As if in answer to his call, the Tree burst into flame. Light flooded the garden and washed the shadows away. Each leaf had become a single tongue of fire, and every one of them fluttered and moved as though rustled by a strong wind. The Tree itself didn't burn; its branches remained un-singed. But it pelted out heat like a furnace. Waves of scorching air knocked Trevor back.

What Trevor was witnessing had not been seen in over a thousand years–not since the Wars of the Subjugation. If he knew Trothward's history better, he would have known what the flames meant. The Guild was under attack.

Meno, Willis, and Drake blinked stupidly at the tree. Then Meno spotted Trevor and pointed. The other two peeled away and came at him.

"What do you want?" shouted Drake, when he was close enough to be heard over the roar of the flames.

"Yeah, what do you want?" Willis added, like usual.

"You can't do this," said Trevor, panting. "That tree is our only protection from the bogeys!"

"Come on, Trevor," Drake said, rolling his eyes.

"You don't understand! Bogeymen aren't our friends! They steal kids from their homes and give them to the Guardians to raise until they're big enough to eat!"

"Trevor, Trevor," Drake said, shaking his head, smiling indulgently. "You and your crazy ideas. Did these Guild people tell you that or did you just make it up?"

"It's the truth! I've seen where kids go when they disappear from the halls! I've been to the Sewers! I've seen the Pantry!"

"Man, what an imagination. I told you the stuff he used to say after lights out, didn't I?" he said to Willis.

"Yeah, what an imagination!" laughed Willis.

"Can't you understand?" Trevor shouted. "We've been stolen from our homes and these people are trying to help us!"

Drake rolled his eyes again. Willis laughed his stupid laugh again. Trevor glanced up and saw that Meno was nearing the Tree. "Hey!" he yelled and lunged forward. Drake and Willis blocked his way. Trevor tried to push between them.

"Get back, you twit," said Willis with a shove that sent Trevor sprawling.

Trevor jumped up, and for the second time that day, something awakened in him. In two steps he was on top of Willis, knocking him to the ground. His fists became hammers and Willis's face became a nail. Slam! Bam! Wham! Each blow made Willis's face flatter.

"Get off!" Drake yelled as he tackled Trevor. But Trevor wasn't the punching bag Drake remembered from their old hall. Trevor instinctively rolled with the blow and turned on him. In a couple of tumbles, Trevor was again on top, swinging away. Willis staggered to his feet, but instead of helping Drake, he stumbled off, holding his face.

"Stop! Stop!" Drake screamed. "I give up! Please, stop!"

Trevor barely heard him. He felt too good. He'd dreamed of this for years. All the anger and the humiliation that had piled up for so long just poured out of him. He was a wild boy, yelling and punching with all his might. Drake, by this time, was covering his face and moaning. Then, as quickly as it began, his rage was spent. Trevor sat up and remembered why he was there.

He saw Meno kneeling over the mysterious box. Springing to his feet, he ran right at the lump of muscle. The distance closed fast and he tackled him at full speed, sending them both somersaulting end-over-end. In spite of that, Meno managed to hold onto the package. When he got to his feet, he scurried back up the little rise at the foot of the Tree. Trevor overtook him from behind.

A struggle began–there were no words–there was nothing to say. There was just the box, and both boys wanted it. There was grasping, flailing, kicking, hitting, biting; finally, it turned into a tug-of-war. Trevor's days in the Ward had done him good, and both he and Meno were surprised at the even odds of the match. But it wasn't a fair fight; it wasn't simply one against one. The box had a will of its own.

Breathing hard, Maggie, Epictetus, and Max burst into the garden. A few paces behind was Ichabod, hobbling with his cane as fast as he could.

"Help the boy!" Epictetus shouted.

The box, which had been twisted and pulled back and forth, finally burst. Like an eruption, a million fine particles flew into the air, showered to the ground and immediately began moving toward the tree. Jumping back, Trevor took a moment to recognize the tiny creatures. They were spiders–thousands of them, moving at tremendous speed, and eerily guided by a single purpose. Meno shrank away. Clearly, whatever he had expected, this wasn't it.

Trevor picked up a stick and tried to smash them, but each time, the branch crashed to the ground harmlessly as the spiders parted before the blow.

Then up the tree they swarmed, thousands of tiny eight-legged crawlies scurrying with unnatural alacrity toward their predetermined goal. The fire didn't stop them. It didn't even hurt them. They passed right through the flames to the luminous fruit where they collected themselves, and with diabolical efficiency began spinning webs. The thread they spewed was thick and dark and seemed to swallow the light it touched. With unthinkable swiftness, one by one the light of the great teardrops dimmed and went out.

Epictetus, Maggie, Max and Ichabod came up behind Trevor.

"Grandfather, what's happening?" Maggie asked, voice quaking.

"Not in my worst nightmares did I envision this," Epictetus said with despair.

Maggie turned on Meno.

"It's all your fault!" she screamed at him.

His beady eyes narrowed. "You're about to be put in your place, slave."

"Not before I put you in yours!" she said, throwing a rock at him.

Her grandfather held her back. "Let him go. He has done all the harm he can, and the harm he's done he can't understand," he said.

A thundering boom echoed through the night, followed by a shout of a thousand inhuman voices.

"It has begun!" said Ichabod. "The enemy is upon us!"

"What should we do, Master?" asked Max.

Epictetus looked up at the Tree. With each passing moment, its light grew dimmer. Some of the fruit were already completely covered in their dark blankets. Many of the spiders had moved on to wrap the Tree itself. The flames that danced along the branches were growing smaller.

"We must do two things at once," said Epictetus, with resolve entering his voice. "Maximus, send word that the women, children and aged must flee. If we win the day, we'll call them back. If not, hopefully they will find refuge among our friends in Olton and beyond. Then send Brendleback with a company of men to the gate. All the others who can wield a sword, send here. For a thousand years, the Tree has protected the Guild. Now the time is come for the Guild to protect the Tree."

Max took off at a sprint, shouting ahead.

Another boom sounded.

"They're trying to break the gate," Ichabod cried out.

"We must be quick then," said the Master Fisher. "Abigail, you and Trevor fetch my sword."

They ran as fast as they could through the archway and into the halls of Trothward. Word was already spreading quickly, and the great house was a frenzy of activity. Most people looked stunned by the suddenness of the crisis. Men of all ages were donning armor and swords on the go, making their way either to the front door or to the Garden. The armor of some was either ill-fitting or rusty or both. Fathers and husbands hurriedly said good-bye to children and wives.

Beneath the clamor of these frantic preparations were other sounds—strange voices shouting faintly in the distance, and a ponderous, rhythmic *boom, boom, boom* that sent tremors through the walls and floors and made dust fall from the rafters.

As they got closer to the front door, the booming grew louder. Before long, Trevor and Maggie were looking out on the courtyard that stood just inside the front door. Trevor remembered it from the outside—a small, unassuming little entryway. *Does it still look that way?* he wondered.

Brendleback was already there, shouting orders, teeth flashing behind his bushy mustache. His men had formed battle lines. Everyone watched as the door trembled with each blow. Trevor overheard a young soldier talking with an old, gray-bearded Alchemist.

"What's happening?" he asked.

"They've got a battering ram," the older man said, as Trevor and Maggie rushed by. "Let 'em pound. That door has the power of the Tree in it. Made from her branches. Never failed, my grandfather told me when I was your age."

Out of breath, Trevor and Maggie finally arrived at the hedge outside Epictetus's chambers.

"Oooh, the maze," Maggie said to herself. "How does it go? Everything's happening so fast. Think, think, let's see...one right, two left; one right...no, no!! That's not it!"

"Slow down, try to think," Trevor said.

"Okay, okay," she said huffing.

After a couple of false starts, she got it right, and they stumbled into the Master Fisher's hearthroom.

Maggie rushed to the mantel. There she found her grandfather's sword—polished, oiled and ready for action—as though its need had been foreseen. She put it in its sheath. She was about to leave, but stopped.

"Wait a minute," she said.

She went to a large chest in the corner and lifted the lid. Inside were a number of items wrapped in cloth. Unfolding one revealed a long, sheathed dagger.

"Here," she said, handing it to Trevor. "Here's one for me, too. Let's go."

After getting out of the maze without mishap, they ran through the corridors to the front door. They arrived just in time to see it buckle and split.

"No! It can't be!" someone shouted.

Through the breach, Trevor saw the massive metal head of the battering ram. When it was drawn back, the orange-red of torch light revealed a sea of bogey faces. A shout rose into the night sky. Brendleback's voice cut the air, "Steady men! The door is narrow! Hold 'em back!"

Trevor looked at Maggie. She stood dumbstruck.

"Come on!" he said, as he pulled her along after him. As they sped out of the courtyard they heard a blast, then the clash of swords.

When they got back to the Garden, the Tree was completely dark. Trevor saw men in the branches, trying to cut the spider thread without success.

Epictetus strode up to them. He wore a breastplate that flashed and shone in the torch light. He seemed taller and younger somehow. His arms and legs were bare and they rippled with sinewy strength. His good eye was hard and eager.

"Master, they've broken the gate!" Trevor told him.

"Courage. The battle has just begun."

Maggie held the sword up to him, handle first. He grasped it with his great hand and drew it. He swung it over his head and let out a battle cry that echoed through the quadrangle. Everywhere men stopped and looked. Then one by one, then all at once, from every corner came an answering cry. Trevor felt his blood warm, and he reached for his dagger.

Epictetus turned and shouted to some men dragging a fortification of hastily-fashioned, wooden spikes, "I want that over here." Trevor noticed now that other men were pounding sharpened stakes into the ground or digging trenches.

"That's the way, men. They'll come here first."

"How could this be happening so fast, Master?" asked a man nearby.

"It only seems sudden, lad! It's been coming a long time, if I don't miss my guess! Let's just hope we can hold 'em off, long enough for Ichabod to cast out the black magic that has stricken the Troth!"

"But where is Master Paracelsus? Shouldn't he be here to help?"

Epictetus said nothing, but Trevor thought he saw the Fisher grimace.

"To the task at hand–do your part," said Epictetus, turning toward the grand arch. "Hurry with those pikes!" he said and strode off.

Trevor looked around. Men had erected a barrier across the face of the archway, but they had also established a path lined on either side by pikes, stakes, and pits that soldiers were filling with oil and beginning to set alight. The path led to an open space well away from the Tree. Smoke from the fires began to fill the air.

Epictetus returned with Max puffing alongside.

"Abigail and Trevor, this is no place for you. Maximus will take you to the passages."

"No! Grandfather, I want to be with you!"

"Abigail, what would your mother want?"

"Please, Grandfather!"

A stern look crossed Epictetus's face. "Child, do what I say. You're not safe here."

Maggie burst into tears. "Grandfather, I don't want to leave you!"

Tears began to form in the old man's eye. He turned away. "My son," he said to Max, "keep them safe."

Suddenly a shout came from the entrance.

"They're coming!"

"To the arch!" commanded Epictetus, as he headed toward the defenses.

"Oh, no you don't, young lady," said Max, as he swooped down and swept Maggie up in one of his big arms. Trevor was too big to pick up, so he grabbed his wrist. "You're not getting away from me this time!"

"No! No! I want to stay. I can fight. Grandfather needs my

help!" screamed Maggie, kicking her feet and swinging her fists. Trevor looked back and saw the survivors of the assault on the front door coming through the battlements. The defenses were closed just in time to turn back the first surge of the enemy. Pikes and spears struck the barriers and were turned aside or broken. A company of archers Trevor hadn't noticed before unleashed a rain of arrows on the attackers. A line of bogeys went down in a wave.

Max reached the far side of the garden and slipped through a hedge. He came to an iron door in the wall. He let Trevor go. "Obey me, boy. Or at least obey the Master's last wish. Don't you go running off!" Trevor was too thunderstruck to try. He just stood and watched. Maggie kept struggling.

"Oooh, let me down! Let me down! Don't just stand there, Trevor, help me! Oooh, I hate you; I hate you both!"

Max paid no attention. He reached into a pocket and produced an ancient key. Into the keyhole it went, but the door swung inward before he could turn the key. "That's right, I didn't have my key with me to lock it after those boys had come in this way," he said to himself.

A short set of steps went down. The only light came from the door, and by it Trevor saw a layer of dust covering the floor. But there were footprints in the dust—two sets going down the steps, but three coming up.

Maggie groaned.

Max turned a worried eye toward her. "What is it, girl? I ain't squeezing you that hard."

"The footprints, that's how they did it! They followed our footprints back, and Grandfather forgot to lock the door!"

A troubled expression came over Max's normally untroubled face. "Well, in we go. The wrongs of the past can't be mended." He pushed Trevor in ahead of him and crossed the threshold.

Then he set Maggie down and threw his shoulder against the door and pushed it shut. "At least we can lock it this time." The little light that came from the keyhole winked out. After a moment, Trevor heard the click of the lock, and the tiny light reappeared. Total darkness surrounded them. "Now you two can't go anywhere, but straight ahead."

Maggie didn't say a thing. Trevor couldn't see her, but he imagined her arms were crossed (which they were) and that she had an angry pout on her face (which she did).

"Max," said Trevor, "where're we going?"

"Away from here. There's a real mess back there, but if anyone can fix it, Epictetus can. Let's hope Ichabod takes care of those spiders! Looks mighty bad, but the Ward has never been taken. If I was a betting man, I'd bet it never will be!" His voice didn't sound as confident as his words.

He took their hands in his thick, calloused ones and led them down the stairs and, after a stumble at the bottom, into the passage. They couldn't see a thing, but the way was straight and the floor was smooth. Occasionally, they veered to the left or the right and grazed the walls, but they made steady progress. The sounds of battle subsided, and before long all they heard were the sounds of their echoing feet and their breathing. The air grew cooler the farther they went.

Maggie hadn't spoken since Max locked the door, but Trevor could feel her frustration through the darkness. Max must have felt it, too, because he tried to comfort them or distract them or maybe both.

"I'm sure everything will be all right, children. That Epictetus is a wonder, he is. He'll clear those bogeys right out, he will. In the meantime, he wants us to go to the woods, he does. Said we should make for Mother Root's. Never met her myself, but she's a powerful woman, I'm told. Epictetus says she'll keep us 'til he comes."

Maggie broke his hold and took off down the tunnel.

"Hey, come back here!"

"No! Grandfather needs me! I can help–I'm no baby!"

Max lumbered after her with Trevor coming along behind.

Can't she see she's only making things worse! Trevor thought.

To keep himself from running into the tunnel walls, he kept his hand on the right one as he went along. From the bumps and "Ows!" ahead, he could tell Max hadn't thought of that. Max kept shouting though, but Maggie didn't answer.

Suddenly, Trevor ran into him. He was standing still, muttering to himself. Trevor noticed that the wall had fallen away to his right.

"Which way did she go? Wait 'til I get my hands on her."

They had come to a fork in the passage.

"Master Epictetus told me to keep to the left. *Left to light and liberty,* he said. But did she go that way?"

"Max, let's listen. Maybe we'll hear her," offered Trevor.

They stood quietly, holding their breath. Then they heard it–the sound of footfalls echoing up the passage on the right.

"That girl is going to get herself lost, and what'll we do then?"

"Max, remember, she came this way before. Maybe she thinks she can get to Epictetus this way?"

"Come on," Max said, with a curse.

They turned down the right path (which was really the wrong path) and went as fast as they could. They stumbled and scraped themselves a few times, but they hadn't gone far when they heard a scream.

"Oh no!" Max said, and started to run. Trevor followed as fast as he could.

Ahead was a red glow. The path bent away to the right, and the glow grew as they got closer. Trevor smelled fire. He hadn't heard anything since the scream.

When they came upon her, they were blinded momentarily by the light. In the time that it took for their eyes to adjust, the bogeymen were on them. Trevor's hand went for his knife, and almost without thinking he stabbed the bogey who had tried to nab him. It screamed and leapt back. Trevor looked up to see that Max had a short sword which he had used to separate a couple of arms from their former owners. They had come upon a company of the enemy. In the middle of them stood Paracelsus. He was holding a hand over Maggie's mouth.

"I don't understand," said Max, holding out his sword uncertainly.

"My dear Maximus, it is not what it seems. Put that thing down. These people are our friends. Come along with us. This needless fighting must stop. I have arranged a lasting peace at last. You will see."

Inspired by Trevor's performance, Maggie found her dagger and plunged it into Paracelsus' arm.

"Aaaiii! Foolish girl!" he screamed, and let her go. "You'll ruin everything!"

"Don't believe him, Uncle Max. He's a traitor!" shouted Maggie.

She ran over to Trevor, and Max stepped between them and the bogey company.

"Run, children! Run! Tell Epictetus!"

Maggie finally obeyed. The last thing they saw as they ran was Max holding the narrow way against half a dozen vicious-looking bogeys. As they went, Maggie was crying and muttering to herself, "It's all my fault; it's all my fault."

"I can't believe it," Trevor said. "I can't believe he's a traitor. He told me he wanted to save children from the bogeys."

"I know," said Maggie, still crying. "But he is. He told me before you came that Meno and those guys are part of his plan!"

Trevor had been numb with shock until that moment; now he felt like he might be sick. He realized with a jolt that he had been part of the plan, too. He was about to say something when he decided to keep his thoughts to himself.

It was completely dark again; and they held hands as they went along, each keeping their other hand on the opposite wall. They came to the fork in the passage and turned left–up to Trothward and the battle.

"What are we going to do?"asked Maggie. "Uncle Max locked the door!"

Trevor hadn't thought of that. What would they do? He imagined being trapped between the door and the bogeys.

In the distance, they saw a line of light shining out from beneath the door. They ran the last stretch and crawled up the steps. When they got to it, they found the door as they had left it–old, thick, rusty, and locked. Desperately, they pulled and tugged. Trevor even tried to pick the lock with his dagger. Nothing worked. Then, the inevitable sound of footfalls echoed up to them from down the passage. The bogeys were coming.

"I hope Uncle Max is all right," Maggie whimpered.

Trevor's mind raced. He hadn't felt despair like this since he had been locked in the Pantry. His mind turned to Zephyr. "If only he were here to help us!" Trevor exclaimed.

"Who?" said Maggie.

"Me," said a tiny voice at their feet.

Both stood wide-eyed before the glowing mouse.

"I thought you would never ask," he remarked.

"Ask for what?" said Trevor stupidly.

"My help, of course," said the mouse. "You almost waited too long. We must act fast. No questions, Trevor–you either, Abigail." Maggie was surprised. "Yes, I know your name. You must do exactly as I say. You understand, right, Trevor?"

Trevor moaned.

"Keep your eyes on me and follow me beneath this door."

"Oh, no! I was afraid you'd say that!" said Maggie.

"It is not the size of the hole that counts, it's the size of the mouse. If you keep your eyes on me, you will do what I do."

Although Trevor had followed Zephyr through the small opening in the door of his cell back in the Pantry, this opening was much smaller.

The doorway was too narrow for them to pass beneath it side by side. "You first," Trevor offered, not because he was feeling chivalrous. "Okay," she said with a weak voice.

"Come along," Zephyr said, with an otherworldly calm. He then squeezed beneath the door. Maggie lowered her face to the ground and looked though the crack.

"I'm waiting," sing-songed the mouse from the other side.

"Go ahead," Trevor prodded.

Maggie crept forward, but as she neared the door a shout came from the passage behind them. She flinched and bumped her head.

"Abigail!" came a commanding voice from the other side of the door. "Look at me and come."

Trevor looked back. Still no bogeys, but he could see a faint, red glow in the distance. They would be there soon. When he looked back at the door, Maggie was gone.

Down he went. He saw Maggie's feet, right next to the mouse. "Trevor, come!"

In a moment, he was on the other side with them.

The sounds of battle crashed upon them. Through the flames and smoke, Trevor saw Ichabod trying vainly to rid the Tree of the dark mass that smothered it in a great black cocoon. Two aged Illuminators held up his arms while he chanted inaudibly from a huge book held before him. Beyond them–in the distance, through the smoke—he saw Maggie's grandfather with Brendleback defending the entrance to the Garden. The way was narrow enough for the smaller force to bottle up the much larger enemy company. Trevor was not a military strategist, but even he could see that the bogeys coming up the passage behind them were enough to turn the battle against them and all would be lost.

"Come on!" he said. Without stopping to thank the mouse, he ran to tell Epictetus the news.

"Grandfather! Grandfather!" Maggie shouted as they ran. They trampled flower beds, once lovingly planted, and pushed through low-lying hedges that only earlier that day the gardeners had trimmed. They thought nothing of them. Everything was at risk and things that seemed precious only hours ago were valueless.

As they ran up huffing and puffing, Epictetus turned and looked at them with dismay. "Children, what are you doing here? Where's Max?! Didn't I command him to take you to safety?"

"Grandfather, I think Uncle Max's hurt. We ran into bogeys in the passage." Maggie didn't mention running away or taking the wrong turn.

"Bogeys? How?" exclaimed Epictetus.

"Master Paracelsus was with them," Trevor said.

Epictetus's face went pale.

"Misguided I called him, but this is suicide," he muttered, shaking his head. "Coming up the passage you say? How long 'til they arrive?"

"They're just on the other side of the door. It's locked," said Trevor.

"Brendleback! Brendleback!" Epictetus shouted.

Brendleback ran up.

"Brend, we must divide our force or we'll be flanked. The enemy is at the rear door. Take some men and keep them bottled in."

"What...the rear door?" the haggard man replied.

It was too late. A blast came from behind them. Trevor looked and saw a smoking gap in the hedge and the door hanging cockeyed by a hinge. Heavily armed bogeys were streaming out of the opening. The men defending the archway saw it, too, and some fell back without an order. A shout came from without. When the attackers saw the defenses weakened, they made a furious press and breached the line. Pandemonium ensued as men turned and fled.

"To the Tree! To the Tree!" Epictetus shouted.

Bogeys poured in like a flood. Small, wiry ones squeezed through cracks, wielding fork-bladed, short-swords. Huge, bull-necked ones lowered themselves and pushed back the pike works like teams of draft horses. Soon these were passed by a surging host of yellow-eyed fiends carrying every kind of spiked mace, or cross-bow, or double-edged sword imaginable. And like a dark wave, they covered the ground with arresting speed behind the fleeing defenders. The slower, older men were overcome. It was a slaughter.

Epictetus leapt upon a rock and called for the ragged survivors to form a ring about the Tree. The few hundred men who had managed to reach him formed a line.

Epictetus quickly conferred with Ichabod as the killing raged in the distance. "How goes it?"

Ichabod looked back and shook his head.

When Epictetus turned to the children, his face was grim. A pause had occurred in the battle as the enemy began taking their positions in preparation for their next assault. The Master Fisher looked at Trevor and Maggie. "Children, be brave. Whatever may happen, let us by our conduct honor those who have gone before us."

"I will," said Maggie, her voice shaky.

Epictetus looked deeply into Trevor's eyes. "I will, sir," he said, fingering the hilt of his knife.

"Good," said the old man, with the trace of a smile.

Flaming arrows began to fall.

"Shields up!" shouted Epictetus.

Trevor and Maggie ducked behind a wall of men. The arrows burned with a devilish fire that burst on impact, engulfing many of the defenders in flames. Throughout the lines, men cast themselves on the ground in the futile attempt to extinguish the fires. Beyond the lines, the bogeys jeered.

Then they charged–first here and then there. The men of the Ward did their best to turn them back. Epictetus ran from place to place, waving his sword and shouting encouragement to the defenders. Once, Trevor saw the line break and several bogeys press through, but Epictetus was upon them in an instant; with marvelous skill he cut them down. Shouts rose from all around, "To the Fisher!" Men came to his aid, and the gap was mended.

Charge after charge the assault continued. Trevor and Maggie helped where they could. Using his dagger, Trevor helped to free a man who had been pinned by a fat bogey. He leapt on its back from behind and silently slipped his blade between the shoulder plate and helmet.

I just killed something, Trevor realized, stunned. But before he could think about it, he had to dodge the shuffling feet of a man and a bogey locked in a match to the death.

With each press of the assault the defender's numbers shrank, and the noose tightened. The attackers were constricted by the shrinking battle line. Wounded and slaughtered bogeys were pulled screaming or senseless back through gaps and replaced by fresh fighters. The defenders didn't have that luxury. Before long, their wounded and dying were underfoot with no place to be taken. When the bogeys advanced over their bodies, a cheer would rise and a frenzy of hacking would follow as fallen men were torn to pieces.

Wave after wave they came, beating the Guildsmen back into a smaller circle. Trevor fought without thinking. Everything came too fast for anything but an instinctive reaction. His arms were soon so weary he thought he couldn't lift them, but still they came, and still he fought. When his right arm could no longer serve because of the cuts he had received and the weariness of the struggle, he discovered his left. He learned that when there is no other choice, what is thought weak discovers its native strength. Finally, after what seemed an eternity of cold, gray steel and warm, red blood, the enemy fell back.

"Have they given up, Grandfather?" asked Maggie, doubled over with her shirt hanging loose, slashed and blood soaking through. Tears were streaming from her eyes.

"No," replied the old man with a cold laugh. Black streaks of ash ran across his face, but he still seemed larger than life and twice as strong as he'd ever seemed. Sweat glistened on his chest and arms, and the sinews of his limbs were swollen with vigor.

A commotion arose from the archway as three huge forms emerged. Each was at least twice the height of a man. Through the fire and smoke, Trevor could see their heavily muscled necks straining against their chains as their handlers directed them with whips and spears. Each demon screamed with rage as it was brought to the front of the battle line. The bogeys quailed and gave way. The defenders grew silent and stared in horror and shock. Many looked to Epictetus, who suddenly rose tall as if he'd heard someone, or something call his name.

"Ogres, men! Ogres!" he shouted.

The bogeys drove the dumb beasts so that they faced the men of the Ward on three sides. Then they stayed behind them at a safe distance. Overcome by despair, some men wept openly.

Epictetus glanced to Ichabod one more time, but the Illuminator just bowed his head. The Master Fisher then strode to the Tree and placed a hand upon its mighty trunk. The eyes of every man were on him, but no one spoke. Finally, he turned to his men and, standing unbowed, he spoke terrible words, hard words that would either crush the hearer or make him strong.

"Brothers," he began. Then he paused and looked slowly around. "As you look out upon the enemy, and as you think about your fallen friends, you may wonder whether you have a choice. The coward in you says, *If fighting is death and surrender is death, what difference does it make?* It is not to this self, but to another I appeal, a deeper and quieter self, but stronger." He paused once more and then his voice rang out like a trumpet. *"You can die a coward or you can die a man!* What will it be? Will you die like cattle or will you die fighting to defend your homes, your loved ones, your sacred trust?"

There was a silence.

Somewhere a man shouted, "We'll fight!"

Then another took up the cry, "We'll fight!"

Then raggedly, but finally all together they cried in unison, "Fight! Fight! Fight!"

The great man held his sword aloft. And following his example, every man did the same, even those whose wounds left them barely able to lift a sword. Trevor and Maggie raised their daggers and shouted with all their might. Trevor felt courage swell in his heart. It was a dark courage drawn from resignation, not hope.

Epictetus strode through his men, grasping the hands of those who reached out to him. The lust for battle was upon him, and his face shone with a terrible splendor. When he reached the front of the line, he raised his eye patch and looked on his men with both eyes–one clear and true, the other ghostly white. "Brothers! I look at you and I see heroes, everyone! It is my pleasure to die with you this day!" Then he took his sword and pointed it at one of the ogres. "Trothward!" his voice rang out. "Let's give those devils something to haunt their dreams!" With a wild cry, he ran forward. All men followed him. Not a single one wavered.

Unable to escape, the ogre at the center of the assault was soon surrounded and shot through with the arrows the defenders had plucked from the dead and dying. In his rage, he blindly swung his club and cut down any Guildsmen who dared to venture too close. It was Epictetus who brought him down, but in doing so he lost more than he gained. The Fisher got to his massive legs and hamstrung the beast with a single, well-placed thrust. But the thing fell awkwardly, crushing him, pinning him to the ground. The surrounding bogeys fell back.

Men were on the creature in an instant, stabbing, and killing it. Then they set to prying Epictetus free–Maggie and Trevor among them. But, inevitably, the bogeys rallied and hemmed them in. The press was furious and swept the men of the Ward back. They broke into small, desperate groups fighting to the death.

Trevor and Maggie lost each other in the confusion. And, although this was terrible for Trevor, things would soon get worse. He spotted a hedge row where he thought he could find cover, and he got low and scrambled for it. Everything was a blur of legs and swords; of men shouting and bogeys laughing. But then his foot got caught and down he went, right next to a motionless body. He turned and looked into the empty eyes of a dead man. Then he heard a dreadfully familiar sound, and the grip on his foot got tighter.

"Sniff, sniff," went the sound; a most unwelcome voice

accompanied it. "I smell something," said a voice. "I smell something–something that reminds me of something." Down by his feet there rose a head even more unwelcome than the voice. It had a hideous nose-filled face, with a broad, toothy, yellow grin. "Ah, yes, I know that smell!" the Snatcher said with glee. "It is my long-lost dinner! I never forget the smell of dinner! Especially a dinner that thinks he could get away!"

"Sabnock!" Trevor cried.

"Ah, Morsel–you remember old Sabnock again, how flattering!" The bogey began to move up Trevor's body. "But morsel, you were such a disappointment the last time we were together. You left without saying goodbye. Now, wasn't that rude? Ol' Sabnock was so sad, he couldn't eat for days. Tsk, tsk–but better late than never, as they say." At that moment, the bogey produced a wicked-looking, double-pronged knife. It looked like a giant fork.

"You keep away from me!" Trevor said, holding up his dagger and trying to pull away.

"Oh, ho! The morsel has a little blade. Well, isn't that delightful. I am so pleased. I like my supper with a little fight in it. It gives a morsel a little extra flavor!"

What happened next happened quicker than it takes to tell. Trevor didn't freeze, like he certainly would have at one time, and he didn't try to get away. Instead, he took his dagger and lunged right at the Snatcher, surprising him. For with his talk about liking supper with a little fight in it, apparently he didn't really mean it. But the bogey knew his business, and Trevor learned the purpose of a forked blade the hard way. With an expert turn of the wrist, he caught Trevor's dagger between his double-knife blades and sent Trevor's blade tumbling through the air.

The bogey bounded on him and forced the air out of his

lungs. Now the Snatcher had Trevor on his back, and his knees were on his arms. Trevor was pinned, and there was nothing he could do. On top of that, the bogey was really angry now.

"Well, morsel," he said, raising his weapon over his head. "Sabnock's going to enjoy gnawing on your bones!"

In that moment, everything seemed to slow down, and Trevor thought about what was happening to him in a strange, detached sort of way–almost as if he were someone else looking upon the scene from a distance, "Thus ends the short, miserable life of one Trevor Upjohn," he thought to himself.

But it didn't end. Instead everything changed. With a whoosh, Sabnock was gone. One second Trevor was looking up into the face of an angry, salivating monster, and the next he saw nothing but sky. He sat up quickly and turned around to see the crumpled form of the bogey lying still on the ground a few feet away.

"What happened?"

"I saved you again, of course," said a familiar voice.

It was Zephyr, and he was standing right by Trevor's dagger.

"Now, hurry. No time for questions. Just pick this thing up and follow me."

Trevor grabbed his knife and followed the mouse to the hedge-row. When he got there, he had no idea what he should do. He didn't know where Maggie had gotten to, and he couldn't see Epictetus any more.

"Well, my boy," said the mouse. "Ready to go home yet?"

"Home? How can I think of home?" he snapped. "Look at what's happening! I can't leave now!"

"Really? I don't think so. You could just up and leave. Nothing to it."

"But I can't leave my friends. Epictetus is in trouble! And what about Maggie? And what will happen to Tubby and everybody?"

"Oh, I see what you mean," said the mouse comprehendingly. "It wouldn't be right to leave now. Yes, yes, I quite agree with that. But what about before? If I recall, you wanted to leave right away, and you were very upset with me when I said you weren't ready."

"But that was different. That was before Trothward and everything."

"Oh, no it wasn't. Nothing was different. Things were bad then; things are bad now. The only difference is you. But now you don't want to go. Very interesting, wouldn't you agree?"

"I don't know. And I don't care. I need to help."

"Excellent," said the mouse, sounding pleased. "We see things from the same side, at last. So, what do you propose to do?"

Trevor didn't know what to say. A couple of times he began to blurt out something, but wisely stopped himself. There was nothing he could do and he knew it.

"Quite a pickle, eh?" said Zephyr. "Well, while you chew on it a bit, let's see what happens next."

The fighting was nearly over. Scattered defenders were surrendering. Guildsmen and bogeys lay dead and dying all around. Bogeys were moving among the wounded, finishing human and bogey alike. Others were already piling bodies. Trevor shuddered when he thought of their fate.

A commotion came from the gate, and a way was made for four small ogres carrying a heavily-draped platform. Darkness was oozing from beneath its curtains.

With the arrival, bogeys scurried to form ranks. Coming behind the platform, captured Guildsmen staggered along. From among them, Trevor picked out Giles nervously glancing about. He had drawn a crowd of ogling bogeys who were admiring his enormous bulk. Ichabod was also there, dejectedly leaning on his walking stick. To one side stood Master Paracelsus, looking remarkably free and at ease. His arm was in a sling.

From the rear emerged a group of bogeys straining to carry a gaudy chair of great weight.

"Gold, no doubt," said Zephyr. "How like him."

"Like who?" whispered Trevor.

"You'll see."

The ogres set the platform down, and its curtains were drawn back. Darkness bellowed forth like smoke. Those near fell to their knees. Trevor started feeling queasy, and he felt an urge to grovel. Zephyr looked unimpressed. He stood on a rock, arms crossed, stroking his whiskers.

A dark, formless hulk emerged slowly and took his seat upon the golden chair. "All cower before his terrible majesty, Lucian the Great!" a voice demanded.

Those still standing fell to their knees as though compelled. Trevor began to get on his.

"Stop that," Zephyr said with an absent wave of his paw. The impulse disappeared.

"Let the sorting begin!" someone cried out.

Bogeymen moved among the humans, pulling them to their feet and bringing them before the dark shroud, one at a time. It was impossible for Trevor to hear what was being said at that distance.

Zephyr turned to Trevor. "My boy, I believe you have a little golden ball in your pocket that should prove quite useful just now. Please bring it out."

"How did you know that?"

"It's the sort of thing a person in my position makes a point of knowing. Just please get it out. I can hear what they are saying perfectly well, but I think you should listen, too."

Trevor reached into a pocket. Yes, despite the violence, it was still buried deeply there. He brought it out and held it to his mouth and said, "I want to know what those people are saying." The orb obliged, and voices started coming from it.

"Quieter ," said the mouse. "We may be discovered."

"Shhh!" Trevor said to the ball. The volume lowered.

"You!" Ichabod's voice shrieked razor-thin from the ball. "How could you?–you, you traitor! What did he promise you? Riches? As if you hadn't enough already! Power? Whatever it is, may it be the death of you! May the name of Paracelsus be forever cursed!"

"Ichabod, Ichabod, you don't understand," said the Alchemist, as though he were correcting a dear, but dimwitted friend. "Just wait, you will see. A new day of prosperity has dawned. Soon you will thank me. Yes, this violence is regrettable, but it was so unnecessary. I tried my best to prevent it. If only you and Epictetus had listened to me, all these dead could have been spared."

"Spared?! Spared?! I was wrong! You're not a traitor–you're a fool!"

"Beware who you call fool, you miserable excuse for a Master!" The Alchemist's mood had changed, and a chilly, accusatory tone entered his voice. "It is you who were foolish! We cannot make reality bend to our wills; we must play the hand we are dealt. We can't bring back the dear old days–as if they ever truly existed, which I doubt. We must change and adapt." Then with an altered tone, like a pocket of warmth on a bitter day, he said, "Come, old friend, will you not now join me? The Troth has brought us prosperity; now it will bring us power and influence! We can make this world a better place, you and I. We can turn it into what the old stories say it once was! We can save children like never before! I have arranged everything! You will see! Think of the good we will accomplish once we have been brought into Lucian's counsels! It's a new day! The old prophesies are coming true, just in an unexpected way!"

For a moment, no sounds came from the ball, and Trevor wondered whether Ichabod might join Paracelsus. But what he had imagined was thoughtful consideration was simply dumfounded shock. "Never! Never!! Get away!" Ichabod said,when he found his voice again.

"So, is this your Master Illuminator?" said a haughty voice that gave Trevor a chill. "My, my, my, from what heights we have fallen. It is sad to see such a noble order reduced to imbecility. This one would not have presumed to sweep my floors in the old days."

"I, I may be an unworthy son, but at least I honor the memory of my ancient order–unlike some I, I..." The Illuminator's voice was cut off.

"Silence, old buffoon," said the voice. "Guard, take this, this thing away."

Trevor saw a couple of bogeys come alongside his former employer. Ichabod, to his credit, raised his stick to hit one of the monsters. But it was a mistake. Before he could strike, the bogey gave him a back-handed blow that sent the frail, old man sprawling. He lay motionless until they dragged him away by his arms.

"Most amusing," said the voice of the hulk, in a most bored and world-weary way. "And now, my dear Alchemist, I, Lucian the Incomparable, thank you for your generous gift."

"Gift, my Lord? I, I don't understand," Paracelsus said, bowing repeatedly before the black mass.

"For centuries, I have looked forward to this day," the darkness said with a new lightness. "Now, at last I stand within the fastness of the Guild and I will finally remove the last vestige of the old world and its reactionary ways."

"I don't understand," Paracelsus said, with dawning apprehension.

"Why, my fellow conspirator, I have come to do away with the Guild, and especially the wild magic at her heart. Again, I say thank you for the gift, but it is a gift which I must dispose of." With that Lucian made a stroke, and a dozen swords fell upon the necks of the remaining Guildsmen.

"My Lord, Lucian," Paracelsus cried out, "This is not what we agreed upon. How can this house serve you without servants? If you take away our ability to make our goods, how will the kingdom prosper?"

"My fair-minded merchant," said the blackness. "You are slow to understand. I do not want the services of this house. I simply want it to go away. As for your precious tree, it is my considered opinion that those so-called goods you derive from it do not constitute enough benefit to the realm to outweigh the risks."

Paracelsus fell to his knees, "Risks? You can't do this! You promised!"

Coarse laughter came from the hulk. "My dear Alchemist, you are deluded if you believe I am bound by promises made to the likes of you. Did you think I would parley with you as if you were my equal? Did you think you could make me perform? You are nothing! I take no thought of you. But, it will amuse me to allow you to see the fate of your precious Troth."

With another wave, some bogeys began driving the ogres toward the Tree. Two bore huge axes in their gnarled hands.

"NO!" screamed Paracelsus.

At last, Zephyr spoke, "It looks like the dear Alchemist and Lucian the Incomparable view risk a bit differently." Changing the subject, he continued, "Come along, my boy. Someone has something he wants to say to you."

"Who?" Trevor said, unable to take his eyes off the drama unfolding in front of him.

"Epictetus. He has been moved. Remember, keep your eyes

fixed on me."

That broke the spell. Trevor looked down at the mouse with new interest.

Zephyr moved quickly from under the cover and out into the open. Trevor scurried to keep up. They didn't set out in the direction he expected, but instead crawled toward the hedges next to the back door. In the distance it appeared to be just a blast-stained hole in the wall, like the mouth of a cave. It took some time to pick their way across the terrain to get to it. When they got there, Trevor found Epictetus with Maggie holding his head on her lap.

He was a shrunken man. Trevor was shocked to see him lying there, so frail and weak. He felt his last bit of hope drain away. Maggie didn't look up to greet them. Tears stained her dirty face.

"Greetings, old friend," said Zephyr. "I am back, and I have brought the boy."

Epictetus weakly raised a hand. "Whenever I have doubted you, I've lived to regret it," he said. "I think today I will not live to do even that."

"Don't say that, Grandfather," Maggie whimpered.

"Granddaughter, I am afraid I can only give cold comfort now. The flame of my spirit burns low."

"Grandfather, what can I do?"

"Just hold my hand, dear child. You shouldn't have come back. If you'd obeyed me you'd be safe–far away by now. This is a bitter end."

"I couldn't leave you," she said, with a sob.

"I know," said the old man, with a wan smile. Then he groaned. His good eye went vacant. "I can no longer see," he said weakly.

"Master Fisher, you fought well and bravely," said the mouse.

"Not well enough, I'm afraid."

"You know as well as I that the battle was lost before you took the field. We both saw this day coming long ago."

"I didn't believe it. I couldn't believe it."

"Nevertheless, it has come."

They were interrupted by sounds coming from the vicinity of the Tree. It was past dawn, and the pale light of an overcast sky revealed a Garden that was wrung and torn from battle. Smoke from dead fires still hung in the air, but through it, they could see that chains had been thrown through the Troth's branches, and that four smaller ogres were being made to pull. Far worse was the sight of the larger ogres, each swinging his mighty axe against the vast trunk. With every blow, a dull chop sounded through the morning air.

Very little seemed to happen. Only small pieces of bark flew up. Trevor, at first, thought perhaps that the Tree could not be toppled. But at the shouts of their keepers, the dull-eyed monsters increased their speed. In their idiocy, they did not see the impossibility of their task and so made slow, but steady progress. Eventually, the white wood beneath the bark was exposed. It glowed in the morning gray. Bogeys shifted nervously. Lucian's voice sliced out, "Faster!" The bogeys whipped the ogres with greater ferocity. Paracelsus babbled and wept on his knees nearby. More and more of the tender wood beneath the surface was chipped away. Their speed increased as the tender middle of the great tree was exposed. Now it trembled with each blow as its inner life was cut away. There came a thunderous crack. Relentlessly, the stupid creatures kept up their hacking. Finally, the Tree started to tilt. A shout of triumph came from the bogeys as it began a slow fall. At the last, it gave way with a snap and fell to the ground with a rustle and a crash.

Trevor and Maggie sat in mute horror. Streams of tears were flowing from Zephyr's eyes.

Emboldened, the bogeys set upon it and began cutting it up. Branches were dragged aside and doused with oil. Soon the quadrangle was lit again by the Tree–this time by a consuming fire.

"A light has passed out of the world," Zephyr said, after a long silence.

Epictetus spoke. "I have failed."

"No, Grandfather!" protested Maggie.

"Yes, Abigail. It's true. I've failed; the Guild has failed."

"There is yet hope; remember our conversation," said Zephyr.

"But where's the *boy*?" he said with a gasp. *"You spoke of a boy."*

"Why, he's right here," said the mouse.

"Trevor?" the Fisher said with disbelief.

"Look, and you will see."

"Trevor," Epictetus said, after a pause, "come near."

Trevor inched forward, unsure what to think.

"Abigail, lift my eye patch."

Numbly, she obeyed.

"Closer, Trevor. Let me have a good look at you."

Trevor was over him now, looking down into the sightless eyes of the old man. His washed-out pupils stared blankly up, searching vainly for something to focus upon.

Trevor swallowed.

"Yes, I can see it now," he said. "How did I miss it before?"

"He is the one," said Zephyr.

Trevor and Maggie looked at each other.

"Trevor, listen to me," Epictetus said weakly. "I have something for you to do–something I think only you can. It is a burden I am loath to place on you, but I've no other choice. I've only heard rumored whispers about it, but if they're true, well...everything will change, *everything*, Trevor." The old Fisher said *everything* with such emphasis, he began coughing fitfully.

Maggie stroked his forehead, and when he regained control, he spoke again. "There is a Fey Brand, I've been told, one of great power," he coughed once more. "It can only be wielded by a boy, if the boy is right. Trevor, you are that boy; you must get the brand."

"Me? Why me?"

The question fell to the ground heavily and silence followed it. For a time no words were spoken. Only the sounds of weeping rose from the small circle. They came from a boy, a girl, and a mouse, and that was all.

END OF BOOK ONE

Who is Mortimus Clay?

Mortimus Clay is the most prolific author writing posthumously in the world today. The modest Clay is not given to sweeping generalizations, but he has this on the highest authority.

While alive Mortimus Clay was, unfortunately, a dismal failure as an author. He was passed over by editors and scorned by fellow writers. Clay spent his life trying to emulate his hero, Charles Dickens, but instead ended up living like a character in a Dickens novel.

During the day Mortimus served as Professor of Arts and Letters at Her Majesty's Knitting College for Wayward Girls, but in the evening he wrote late into the night in his unheated Manchester flat. The professor never married. When asked he declared, "I have my art! Who has time for a wife?"

After fifty years of teaching *Beowulf* and *The Faerie Queene* to unappreciative knitters, Professor Clay died in 1885, half-starved and grasping the shards of a badly crafted poem entitled, "Ode on a Grecian Fern." It was the best thing that ever happened to the old boy as his writing took an immediate turn for the better.

....

The Weirdling Cycle continues with Book 2–
The Quest For the Fey Brand,
available in better book stores in 2010!